T RAIBON 1

The Prince's Priest

TRAIBON FAMILY SAGA

The Prince's Priest

V. C. WILLIS

4 Horsemen
Publications, Inc.

Daemon, Daimon, or Demon

Pronunciation /`diːmən/

1. a divinity, spirit, or supernatural being considered part god and part human.

2. An inner, attendant, or guardian spirit; inspiring force.

3. Ancient Greek and Latin for "godlike", "power", "fate"

TABLE OF CONTENTS

CHAPTER 1

The Fanged Lady

I gripped the silver dagger, *La Dame d'Croc*, tighter. Like droplets of blood across the blade, my eyes reflected my desire for its destruction. The ornate hilt's laughing skulls and vines dug into my palm. With a tilt of the keen blade, a long-forgotten language made itself known. This was the tool for the rite of passage for the next generation of bloodeaters. It was my duty, the next in-line to be King of *The Court,* to protect it with my life. I didn't care to inherit the wretched thing.

Tonight, in my honor, a masquerade party whispered from the lower levels of the manor. The sense of jubilation resonating from the guests was a growing friction of heat against my soul. I intended on ending the centuries-old tradition of bloodeating with my abdication from the throne. My father's advisors would likely imprison me if they knew of my intentions. They would claim the pacifist daemons of *The Court* or even human ideals from *The Tower* were to blame. The truth was simpler. What little historical records survived amongst the royal library told me the story of betrayal and ascension to a never-ending civil war. *The House* had turned on those it promised to protect and devoured them for their power. Thus, the tradition of eating the blood of humans was born with the use of the magical blade in my hand—and I wanted nothing to do with it.

"Are you not joining the celebration, Dante?" The voice belonged to Viceroy Falco, a sinister bastard who was also a revered war hero. "Ah, I see they handed the *La Dame d'Croc* over to you. Mmm, *Fanged Lady,* such a wonderful name for a blade."

Glancing over my shoulder, I saw that his lips were tight and a scornful flare in his eyes told me what I already knew. "I'm sorry my father didn't hand it to you, Viceroy Falco."

By human standards, Viceroy Falco was in his mid-twenties, but he had been walking this world for at least two centuries. He fought in the front lines when the civil war reached a peak pressing for territory. They pushed *The Court* and its non-bloodeater daemons to the mountains over a hundred years ago. It was obnoxious how he towered over me, despite my superior ranking. He was broad-shouldered, carried a sword, and the white strands of his hair looming across his maroon eyes added to the deceitful atmosphere that never left him. With each step, Viceroy Falco's armor clacked as the golden devils and chains knocked against the black lacquer of the ceremonial armor on his shoulder and chest. It was more of a fashion statement than practical for battle when he wore the black steel equivalent.

"It's only because you're the King's last surviving son," he snorted, stepping closer to inspect the skulls on the hilt. "You are still too young and naïve to wield such a sacred artifact. A mistake, no offense, my dear prince."

"Twenty-eight is old in human terms." It earned me a sneer, his fangs clenched as I covered the blade with its black silken cloth. "I'm old enough to know not to misplace this into the wrong hands." He stiffened, feeling the verbal stabs aimed in his direction. "As its protector, no one is to touch it."

Despite my age, I appeared to be nothing more than a young boy of eighteen. Besides the fangs hidden behind my lips, the ever-present maroon eyes of a daemon were the signs of what I was: not human. Earlier in the war, it'd been a malicious tactic to send out younger daemons to use their childlike appearances to infiltrate various noble households serving *The Tower.* Many hadn't come home after being discovered, including a few cousins and a sister far before my conception. Daemons that young had no power, not yet come of age to join the ritual of the blade where cutting of flesh and their first feeding unlocked a lifetime of thirst.

The first blood must be taken from a cut brandished by *La Dame d'Croc* or the daemon faced the Madness, a curse which drove human and daemon into insanity of wanting to devour the meat of their fellow men and sometimes, themselves. When the Madness peaked, they would foam at the mouth, eyes rolled back in their heads, berserking until their hearts beat themselves to death. The magic ritual passed down to *The House* cleansed both vessels, bloodeater and prey, allowing the art to be feasible. Viceroy Falco had sent many humans and opposing daemons in battle into the Madness with relentless bites, earning him the title of *Le Chien Enragé* or *The Rabid Dog.*

"Watch your words," Viceroy Falco hissed. Turning on his heel, tugging his mask back on, he paused as if regaining his composure. "If I didn't know better, you were accusing me of being a thief, Dante."

"Don't fool yourself, Falco." I didn't fear the monster standing before me, my eyes hitting his own with knowing supremacy. "If I wanted, I could end your life here. We both know you've stolen enough from me, but you will not have this."

"A lot of talk for a daemon who has fought one tiny battle and has yet to drink human blood." Gripping his sword, he finished his warning for me, "I slayed armies of men before your conception. A day will come, and I *will* take what's rightfully mine."

"And *I* will be there to watch you fail." I watched him march away, the sway of his fourteen-knot braid reflecting his position as a Viceroy.

"The scorned lover look doesn't suit you, my dear prince." Laughter rolled from him as he vanished down the hall.

I glared at my braid laying across my shoulder; sixteen knots marked me a prince of Glensdale, one of three kingdoms in Grandemere. Only Kings held eighteen knots and Queens seventeen. From there, the caste system continued, ending with the braidless servants and the bald shaven heads of slaves. Cutting one's braid was distasteful, a sinful way of disrespecting your status and birthright, whether you served *The House, The Court,* or even *The Tower* and *The Church.* It had been this way for a long time among humans and daemons.

I will not become one of them. I will not become the Blood Prince they expect me to be.

Tucking the dagger into my white leather tunic, I gripped the cold marble railing of the balcony. Looking down, it was two-stories high. Snow lay heavy across the ground and topiary. Winter was at its peak, the days more dark than light and the icy air a reminder of the harsh desires held by *The House.* With little effort, I hoisted myself over the railing, falling through the freezing bite of the wind. Landing in silence, I peered at the lights and shadows from the nearby ballroom. A great weight was lifting, and with no remorse, I surged into the forest, leaving nothing but the shattered mask of a Prince in the snow.

Chapter 2

The Old Farmer

Deafened by my thoughts, I sat there on the wet boulder for hours. The ancient mountain forest encased me, tall and dark, the embodiment of solitude. Flurries started to fall, and I lost sight of the glow from the city braziers. I traveled far beyond the territory of *The House*, well into the sacred grounds of the Old Farmer, a forbidden place. Rumors about the old man say he would kill a daemon for trespassing. Much to my amusement, one record written in the royal ledger states he is the only man to have ever faced Viceroy Falco and survive. In fact, they claim my father had rewarded the man this property to persuade him to lay down his sword and leave the war.

What does it matter if I die here? I would rather die by this man's hand than give that pleasure to Le Chien Enragé. *I have served my purpose, haven't I?*

I prevented more bloodeaters from being created, thus stopping the source of the Madness; I had fulfilled my one desire in life. Snow covered my head and back in a thick layer. One could have mistaken me for a statue. My heart was heavy with remorse wondering what my father's state would be with his last living heir gone. I stared at my pale hands bitterly. The older I got, the slower I would age, making it rare for my kind to die of old age. These near-immortal vessels had performed my taboo in the secrecy of nature's sanctuary. *Betrayal.* The steam from my breath cleared from my sight, and I glared at what I held.

These things belong in the past I've abandoned, forevermore. Au revoir, cher Prince.

My left hand held *La Dame d'Croc* with its blade melting the flurries landing on it. In my other hand, I gripped my sixteen-knot braid of chestnut brown hair. I had been proud of this rope and the number of knots it carried, not realizing I would have to sacrifice who I was to keep it. My status on the social pyramid had fallen to the bottom tier with one tug of the dagger. With this gone, my status was no longer above all others in *The House* or the land of Grandemere.

What do I want? Am I not free to choose my own path now?

I didn't regret leaving my burdens behind to someone more willing. Without a single knot to elevate my status, these responsibilities were forbidden to me. Nothing more than a braidless servant. I was no longer a worthy citizen without the care of a *keeper* or *master*. Common citizens and the lower class held a dignified one- to three-knot braid. No one owned them, not like the shaven and hairless ones. Those above them with no braid were said to voluntarily devote their lives to a person, an assortment of maids, butlers, laborers, and even farmhands.

A keeper. Whom shall I serve to atone for my sins? I want to protect them from the darkness I drowned in for years. This person will become everything my life stands for, and strangely, the thought makes me happy. They need to be human, someone unaware of who I am, someone who can gain nothing from knowing my past. Where shall I find a person worthy?

"Aren't you cold?" A masculine voice took me from my thoughts as I maintained my glare on the dagger. "Are you lost?"

I willed my eyes to look in the direction of the concerned voice. He was a human boy and appeared to be the same age physically. Tufts of his blonde hair pushed out of his wool cap as he stared astonished at me. His blue eyes were bright with the innocence of his kindhearted nature. Behind him was a toboggan filled with kindling. Dropping the rope, he shuffled to pull his hands free of his thick mittens and struggled to take his coat off. Looking down, I'd forgotten I was wearing nothing more than my brown leather capris, a horridly thin white blouse, and a white leather waistcoat. I smiled. *Yes, this boy would be a worthy keeper, no?*

"I'm not cold." My response confused the boy, his cheeks and nose red from the frigid night air. "Isn't it awfully late for you to be out here? Dangerous to be all by yourself? I didn't gather enough wood, so Grandpa Paul sent me out for more. He says his old bones don't handle the cold well these days and I need to be more aware of what I'm doing, er, not doing in this case." He fought to close his coat, his numb fingers struggling to hold the buttons. "I was on my way back. If you want to come, there's a fire waiting. Besides, aren't you freezing?"

"A fire sounds inviting. I can help you collect more wood and earn my keep to stay until daybreak." Tightening my grip on the dagger and my braid, I gave them one last sorrowful look before dropping them at the base of the old rock. "Your Grandpa wouldn't be the one they call Old Farmer, is he?"

"Some traders call him that." I brushed his hands to the side and fixed his coat, closing it again as he continued, cheeks glowing, "They tell me Grandpa's been here since they were kids, and no one dares to mess with him, not even the daemons. I don't know why, but no one will tell me the

7

story of how he ended up here. There's nothing out here, but I know it has to do with the war and the scars." I finished the last button and we froze, staring into each other's eyes. "You, you have unusual eyes..." he muttered, abandoning his anxious chatter.

"As do you." Looking away, he pulled his mittens back on and I grabbed the toboggan, waiting for him. "I suppose I'll ask your Grandpa to teach me to become a farmer. You think he'd take me on as an apprentice? I've always wanted to learn how to grow things and live off the land. It seems like a peaceful life."

"Oh, he'd like that very much. He tries to teach me, but it doesn't interest me. I have other plans." His excitement was comforting, but he looked back at the snow-covered boulder where he'd found me. "Don't you want to grab your things?"

"No." Sighing, I motioned for him to lead the way. "If I ever need them, I can find them here."

"I don't know, a lot of people get lost out here." Using his mittens, he did his best to warm up his nose and cheeks. Steam rolling over his face did nothing to dim the brilliance of his blue eyes. "My name's John Thompson. What's yours?"

"Dante Traî– Just Dante." Grabbing branches at my feet, I followed him through the labyrinth of trees by the yellow flicker of his lantern. "John, what happened to your parents?"

"I was too young to remember much. A man in black with hair white as snow came one night. They say he attacked my parents like a rapid dog, and well, the Madness took them. I'd crawled under a bed, closed my eyes, and covered my ears. I don't know how long I hid there, but by the time Grandpa pulled me out..." John's words fell away, his shoulders slumping.

How far does your malice reach, Viceroy Falco?

"I'm sorry. I didn't mean to bring up sour memories for you, John."

"Grandpa is mad at me, Dante." It was a curious thing for someone to say to a stranger, but then again, in his eyes, I was just another eighteen-year-old boy. Perhaps he'd longed for a friend of the same age for some time before I came along. "I feel us meeting tonight was fate. That we were meant to be here, you and I, for some greater cause."

"Fate." *How can I confess I feel the same?* "I'm sure with this much wood your grandfather will forgive your misjudgment." He paused in his steps and with those soulful eyes, I found my cheeks hot and my heart aflutter. "What's wrong?"

"It has nothing to do with the kindling." He gave me a grave look, his brow furrowed as he spoke, "He's upset that I want to become a priest."

I smiled. Never had I met someone so young so sure of his chosen path as John. His tone was strong, his decision an unmovable mountain. I couldn't say if he knew how dangerous it was to be part of *The Church.* Many thought the life of a priest or nun to be suicide. Their mission was to cleanse the world of the Madness, to fight for cures and better practices for bloodeaters. We stood there in the snow, exchanging stern glares. My decision was final. If this eighteen-year-old boy could choose a reckless path, I could decide on my own destiny.

I shall devote my life to this future priest, John. He shall be my keeper.

"The title of priest fits you well, John. You're kind and charitable in every sense." He held amazing power in his eyes. "It's a good path to follow. I wish you the best of luck."

"It feels right." He huffed and steam blocked his face as he turned away.

It wasn't much farther down the hillside before the glow of a cottage peaked between the shadows of the trees. We came out into a clearing and the smell of a fire greeted my nose. Obedient, I followed John to the side of the cottage. He continued talking about his plans of being a priest, a means of changing the world for the better. I stacked the branches onto the understocked pile listening to him. We finished and it was time to face the Old Farmer. I shadowed John onto the porch where we stomped the snow from our feet. Opening the door, the heat inside welcoming, but the stare from the old man wiped the smile off my face.

The Old Farmer sat in a rocking chair, facing the fire gnawing on his pipe. There was no fooling the educated, the old man knew I was a daemon, unlike the naïve John. Though he shared similar blue eyes, they lacked the glow of his grandson's own. A scar snaked out from behind his left ear, across the side of his neck and disappeared under his long white beard. Rubbing his crooked nose, he assessed my appearance as John explained how he found me. I doubt he cared for anything the boy had to say.

I kept silent, waiting for the veteran warrior to reveal what sort of man he was. He held out a hand, inviting John and I to sit. Stroking his beard, staring me down, he gathered his thoughts. Broad-shouldered and gnarled, this man had fought in the war. Judging by the braid swaying behind the chair, he sat far higher in the caste system than I expected. Twelve white knots marked him a Lord Knight, a general of a legion which meant he led five to six thousand men at one time, *impressive*. If he had been a farmer, there would have only been one knot, never more, never less. Neither of us were what we appeared to be. Our eyes met. He knew I was aware of his rank. *Which of us has the advantage now? Are we both looking for an escape from society?* Glancing to John and back to Paul, the question weighing on my mind left my chest aching.

Will he allow me to follow in John's footsteps?

Taking one last puff of his pipe, billowing the pungent smoke into the cabin, he spoke in a deep throaty tone, "What brings you this far south?"

"I wish to be a farmer." My words were solid. I wanted my resolve to carry the same impact John's had hours before.

"A farmer?" Paul snorted as he glared at the fire, anger seeping into his voice, "Why didn't you ask someone back home to teach you?"

"None will relinquish their pride to lower themselves to get their hands dirty. They prefer to be served on silver platters. I'm sure you're aware of that fact." I wanted to make it clear we both knew who we were without dragging John into the middle. "John mentioned you were the best, and the only one who has ever tamed these woods."

Another grunt escaped the old man. Teeth clacked on his pipe and short frustrated puffs came from his mouth as the fire reflected in his eyes. The silence was painful awaiting his judgment. Not only had I misled his grandson, but we spoke in front of him in a shielding manner, keeping the secrets of daemon and Lord Knight in the dark. John had been sheltered, knowing little of what danger sat next to him.

It doesn't matter if he casts me out. I've decided to watch over John and will do so from the shadows if I must.

John's left leg rocked back and forth underneath the table, and he bit his bottom lip. It was clear he was questioning if he'd been wrong to bring me here. I stood up. There wasn't any point in punishing John for the principles he displayed. These actions were done in support of the fate he had chosen to become a priest. The wooden chair screeched as I pushed it away and started for the door.

Let this be my first act in serving John. He shouldn't be punished for my deceit.

"Wait." I froze at the sound of the old man's bellow. "Are you not one of them?"

I looked over at John's questioning blue eyes. He didn't know to distinguish my maroon eyes as a sign of a *daemon*.

Taking a deep breath, I turned and faced his grandfather's piercing glare. "Yes. I am one of *them*." He intentionally avoided the word, so I followed his lead.

The Old Farmer remained silent. John furrowed his brow and he stared in pure confusion back and forth between us. It didn't ease the pressure on my soul. John's eyes widened; he had put some of the pieces together. His body tightened, making him stand. The chair behind him knocked over in a painful clatter.

"I apologize for misleading you." Our eyes locked, and he gave my own a deeper evaluation.

"Daemon," he whispered, paling.

"I didn't aim to trick you, John. I'm sorry. I'll leave." I turned. I had squandered my chance to do something good. *Dammit...*

"Dante." I stopped. John gripped my wrist, sending my heart racing. "You want to be a farmer? Did you mean it? Was that why you came here?"

The heat from his touch was exhilarating. Emotions stirred in my heart and I swallowed them down, "Yes, I want to be here." The Old Farmer's face softened, and I caught myself smiling, "I wish to live out my days away from society. To be proud of a day's work, happy for the blisters on my hands."

"Please, sit. I'm making my decision." I did as Paul commanded, picking up John's chair before sitting in my own. "John wants to join *The Church*, you know. You'll be living here with only me for quite some time."

"I understand, but you are the one who will teach me to be a farmer while he's away being a priest, no?" He smirked at his grandson, amused at the situation as I continued, "I think it suits him. He's kindhearted and charitable in his actions."

"Let's be honest, Dante. I won't live long enough to see him come home from his studies. He'll be heading south to Captiva City soon and devote his life to *The Church* for seven or more years." Stroking his beard again, he struggled pass the rattle in his voice caused by the wartime scar on his neck. "I will need you to tend to the farm while he is away. Someone will need to maintain this place so he can return home. After that, he'll be far too busy once he starts his own clergy and maintaining his flock. Priest don't marry. They take an oath of celibacy, forfeiting love for man or woman in exchange for their love to the cause for peace. Would you be able to look after him when I leave this world?"

John sat silently, holding his breath while waiting for my answer.

"I understand." A great weight lifted from my chest. I'd found a new home and a new purpose. "It would be an honor to serve John in your absence. Thank you for accepting my request."

A rushed exhale left John's lips, a smile stretching across his face. "Welcome to the family."

"Know this, Dante." Paul pulled the pipe from his lips, leaning forward in his chair. "I never thought I would meet the Prince of the same kingdom who once tried to strike me down." My eyes fell on the ragged scar, realizing it was a failed assassination. "But Falco is too prideful to share his failures with royalty, I imagine."

My eyes widened. My destiny had dealt me an unusual hand. "I see. You are the Lord Knight Paul who overtook Falco. Not once, but twice."

"Wait? Prince? Lord Knight?" Red-faced, John realized how far removed he had been in the conversation. "What's going on?"

Paul's throat rattled with a broken laugh and a sparkle came to his eyes. "So, my name even reached you, I see. My dear grandson, I have given up on the life of a Lord Knight shortly after you were born. Ah, and the man you have brought into our home, well that's Dante's choice to tell you some day."

"No wonder no one comes here," groaned John, baffled by the old man. "I knew you had a rather big braid for a farmer, just thought you were a Count who had lost all his money or something."

"That's eleven knots, John," snorted Paul, smoke boiling out of his lips and nose. "One shy of my status."

Leaving my chair, I knelt before the old man. "Let me have the honor to study under you, Lord Knight Paul, as your apprentice. If I am to protect John, let it be by your guidance that I achieve this. I will protect his home, and with your mentorship, protect his life in the same fashion you carried your blade."

"You know how to use a sword and never taught me?" As he leaned over the table, John's chair fell behind him once more. "Grandfather, how many secrets do you keep from me still?"

"Then, I will allow John to be your keeper." Paul dismissed his grandson's outburst.

Looking over my shoulder, I waited for John's approval. "Agreed?"

"Fine." Pulling himself off the table, he stormed for one of the adjacent doors and slammed it.

"Will he be okay after all this?" I sighed, my purpose found and secured. "I feel guilty about this..."

"Go grab more wood for the fire," Paul grumbled, rocking his chair and staring back at the flames dwindling in the hearth. "He'll learn soon enough this world is full of dark secrets."

The sun peeked through the trees. There was no mistaking the fact Paul knew my name the moment I walked through his door. It wasn't a child's request to run away from home, but a daemon who wished to escape the violent ways of *The House*. If John still wanted to return to this place, I would become his Sword and Shield in order to protect him from the northern tyrants of Glensdale, especially Falco. Even if it cost me my life, to be a guardian spirit for a human was our first purpose according to the old folktales. My thoughts reeled as I took off the white leather tunic and rolled up my sleeves. Work allowed me time to reflect on the world I left behind.

Daemons were different yet similar to humans in a few ways. Our physical tells were the maroon eyes and pale skin. Limitless stamina and greater strength allowed us to carry more weight further, and during war, we could fight longer with more power behind our sword strikes. We were immortal besides the threat of the Madness or death by another's hand. Our resistance to illness and disease made us seem indestructible, though we couldn't conceive children as easily as humans, so population was slow growing if at all.

The House was a faction of daemons who broke away from the core foundation called *The Court*. Unlike their relatives, members of *The House* practiced the forbidden art of eating blood of humans, earning them the nickname *bloodeaters*. We were protectors according to the tales, but there were others who desired to rule. The founders of *The House* discovered a means to gain power and took over substantial portions of Grandemere. Civil war broke out and it took decades of years before the territories were established. In fact, they still push at one another trying to claim territory when they can.

The Tower, the human monarchy, allied with *The Court* to overturn *The House*, but failed. Bloodeaters outlived the average daemon by threefold. Many of the warriors and knights fighting the veterans of *The House* were new generations. They were children facing the same bloodthirsty tyrants their great grandfathers had failed to subdue. Faster, stronger, and worse off, being addicted to the taste of blood only gave them power beyond the peacekeepers or citizens of *The Court*.

The Madness plaguing the world comprised of a terrible

hunger and it didn't matter if they were devouring the dead or living. Humans either died within days of being bitten or worse, suffered from fits of madness. It was a plague taking down entire units when the war first started. Daemons serving *The Court* suffered with the illness too. Maddening cravings sent most begging for an end by their fellow soldier's sword.

The Church vowed to find cures, despite devotion to being a neutral entity with no territory. It was an injustice in their eyes. The illness the devils from *The House* plagued the world with needed to be stopped, at all costs. The only known cure was the black arts from which *The House* had started the curse itself. As far as anyone knew, this was a practice only usable by a bloodeater or with the use of a sacred blade. As to how one would cast a cure or spell to counter the Madness, the secret was lost to the world centuries ago. The only magic known was the ancient chant said to absorb the curse into the daemon's body, taking in the corruption into themselves and cleansing it with the magic given from the first feeding. It was normal for noblemen in Glensdale to have slaves who never experienced the Madness their whole lifetime, despite daily feedings.

Grabbing the toboggan rope, I aimed for the woods nearby. A smile was written on my face and I was left with a glorious thought: *My actions tonight are the beginning of ending a war, a disease, and maybe, reuniting the kingdoms. Today, I become a stepping stone to a better future where rabid dogs no longer feed upon the mothers and fathers of children. Your world is ending, Falco.*

CHAPTER 3

Learning to Farm

Over the next several weeks, the old man and John gave me a crash course on maintaining the farm. During the winter, the focus was around keeping the cold out and the heat in. All the preparations happened during harvest time when the food was packed into the cellar, the field stripped to aid melting snow in spring, hay used to provide insulation for chickens, not to mention stockpiling the woodpile. Granted, John had gone lazy on this matter, and we found ourselves in the snow, chopping down ice-covered saplings and having to dry them out beside the hearth.

At night, I spent my days helping John learn to read and write. It was the one thing Old Farmer Paul couldn't teach him, despite his position as a Lord Knight. If John wanted to be a priest, he needed to master these skills before he dared step foot in Captiva City and walk through the Abbey doors. It wasn't that the old man couldn't read and write, but teaching it had been something he failed to do time and time again with John. Which of the two would grow too frustrated with the other first and derail their efforts was hard to say.

Watching them all this time, I saw that they both had the same stubborn glare when they refused to speak further on any of the disagreements that unfolded between them far too often. I had found myself using my "gift of diplomacy" just to get them to part their lips to answer me, dancing between them, playing the peacekeeper.

Spring came and the arguments quelled. Perhaps being trapped indoors had been part of the issue after all. The snow had barely melted, the field brown and muddy with ice, when the Old Farmer insisted we break it up.

"It's half-frozen." John crossed his arms, the exchange of glares sharp enough to cut the air itself. "I'm not going to break my back over it."

The Old Farmer's eyes danced between us as he gnawed on his pipe, mulling over the thoughts in his mind. I'd learned over the winter this never boded well for John.

"Look," John's arms unfolded, and his tone softened. "I'm going to check the meadow—see if it's thawed out yet. We both know you wanted some of the wild carrots and Indian tobacco for the garden this year."

I lifted an eyebrow, "Are we learning to compromise?"

John's face flushed; he had been caught stealing my method of peace-keeping during the winter. "It just works out best for everyone." He spun on his heel, leaving me with his back and hiding his face. "I'll grab the bucket and be back with whatever I find."

We disappeared and the weight of being alone with the old man hit me. During the snow and blizzards, I'd been busy entertaining and learning more about John. Looking up at the old blue eyes, a sobering realization hit me. My future would be with him, not John. Swallowing, I waited in silence, unsure what to say or do.

"He likes you." A billow of smoke poured out of the Old Farmer's lips as he sighed, sitting on the edge of the porch.

"I like him t..." I paused, catching the look in his eyes as the smoke cleared between us. "He's going to make a fine priest."

Is he mad? He can't mean...

"Take the hoe there." We both evaded the topic. Paul gestured to the tool John had left leaning on the post. "Start breaking it up."

"But I thought it was half frozen?" I grabbed the hoe, walking to the edge of where the mud hinted the start of the field's edge. Tapping it against the slush, the ground was frozen except for the top layer melted down by the sun. "Yup, it's still frozen."

"I said break it." The tone and glare from Paul made me flinch and he could see the question lingering in my mind. "You've got to build up the muscles before we can train the muscle."

My eyes widened. "Training, huh?"

He nodded, puffing on his pipe with short, impatient sucks.

"As you wish, Lord Knight."

Holding the hoe, I peered down at the frozen mud with a scowl. Blisters and callouses hinted their displeasure. I earned them chopping frozen saplings, and here I stood before a task John didn't even dare to attempt. With a heave, I brought the hoe down. The metal piece bounced off the ice, jarring my arms and shoulders. I let go of the hoe in alarm, pumping my fist to fight the numbness the impact brought on. It was a horrible sensation, lasting far longer than I had expected.

"Pick it up." It was a command worthy of his title; Paul rose to his feet, adding to the authoritative presence. "If you hit a shield hard enough, it'll jar you like that. Get a worthy opponent and lock blades, it'll jar you again. That mud is your enemy, and you're John's shield. Don't let me see you drop that hoe again until it breaks."

My heart dropped, his words stabbing deep. I swallowed,

picking the hoe off the ground. The mud gained a new level of intimidation.

John's shield. No, I want to be his sword. I don't want to just take blows but deal them; I want to cut a path for John to walk so he can move forward with his dream.

Gripping the hoe tight, I brought it down hard. It bounced off once more, jarring vibrations threatened to rip the hoe free, and I pulled it back to me. With another motion, I swung it back around and leaned into the strike. The hoe stuck and I froze, surprised.

"There you go." The Old Farmer sat down, pleased with my response to his words. "You gotta put your weight in there. If you've been jarred, you put that energy back into the next swing. You've got good instincts, Prince..."

Meeting eyes, the old man and I paled.

"Don't," I whispered. *I've kept it quiet, avoided it at every turn during the winter. Don't you dare slip up now, old man. We both know if John figures it out, who I really am, our plans to live out our days here lost to the world will be over, or at least for me.*

Sighing, he confessed, "It's hard, ya know. Being my age, knowing my place from your place, but here we are, a Lord Knight teaching a Prince to be a farmer."

There was a humor about it, and we both couldn't keep the smiles from creeping between us.

"Just don't tell John."

"No, it's your place to tell John," he added before motioning for me to continue. "He might have figured it out, but he'll want to hear it from the horse's mouth."

I tugged the hoe free and shifted my stance, avoiding the subject. If breaking the frozen ground called for my weight to be thrown, then so be it. Again, I brought it down, yet this time I broke the ground. A tug toward me, and I flipped a patch. Another strike and again the jarring rung into my elbows and sent my muscles aching. Numb fingers clung to the wood. Taking in his words, I repurposed the energy and added to my next swing. The hoe struck closer to the already broken ground. It gave way, sinking deeper. My body was on fire with the feat of only a few strikes. Inhaling deep, I took in the aroma of dirt filling the air, a satisfying scent that brought proof of the work unfolding. I found my enemies' weakness, but aiming close to the last strike would prove hard with numbing hands, wrecked joints, and burning muscles.

I reached from one end of the field to the other, a single rupture of mud between me and the porch where the Old Farmer sat, silent. Sweat dripped from my chin and my body was sore. *No wonder John refused.* Panting, I took a moment to catch my breath and pulled off my shirt. The cool air of early spring gave me the reprieve I hoped it would bring. Burning muscles fought the cold shiver on my skin, sending goose-bumps across my pale body. Snorting as I saw I was white as the snow dabbling the ground, I thought my flushed arms from my efforts only added to my pitiful appearance.

Looking to the sky, I saw that noon had passed me by, but I wanted to keep working. I broke ground on the second line. The jarring dulled, or I accepted it. My strikes were more consistent, though as I crept closer to the porch, my misses were increasing. Frustrated with my results, I pivoted and began the third row. Quicker now, my strikes tightened closer once more. I hit the end and turned again, coming back toward the house in the fading light. A whip-poor-will chirped in the woods as I landed the hoe on the last strike. I realized it had grown dark, a lamp lit there on the porch between Paul and John.

My face reddened deeper on top of the flushed exhaustion. "W-when did you get back?"

"Two rows ago," John answered, his eyes on the field. "I could have helped you, Dante."

My eyes skirted to the old man who said nothing. "I've

never swung a hoe before, so I figured it was good to start."

"You lie." John's eye shot up, catching my own in their fiery blue gaze. "No one swings like that on their first try. You've done similar work."

Slumping my shoulders, I sat down on the porch next to him, staring at the field. "You're right. I've mucked my share of horse stalls and cleaned out some pretty big hearths."

"He's no stranger to hard work, John." The old man stood, pausing at the door. "I'll make supper. You rest and get some water in you, Dante." And the door shut.

Silence fell between us. Afraid to peer at John, I tried to pull myself to my feet only for the world to spin and my balance waver. John's hand gripped my upper arm, and I hissed, the muscles sore and burning under the heat of his grip. He eased me down, and the worry written on his face swept my breath away. Before words could be exchanged, he rushed away, around the corner of the porch where the squeak of the water pump echoed in the dark of night. Leaning forward, I cupped my face into my hands, fighting with my body and my heart. I could still feel the heat of his fingers on my arm and it sent my stomach fluttering.

I'm just tired. So much has happened, and I didn't stop for water or food. It's just exhaustion... isn't it?

"Here. Drink." John sat next to me with a dented metal cup and bucket of fresh water. "Next time, at least drink something after running a row. That's what I do."

Nodding, I gulped down one cup full, then another. "I've never been so thirsty in all my life."

John laughed, "You work that hard in the summer, and you'll find today not so bad. It's good to hydrate, especially a guy with little muscle like you."

Another slurping of water and I mocked him, "So you noticed I wasn't much of a hard worker?"

"How could I not?" His eyebrows rose high, smirking.

"You're so pale. I thought a ghost was breaking the field."

We both laughed. "I can't argue on that. That was my thought when I took my shirt off."

"Tomorrow I will help you." John stood, offering a hand to help me to my feet.

"No." I ignored the extended hand, standing with renewed vigor. "You need to be prepping for joining *The Church*. Let me take care of things, learn and do for myself."

"You're going to kill yourself being this stubborn." His tone soured.

"I could say the same for you and your grandfather," I snorted, reaching the front door. "I may look fragile, pale and soft even, but remember, I'm not human John. I'm not the same as you."

Pushing through the doorway, I evaded him.

All I can ever be is your sword, your shield, and maybe, if I'm lucky, you'll come home and ask me to be your wall.

Sitting at the dinner table, I scowled. My body throbbed, and even the hairs across my arm seemed to scream in pain. To beat across frozen mud had been more taxing than surviving a day out on the battlefield. I had only done that once in my short-lived reign as Prince. I had nearly taken an arrow to the chest, but a masked warrior cut it from the sky. My horse had shied away from the shattered arrow, and by the time I looked back, the horse and warrior vanished like phantoms. While I was shaking my head free of the memory, John had come in, lugging the bucket of water.

He sat it beside me, slamming a cup full of water in front of me, "Drink."

"I won't have any room left for dinner if I do," I retorted.

His face reddened, "You have an answer for everything, don't you?"

Shrugging, I ran my hand over my head and paused where I cut my braid.

"How many knots did you have?" John's words were barely audible as he muttered across the table, glaring at me.

"I don't remember." *Not this again...*

"Liar." His forehead creased. "Why don't you just grow it back?"

"I suppose I could." There was no hiding the fact I wouldn't and couldn't tell him. *16 knots. The braid of a Prince. Cut off to a servant's level. Treason by many standards.* "But I don't know if I deserve to have it back."

"Grow it back." John's tone snapped me from my exhausted daze.

"Is that an order from my keeper?" I mused.

"It's my only order. Grow it back by the time I come home as a priest." His chair screeched as he stood. "I'll eat in the morning," and his door slammed shut.

"How selfish," I muttered at the shut door.

"Is it?" Paul dropped a bowl of stew in front of me. "The same could be said about your own actions and secrets, Dante."

Groaning, I relented to silence, unwilling to reveal how right he was on the matter. Unwilling to talk, I leaned over the bowl and shoveled the food into my mouth. My body felt starved, the energy I took in still miles from what I spent out in the field. Seeing the bottom of the bowl lasted only seconds before the old man scooped another helping into it. I looked up at him and he smirked, a softness in his eyes I had only seen him give John.

"But..." I wanted it, the potatoes and carrots with hunks of meat.

"But—nothing," he retorted. "Eat. I need you to keep your energy high and building muscle fast." He placed the pot on the stove and eased into a chair with his own bowl. "I want to be able to train you properly, but we're on borrowed time. Claymores are heavy, unlike that hoe. You think the jarring on frozen mud bad, then you haven't felt nothing until your claymore hits a sturdy shield in the wrong spot."

"R-right." I scooped a few bites up and pondered on the matter. "Why the claymore?"

"It doesn't just cleave through things; it can take off limbs."

My stomach turned. I remembered being in a medical tent for bloodeaters. Every severe injury was a case of missing or mangled limbs. "I see. It's the best weapon against the opponent you faced."

"Falco has a scar," the old man said. I paled, my mind seeing his naked form and remembering the way he snarled when I asked about the purple line stretching across his ribs on the right and wrapping down toward his lower back. "Did you know I landed a nearly fatal wound on the Viceroy?"

"That was you?" Dropping my spoon, I locked eyes with cheeks red, a sobering expression on my face. "He never told anyone what happened."

"You've seen it?" Paul's frown deepened and I could feel the old man peering into my soul as if he could see my regrets. "He's manipulative. You're not the only one he's spun into his web of lies. If I had known..."

Shaking my head, I raised a hand. "I was young and blind. Looking back, I should've seen it or accepted what I knew at heart. Let's just not talk about how or why I know of the scar."

"And what do you intend to do with him?" The Old Farmer pointed a spoon at John's door.

"Nothing." My voice was low, weak as my heart ached. "He will be a priest, taking a vow of celibacy. I have no intentions of falling in love with your grandson..."

The spoon slammed on the table, jerking my eyes back up. "Are you deaf, boy?"

I could hear his words from earlier echo through my mind: *He likes you.*

Standing, I leaned over the table, my eyes on his as I whispered my answer, "You want me to be his shield. I want to be his sword. When John leaves this place, I will be just that. Nothing more, nothing less. His mind will be filled with teachings and learning of a world far greater than me or this farm. I am a tool for him and him alone, left behind as a parting gift by his grandfather to ensure he succeeds with his life intact."

The old man's face twisted, and he nodded.

CHAPTER 4

John is Leaving

I managed to break the rest of the field in a week, only to be told to break it again, twice over. What once were sore muscles hardened and grew, swelling and making the skin on my back and arms taut and strange to me. As I came to the end of the third pass, my skin was no longer pale, but peachy and red, a constant tanning and sunburnt state. The last of the ice and snow melted away, insects and small creatures making themselves known, including the occasional house mouse. I had no idea how lively the dense forest could be, but it was far from feeling isolated like during winter when so much life stayed hidden, warm, and hibernating. The old man put us back on the field, demanding we make up for lost time. John muttered curses under his breath as he sprinkled seed in the row I furrowed out.

"That's not how a priest should talk, now is it?" I teased, following on his heels as I kicked the dirt in and slapped water from my bucket over freshly-planted seed.

"I'm not a priest... yet," he huffed, reaching the end of the line. "Let's do this again. So, sixteen to eighteen knots in the

27

braid is royalty?"

"If you phrase it that way, you should include those with fifteen knots." Another slosh of water and I paused, musing over the difficulty this brought him. "I can't believe this is so hard for you to remember."

He waved a hand at me as if my words were a swarm of gnats before starting down the next row. "Fifteen knots means they're a subfamily, right?"

"That's right. They are often guardians and city guards. More accurately, cousins to the Princes and Princesses." I emptied my bucket and circled back to the pump. As I passed John mid-field, I quizzed him further. "And what do twelve to fourteen knots have in common?"

"Let's see," He paused, wiping sweat from his forehead with a forearm while he marched back to where I left off. "That's Lord Knights like grandpa, Dukes, and then Viceroys at fourteen knots. They all have authority in the army or control territories. Viceroys often manage a town or city."

"Good!" I finished watering the row and joined John on the next. "Keep going. You're doing better."

"Uh, nine to eleven knots, that's Lords, Bishops, and Counts." He started dropping seed again. "They are often in charge of businesses or serve the high tiers in some way. Bishops often manage entire territories on behalf of *The Church* and are in charge of leading several priests and their flocks. After that, anyone who owns property or have some sort of connection to the above tiers can wear eight knots. Then seven knots is strictly for priests." Pausing, he smirked. "I wonder which of us will have the longer braid when I get back?"

I paled, the idea of it making me overshoot water by a longshot. John glared at me, and I refused to meet his gaze. Tightening my grip on the bucket, I sloshed the water on the intended spot, unwilling to react.

Does he know? How many times do I have to evade this?

"It was an order." His tone darkened and it was enough to make me lock eyes.

"I know," I replied weakly.

"Six knots," he broke his stare, cheeks red. "Acolytes?"

Sighing, I sat the bucket down and stretched, waiting for him to gain a bigger lead. "Yes. You'll be changing your three knots in for six if you are accepted." My eyes glared at the golden tail of hair falling between his bare shoulder blades. He knotted it three rows before letting a long streak cascade down like a ponytail to midway down his spine. "Here's a good question that might be asked of you. Why are you worthy of three knots when a farmer traditionally has one?"

"We don't work on someone's land." His jaw twitched as he pivoted and started down the next row, now planting the dried bulbs from his satchel. "We own land, we don't borrow money, and we trade in surplus or sell it. Two knots if we didn't sell, one knot if we worked on someone else's farm."

"That's right. What defines upper class?" My muscles burning, I returned to the task at hand. "What's the difference between four and five knots?"

"Four knots are for those who can afford to live in the city and often they work for those with five knots. Traditionally shop owners have five or eight knots, whereas four and below might have a tent or stall in the streets." He crept along the line, his back kept to me. "What if it takes me longer?"

"To learn this?" I kicked down the last of the dirt over the tiny seeds, sloshing the last of the water. "I think you've got it down."

"I mean the time it will take me to become a priest." He kept going, not missing a beat as he spoke in a hard tone. "It's supposed to take seven years, but..."

Heading to the pump, I glanced over my shoulder and stole a peek at the scowl on his face. "I'm not going anywhere. You're my keeper. My orders are to stay here, keep the farm in working order, and tend to your grandpa's needs."

"Don't let him hurt you." John's face flushed, but he spun down the next row, his golden tail of hair flashing like metal in the sunlight. "He's training you to fight his way, isn't he?"

"No, not yet." I started pumping the water once more, the whine and gurgle keeping the edge off the silence. "You know, he may change his mind; I was the one who asked him."

John's hand searched the satchel but came up empty-handed. "That's the last of it."

"Take a break. I'll finish." Before I could finish at the pump, John was through the door of the house.

He's going to press the old man about teaching him how to use the sword again.

Slumping my shoulders, I finished covering the bulbs and watering the rows. Circling back, I did one more round for good measure, ignoring the shouting match unfolding inside the cabin. I had nearly finished when John shot out the door. Pausing, I watched him march off and lost him in the scores of tree trunks. After a minute or two, the old man came out on the porch, leaning a shoulder on a post as he lit his pipe. Hanging up the bucket, I came to attention in front of him, eyebrows high.

"Don't you look at me like that." His teeth chattered against the pipe. "Grab the scythe and go mulch out some grass for the piglets."

"When did we get piglets?" I marveled.

"Doesn't matter. Now go mulch." With that, he turned and dove back into the house.

It took a moment for me to sort through the tool shed to find where John tossed it. Picking the scythe up, I hadn't realized how much it weighed and the overall awkward feel of the tool. Marching out to the edge of the clearing, I stopped where John mulched a chunk out for the chickens the day before. It wasn't a task I had performed yet. Mimicking how

I thought John held the contraption, I attempted a swing, failing miserably. Scoffing, I adjusted and tried again, barely doing anything but laying the grass flat.

"You look pitiful," John laughed from where he leaned against a tree.

"How long were you going to just watch me struggle?" Furrowing my brow, I ignored him and tried again, failing. "You made this look so easy."

"Because it is. You're trying too hard." Pulling himself off the tree, he continued, "You're holding the snath all wrong."

"The what?" I stood up and found John practically on top of me, gripping my right wrist and shoving my hand on the handle again.

"Take this hand and grab the lower nib on the snath, then this hand on the upper nib." I regretted all the times I mused over his frustrations in our studies as I found myself the student. "Straddle your legs."

"Like this?" I shifted my stance.

"No, more like…" He was tapping my feet, kneeing my legs, and my face flushed. "Good, that's better. Now put the heel down."

"Heel?" Swallowing, I couldn't ignore the beating of my heart and the heat rising in my face. *What's wrong with me?*

"The blade, Dante." John's face was focused on the tool and task at hand. "There," he took a step back. "Now give it a sweep." I started to twist back but found him up against my back, like a puppeteer moving a doll. "No, not like that. You'll wrench your back out."

His hands cupped my own. The speed in which he took control and how easily I allowed it startled me, my beating heart aching in my chest. His arms matched my own in length with my elbows nestled in his. The heat of his body, sweaty against my bare back, stirred emotions I had been denying existed.

He likes you... I like him... echoes from months ago made my heart ache.

I tried to step away, but his knee caught mine, and we leaned forward together. My breath caught, his body dominating my own as we moved our hips and arms one way, sweeping the scythe with ease to the other side. *If it wasn't for the tool in our hands, I would have thought...*

"Like this," his voice was soft and sultry as it rolled over my shoulder. "You rotate the hips and sweep your arms. Just bring the scythe with your arms. See."

I nodded and he broke away from me, sending chills across my body. "Like this?"

"Perfect. Just two or three more should be enough." He grabbed up the mulch we had cut as one and headed for the pig pen. "They don't need much."

"Right." I finished the sweeps and leaned on the scythe, covering my mouth.

I know better. Haven't I learned nothing good comes from following my heart? He's becoming a priest, and I'm a runaway Prince. Our worlds should never cross paths like this. I didn't come here for love; I came here to live. Is the old man right, that John...?

"Dante?" John's voice brought my gaze to him, and he creased his forehead, still wearing the scowl from before. "That's it. You're done for the day." He tossed the last of the mulch in the pig pen. "Come on. No more." He ripped the scythe from my hands and tossed it to the ground. "I've got a parting gift for you."

Again, the swelling ache ripped across my soul as he gripped my wrist and tugged me along. My feet followed, my mind and heart in battle and unable to deny him anything. We passed the water pump and faded into the forest. Soon the uphill climb and increasing boulders forced John to let go, though the warmth of it lingered with a haunting want I hadn't ever known even with Falco. Despair weighed down on me, watching the fluttering of that golden braid.

I'm not supposed to feel this way. He will be swearing celibacy. I can't be the reason he abandons that dream.

John looked over his shoulder, smirking. I frowned, and his smile faltered. The moment made my chest ache, I had hurt him in that instance, but he couldn't possibly understand. He waved me ahead and pointed toward the sound of rushing water. There, pooled in a circle of boulders, was a spot perfect for bathing.

"I found it when I had to fix the pump's waterline." He sat on the boulder, watching my excitement. "Grandpa's not much of a bather, if you haven't noticed. That doesn't mean you have to be. Figured, with the way you dressed and looked, you'd want to know you had some place to scrub clean other than the water spout and rain barrels."

Abandoning all reason, I kicked off my shoes and dove in with a big splash. I surfaced, taking in a deep breath, feeling refreshed. The cool water eased the aching muscles and sunburnt skin. Laughing, it was a luxury I had thought no longer viable in this new way of living. John smiled, our eyes locking for a few seconds before his smile broke. He frowned, a sadness taking hold in those blue eyes before he sighed, leaving me alone. I cursed myself for even letting my emotions run away with me.

I took my time before making the walk back, shoes in hand, pants soaked as water dripped off me. The old man was on the porch in his chair. It didn't take long for the dread to hit me. Dropping my shoes, I rushed into the house, throwing open John's bedroom door. The bags and stack of books, all of it was gone. I spun back to the front door and glared at the old man.

"Why didn't you say something?" I hissed, anger seeping forward.

"Wasn't my place." He didn't bother to look at me, puffing on the pipe. "John said he had one last thing to teach you, the scythe. He did that and went on to do what he intended to do long before you showed up, Dante."

Dropping my head, I whispered, "He'll be back in seven years, right?"

"Only time will tell. If he takes longer, will you wait for him?" He gnawed on the pipe.

"We both know I will wait for him twice as long if that's what it takes." I punched the door frame and faded into the house, exhaustion and heartache eating me alive.

CHAPTER 5

The Lord Knight's Gift

Blood dripped from my busted knuckles. Panting, I scowled at the old man who stood far out of reach from the wooden claymore I carried. In his hand, he held a rapier, its blade and handguard glittering in the sunlight. He nicked me several times, lines painting my skin like red ribbons pinned on a tan curtain. Trying to catch my breath, I shoved the blunt tip into the ground and leaned on the hilt, cursing the lead that weighed it down. My braid stuck to my shoulder and neck, and I slung it back over my shoulder, annoyed that eleven knots didn't weigh down the same as my old sixteen knot braid.

"You can't take a break in battle!" he roared from where he stood, and I smirked.

"Good thing I'm just training with a stubborn old knight." I ran my palm down my face, flicking the sweat off to the side. "Summer time is hell for this."

"Pick it up." He took an offensive stance. "Once more."

Grunting, I heaved the claymore up with both hands, my muscles straining from its weight. It was twice as heavy as the real thing, but its intention was for building enough muscle to swing and move with greater speed. With a roar, I ran toward the old man, slicing across. He sidled out of striking radius and jabbed the rapier's point against my ribs. I spun, letting the blade slice as I swung around with greater momentum. The rapier's tip lost its aim as my body rolled along the blade; the old knight's blue eyes widened. Every muscle tightened, a rapier dropping at my feet and the knight on the ground was stunned. The wooden blade stopped shy of hitting him if he had been still standing. Despite the soreness, the exhaustion, the muscles in my arm held it still as the wind of its potential force waved over the Old Farmer. I panted, staring down at him, holding the dreaded anchor still, its shadow cast across him like a tree.

It took him a while to regain his wit, and he smiled, "You've figured it out."

Slowly, I dropped the wooden claymore's tip to the ground and leaned on it. I grabbed my side, the slice stinging to life as salty sweat crawled down and in. My hand came back bloody, and I grumbled, annoyed.

"You think this one needs stitches, old man?" Leaning down, I used the claymore for support and picked up the bejeweled rapier. "And please, don't drop this. You said you wanted to give it to John, right?"

Grabbing it from me, he used his pants to clean my blood from the blade. "I would, but I'd be happy if he would choose any of them."

"Did he know that you had an arsenal in the cellar?" I offered a hand, and after a short internal battle, he caved and took it.

"No," he grunted as I heaved him to his feet. "So, was that instinct or your head thinking?"

"Which part?" I pressed against my side, blood still seeping and my heart thumping hard against my chest. "I don't do much thinking when I'm exhausted like this."

"Instinctual fighters live longer." He motioned for me to head to the house. "It'll need stitches if it's bleeding like that, but I got to take a close look. Your blood's boiling after that strike. What you did there, rolling and redirecting the rapier so you could make a counterstrike, is good."

"It doesn't feel good." Snorting, I dragged the claymore behind me, abandoning it on the porch so I could lean on a post. "Plus, weren't you the one that told me that a claymore user had to be willing to take a hit to cleave a head?"

"Take a hit, cleave a head," he echoed, grabbing a scoop of water. "Now move your hand."

Sighing, I did so and was met with water slapping across the cut. I scoffed but remained unflinching as the old man leaned in, taking a closer look.

"Well?" It had been a few weeks since I let a gash this large be written across my skin, the pink and purple sunburnt scar on my arm a sour reminder. "Is it as bad as me catching the strike on my arm like last month?"

"You know," he laughed and digging into a tin, "it's just skin deep. Some ointment and a proper wrap should do the trick."

"Ointment. More like a wad of rotten vegetables that even the pigs won't eat." The cold, pungent mush landed on my side, and I scrunched my face in response. "So only skin deep. Is that significant? You seem rather pleased with that."

Another helping of the ointment slid across my ribs and numbed the cut. "It means you've hardened those muscles just right. How many hands do you need to hold a claymore?"

Furrowing my brow, I answered, "Two."

"I said you." He closed the tin and now began circling my torso in a cloth bandage.

"Two?" I wasn't sure where the old knight was going with this. "It's hard swinging a tree trunk weighed down with that much lead."

"I said claymore." Tying the bandage tight, he smacked my shoulder and commanded I follow.

"You sound crazier each day, old man." Running my hand over my head, I brushed back long strands of hair that escaped my braid.

He laughed, edging down into the cellar. We both weaved through shelves until the indoor training area revealed itself. The Lord Knight was smiling, something I had rarely seen him do in the three years I had been there. He pointed to a display of armor and other armaments. The item in question leaned on a shelf there, too large to fit into his chest of swords. The Claymore's blade was etched and polished to be worthy of a Royal Guard or Prince. It was beautiful in the brazier's light.

"You can have it if..." he paused.

"If?" I finally gave him my attention.

"If you can wield it one-handed," his smile crept across his face like a snake.

I frowned, "How ridiculous."

"Dante, I've seen you carry a bale of hay with one arm." He sat down on the chest. "Go on, with one hand."

"You do know that's a claymore, not a broadsword." I walked closer, taking in the detail of it all. "Was this...?" *Falco.*

"Yes, it's the very same blade."

I closed my eyes, thankful for a change the old knight had a way of reading me. Inhaling deeply, gripping the hilt, I readied myself. The grip was smaller in length compared to claymores I had seen in the past, and swallowing, I pulled it up off the shelf and ground. It came with little resistance and the weight half that of the wooden one I used out front. I gave it a swing, the weight only slightly cumbersome as a heavy broadsword. The balance in the claymore had been altered, repurposed for just this reason. I held the blade flat, at eye level, admiring the thickness and how straight it had been despite facing battle.

"It's gorgeous," I muttered.

"I call her the Duchess." Paul broke into a rash of coughs, wheezing to catch his breath.

"You need to head back upstairs. This damp air doesn't do your lungs any good and neither does that pipe." I switched hands, pleased at the ease I had with my less dominant hand. "The balance in this is uncanny. Where did you find a black-smith so talented?"

"In Prevera." He caught his breath.

"Why does this not surprise me?" I took a swing, the speed making my muscles flinch. "It'll take some time to master this one."

"You can abandon the axe and use that to cut down sap-lings and the likes." He shuffled on his perch, rubbing his chest. "It's how I trained on it. It's all about repetition now, Dante. I've taught you all I know. You've got the instincts, you can read the books here for more, but as for my skill and my blade, you now know my secret. Never let them know you can carry it with one hand."

"A farmer turned Lord Knight," I breathed. "Let's get you back upstairs."

"No, go give it a good swing. I'll get myself up there." He gave me a mournful look. "I'm sorry, Dante."

"What for?" I smiled, turning back to him.

Paul grimaced, his hand gripping his shirt as he fell for-ward. I abandoned the claymore, barely catching his shoulders under me. His body went rigid, his jaw clenching. Panic took hold, *no, don't leave me.* He wasn't breathing. Wrenching his hand off his chest, I laid him down on the ground and pressed my ear against it. *Nothing.* The warmth was already leaving his body and my stomach twisted. His heart had stopped.

I rocked back on my heels, covering my face as the weight of it settled. The old man knew, *I'm on borrowed time.* He had said it time and time again. The pain wrecking my body wasn't physical; it was pure heartbreak. I was the child, no, next heir to an enemy country, and yet he treated me as if I were family. He never once caved to John's whims about who I was exactly, or why he would teach me over him. My life was expendable, and if anything, it would right a wrong of what happened to John's parents from a Viceroy who served in my name, my father's name.

A frustrated roar escaped my lips, the cellar dampening it. Winter was a long way off, so I had time to bury him, to choose the spot and plant a tree as a marker. John wouldn't get to see his grandpa one last time. Paul wouldn't get to see his grandson returned a priest.

And me, where does that leave me?

"Three years is all you had."

Pulling my hands from my face, he looked so peaceful for once. Again, a pain struck my chest as my eyes looked to the claymore on the floor.

"I'll finish training with it, but after that, it gets stored away until I truly need it. Thank you. It's a wonderful gift." I rolled to my feet, picking it up and brushing the dirt off. Looking back at the lifeless vessel, I sighed, "Don't worry. I'll wait for him and make sure he receives his gift when he's ready."

Come home soon, John.

Chapter 6

Ten Years & Counting

The smell of freshly-broken ground filled the air, overpowering the hint of wild cherry blossoms. Spring was creeping into summer, and the ground defrosted enough to plow the field. Churning the soil and lugging the hand plow along was back-breaking work, even for a daemon. The sun rose ever higher, and by noon, I finished the last row. The seeds were still in the cabin where the birds wouldn't eat their fill, a lesson I learned the hard way my first year in charge of all the work. Sweat trickled down my back as it slid between my shoulders and down my spine. Despite the shade from my straw hat, nothing could keep the heat of the day from beating down on me.

Putting the plow off to the side of the field, I marched for the water pump. My mouth begged to have its thirst quenched. Opening and closing my hands, I tried to shake the lingering ache from gripping the plow for so long. Callouses made their home across the top of my palm and along my fingers, badges of years spent working as a farmer. I wasn't the soft pale Prince anymore, but a broken-in workhorse. Touching the metal handle of the water pump, I jerked my hand back.

"Dammit, that is hot!" The sun turned it into a frying pan. "I never learn, do I?"

Agitated, I pulled off my sweat-soaked shirt. Wrapping it around the handle, I raised and lowered the lever to draw water from the mountain stream somewhere uphill. My biceps and forearms were sore, but my want for the cool water won out. *Three, four, and...* The pump grumbled, sputtering, then nothing. Leaning on the trough, I sighed.

"Days like these make me miss you, old man." Looking up, I glared at the menacing woods between me and the unknown water source. "You never did tell me. Always mumbling *uphill* at me when I asked where it came from."

Inhaling deep, I saw this was another example of having to learn as I went. There had been heaps taught to me, but I never imagined so much hadn't been covered for the everyday troubleshooting. I found myself struggling from time to time. Still I smirked, glancing down at my newly tanned arms, dark from all the outside work I'd been doing since the farm had become home. Granted, my bronze skin was painted with scar lines of white, pink, and purple. Those were also badges, ones earned in the relentless episodes of sword practice bittersweet with memories. The Lord Knight was old but not lacking in the ability to be ruthless during training.

"*Who knew a daemon could tan?* Isn't that what you fussed about? I think it's darker than that last year you sat on the porch making remarks about how I cut your field wrong." Chuckling, I followed the piping up through the trees until it faded into the dirt. "Old man, you buried most of this line out here so no one could use it to find you. How am I to fix something I can't see?"

I'm sorry, Dante. It was a bittersweet echo.

All I could do was guess, but before long I heard a trickling of a stream. Deviating from my path, I would have had better luck finding the unburied backend of the line leading into the water. A breeze flowed through the trees, sending shivers across my bare back, reminding me I left my shirt behind. The farther I walked upstream, the bigger the rocks became, making it hard to find solid footing. A glance ahead told me I would have better luck walking in the stream at this rate. Kicking off my shoes, I hoped they would at least mark when I neared the cabin again. From where I entered, the stream proved deeper than I expected, coming up a little higher than my belly button.

John's parting gift. I haven't visited this spot since he left.

"Where have you been?" Cooing to the water, I slung my hat onto the shore and dunked my head under. Scrubbing my long auburn hair free of the sweat and mud, I burst through the surface with a great roar. "I can't remember the last time I could take a proper bath. Oh, I will be back later, but I have work to do."

Running my fingers over my head, I shoved the long loose locks behind my ears, sixteen loose knots heavy with water. I allowed it to grow out with encouragement from the old man. Yes, I promised John, but the old knight believed no one should abandon their status nor their past. It wasn't much farther before I caught a glimpse of the pipe running parallel to the shore in the shallows. I chased the pipe, picking up pace until at last I found the problem. Boulders had rolled into the stream, redirecting the flow of water and leaving the pipe in still waters. Shoving the pipe end into the flow solved the problem, but I wasn't satisfied. To add security, I rearranged the larger boulders until I was content they would preserve the pipe end and its location.

"I'm lucky it didn't smash this." Looking up through the branches, I realized I had wasted a lot of time. "I've managed not to need to visit town or contact the traders since you left, Paul, but how much longer can I limp by without John here?

You think he's really coming back home?"

The walk back was a sour one. With each knock of my wet braid at my back, I couldn't help but revisit my past. No one would have expected the pale, scrawny Prince to be living a life like this. I now carried broad shoulders and thick muscled from years of what many would label peasant's work and had grown taller. *He's a late bloomer,* my father would chuckle. When I left, I was barely to Viceroy Falco's shoulders, but I imagined we'd be eye level at best by now.

I wonder how tall John... I retracted the thought, my chest stinging at allowing my mind to wander so freely.

Climbing out of the stream, I pulled on my shoes and grabbed up my hat. The walk downhill was effortless, but glancing at the scars on my knuckles, I found my chest aching again. They were from a time when I had endured cruel training and the old Lord Knight no longer could walk far from the cabin. Those were our last days together, and after he passed, I had taken my rage out on the trees until my knuckles bled.

If you hit a shield hard enough, it'll jar you like that. It was the first lesson he ever taught me.

Blaring sunlight greeted me as I came into the small opening where the cabin and field waited. Coming around the corner of the cabin, I froze. There sat the bag John had left with over ten years ago. It carried what little he owned back then. A stack of books sat on the chair next to the door made up of texts associated with *The Church.* My face flushed and my heart pounded in my ears. I took a step closer but stopped. The wind rustled the leaves, and a shiver crawled across my skin. Dread poured over me.

I can't greet him looking like this; no shirt, pants drenched. He's a priest now. It's frowned upon to approach one like this. You came back, John, but I don't want you to see all these scars. I don't want you to blame yourself for this outcome.

Without hesitation, I backtracked to the water pump. My shirt was still wrapped around the handle. Unravelling it with haste, I sniffed it, then pulled it away. It was dry, but with the soured smell of sweat. Working the pump handle, I prayed I fixed the wretched thing. *One, two, three...* Gurgling sounds of water were echoing out of the nozzle. *Four...* Water was dribbling out. *Five!* And the spout gushed water into the trough. Satisfied plenty of water had been pulled, I scrubbed the shirt, grabbing the bar of soap I made of fat and lavender.

What am I going to do? Wear a wet shirt? Why do I care...? It's been over ten years. Will he even let me stay here? Does he remember he is my keeper and I am his servant? How much has he changed? Not just mentally, but... humans age so much faster. Dammit, what the hell is wrong with me? Why am I panicking?

Groaning, I rinsed the soap out. At least the wet shirt would match the wet pants. Tugging on my braid, I slid my hair out of my collar and it slapped heavy against my back. Again, I froze, looming over the trough with doubts gnawing at me. My stomach twisted. John left as an eighteen-year-old, but now, he would be twenty-eight. *What does he even look like after being away and part of* The Church?

"I heard the pump." The muscles in my back flinched, tightening at the sound of his voice. "It's been a long time, Dante."

"John." I lost my words, my ears relieved to hear the more seasoned tone of his voice, relishing my own name. "I was starting to think you weren't coming back." Still, I couldn't force myself to turn and look at him. "Was there much trouble making it back?"

"No..." His steps moved closer, his fingers brushing my back and lifting my braid. "I didn't think you would ever wear your braid again. It feels like yesterday when you sat there in the dead of winter and dropped it on the ground."

Spinning, I found myself eye to eye with those blue eyes now bordered by crow's feet. "This was temporary. Hard to fix the waterline with wet hair flopping in my way." My face flushed. He had lost all those boyish features and was still wider in the chest than myself.

He smiled, the blonde short beard fitting his square jaw with finesse. "Indeed, it would be. I like seeing it like this; it seems more fitting." His hand and fingers were so much larger than I recalled as he let go. "I've earned the right to wear seven knots. You know what that means, right?"

"You're a priest," I laughed. "Impressive, John! Not many can say they aimed and achieved their dreams. Though it may not have seemed like it, Paul would have been proud of you."

"Thank you for taking care of my grandfather." His arms wrapped around me, the hug full of warmth and strength. "The farm and house are in good shape thanks to you. Why don't you rest up while I finish seeding and watering? Isn't that what needs to be done next? I saw the bag in the house."

"Can't let a priest do dirty work." I broke the hug and held him at arm's length, gripping his shoulders while another wave of heat hit my face. "Sorry, I've gotten you all wet."

"You did say you were working on the waterline. Now, I've already rolled up my sleeves. At least let me lend you a hand." With a forearm, he shoved my hands off and away. "Maybe even visit the old man if it's not too late."

Swallowing, I grabbed the buckets out from under the trough. "I'll get the watering done, you lay the seed down? Like old times?"

"Yeah, you're already wet." He chuckled, walking back into the house and returning with the satchel of seeds.

Silence fell hard between us. Part of me wanted to write it off as just extreme focus on the work before us, but I knew better. I trailed behind him, kicking dirt over the seed and sloshing the water over it to start the germination process. Staring at his back, I watched how his braid caught the sunlight and glimmered like gold. His hair was thicker than I remembered. John would glance over his shoulder, shaking me from my admiration, and I would drop my eyes to the ground again. I emptied the two buckets by the fourth row. Turning, I went back to the pump, but when I started back, I found John had stopped to stare at me. I flinched, unsure what to think of it. Rolling my shoulders back, I tightened my grip and came marching back.

"Where on earth did you get all those scars from?" John's voice cut through me as he continued spreading seed. "Was that from training with grandpa?"

"Y-yeah." Another kick, stomp, and splash of water. *He noticed them after all...*

"Grandpa was always one to teach the hard way." The tone of his voice was meek, but it was me who failed to realize a wet white shirt wouldn't hide them. "I owe you a lot, Dante."

"It was my choice, my request." John paused, almost as if he meant to turn to say something. "Like you, I came here with a dream, though not as glamorous as your own."

"You never told me where you... never mind." He shook his head, returning to the task in front of him without another word.

I opened my mouth, but I wasn't ready to tell him whom I used to be. That day and time hadn't come. Part of me hoped he understood the weight it would bring him to know my true title, my braid betraying where I ranked in this world.

I'm royalty. He knows that much without a doubt now.

By the last row, John was taking a bucket from me, and we worked from both ends until water sloshed across each other's boots. John gave me a hearty pat on the shoulder, taking my bucket and heading back to the water pump. Again, he refilled them and handed one to me.

"There's not much daylight left. Let's go see the old man." He mustered a smile, but I could see in those blue eyes he was pained. "You planted a tree where he was buried, right?"

Nodding, I led the way through the forest in silence. The trees grew darker with every step, adding to the weight of John trailing so close behind me. Breaking into a small clearing, a big cherry tree took up the center. The air filled with the scent of its bloom; white flowers in long clumps bounced in the wind. I splashed my bucket at its base and flipped it upside down and took a seat, leaning on my knees. John mirrored my actions. Crickets chirped, announcing the night was creeping closer, and the air would soon cool. Taking in a deep inhale, I looked over at John. He was finishing a prayer, his closed eyes shedding a tear. A smile grew on his face, his eyebrows lifting.

What on earth is he thinking?

Opening his eyes, he turned to me, chuckling. "He hated cherries." He shook his head in amusement. "What possessed you to plant a cherry tree on his grave?"

I grinned, "It was payback for the scars."

We broke into laughter, the tension breaking as we headed back in time for night to take over.

CHAPTER 7

The Time Apart

I began cooking the stew I had learned from the old man, watching John over my shoulder. He had been reading a book since we returned, the silence between us back. Stolen glances made both of us aware of how curious and intrigued we were to see how much we had changed in the time apart. Somewhere in the black night, a nightingale sang loud and true, drowning out the pops and crackling of the hearth's fire. John slammed the book shut, and I flinched. We locked eyes, and he gave me a smirk as he rose to his feet.

"So no one touched my room when I left?" John walked over, pushing the door open and walking in, then he placed his belongings on his bed.

"No." My voice came out softer than I had intended.

"There isn't dust. The bed stuffing is fresh." His fore-head creased, more lines than I remembered across his brow. "You've been keeping everything in shape this whole time? Alone?"

"Yes." I kept my eyes on the stew, grabbing a knife and carrot.

"Alone for how long?" His voice deepened, and my breath caught.

Slicing carrots, I wasn't sure how to answer the question.

"How long, Dante?" He had a talent to sound demanding, but in a seasoned voice, it was startling.

"Seven." I cursed under my breath, cutting my thumb slightly.

"Seven years," he echoed in a gentle whisper. "I'm sorry, Dante."

"And those were his last words to me." Slumping my shoulders, I kept moving. The cut was too shallow to bother with. "He was on borrowed time."

"I know. He was always quick to remind me." John walked into his room and slammed the door.

I remembered to breathe again, leaning on the water barrel beside the stove. It was a conversation I knew would come, but it stung on so many levels. Catching a flicker of maroon reflecting on the water's surface, I glared at myself. Never did I think someone would shake me to my core like he did. Pulling away, I lost myself to the task at hand. Again, only the song of a lone bird outside filled the quiet wall building in the space between us. I scooped a bowl for John and placed it on the table and one for myself. John's door opened, and he sat down, waiting for me to do the same. Nodding, we began eating, though it all felt strange without the old man.

"How did you like Captiva City?" I couldn't bear the silence any longer.

"It was fine." He took a large bite, then shook his head. "It tastes the same."

"The stew?" I paused looking at him.

"It's the same as his." Sighing, he started scooping up the next bite. "Thank you."

"It's the only recipe I know," I confessed.

A smile broke out on both our faces.

Swallowing, I pushed him further, wanting to hear about his time away. "Did you make friends with anyone?"

Nodding, he smirked. "Of course I did. A knight named Valiente who serves under our friend Sonja, a Mother Superior of the Nuns. Then there's Bishop Montgomery in records and the guardian of the catacombs."

"Catacombs?" I lifted an eyebrow.

"Some of the oldest texts are kept there." He didn't look at me as he spoke. "It's why it took so long for me to return."

I froze. "What do the catacombs have to do with how long you took?"

"You have to be a priest to gain access to them," he answered flatly.

"So, you read musky scrolls and books for three years before coming home?" My spoon dropped, clacking loud against the metal bowl. "What was so interesting to keep you enthralled for that long?"

He paused, glaring at this stew before looking up. "I'll tell you another time."

My face twisted and he snorted. It was his way of jabbing me about my own secret. With a sigh, I opened my mouth to continue the conversation. My words failed as he slid his empty bowl to the center of the table and stood.

"Forgive me." He spun away, headed for his room. "I'm exhausted. We'll talk more in the morning." And his door shut.

Glaring at the door, so many memories of him doing this very move to his grandpa came crashing back. It made me smile, but it faltered. He was now avoiding me. My chest swelled.

He doesn't want to talk about Captiva City. Something happened, and sadly, his shield and sword was here, unable to help him.

I pushed down the thought, chills rolling across my skin. It was unnerving to not know what his life had been like in these ten years apart. I finished cleaning up and pushed into what used to be the old man's room. I hadn't really made it my own, keeping the cabin in the exact state it had been when John left. Sitting on the bed, I covered my face in frustration. Parts of my clothes were still damp. I hadn't stopped or deviated from being the lost puppy at John's heels.

Sleep was impossible. Knowing John was there on the other side of the wall after spending so long wondering if he was ever coming back. *He is back. Now what?* The thought felt like a jab from beyond the grave. *He likes you...* the old man had said once. *He can't possibly be like that now,* I retorted, part of me bitter to even have to think about it at all. Morning came, and I dressed, eager to dive into chores and not think for a change.

John was sitting in the chair, reading once more. I froze. I hadn't heard his door open and wondered if he had been as sleepless as I was. Without a word, I walked past him and made my usual trip to the cellar. I returned with eggs and the last of cured bacon I had been saving. At the stove, I brought the fire in its belly to life once more. Bacon sizzled on the cast iron skillet and I cracked eggs to fry. The smell of it all filled the tiny cabin in an instant.

"Liar." John's voice made my heart drop.

I turned to him, wide-eyed. *Liar?*

Twisting to steal a glance, I realized he was hovering over my shoulder to see what I was cooking. The heat of his hand rested on my shoulder, and he grinned at what he saw in the skillet. The moment he let go, I remembered to inhale and exhale, almost burning an egg needing to be flipped. The last time he said that word to me, we were talking about who I was and my braid.

"You know more than one recipe," he added, much to my relief. "You're a good cook, Dante. I'm surprised."

"I wouldn't call heating meat and eggs to an edible

temperature a recipe," I retorted.

"Some folks can't even do that," he added, opening his book.

I slid eggs and bacon into the two bowls, one for John and one for myself as I joined him at the table. We ate, not like it had been before he left. At this point, he would either challenge me or the old man on a matter before we had our first bite. By the third bite, an argument would erupt and insults began flying. At this point, halfway through a plate or nearly finishing my plate, either I would have to play peacemaker, or John would tire of the circles I spun and marched off to his room. Then again, he wasn't an eighteen-year-old boy anymore. Across from me was a man who still held that light I saw the very first time we found each other. My food slid off my fork and slapped back into my plate. John peered up from his book, his eyebrows high. A heat rose in my cheeks, and I scooped it back up, speeding myself along.

Does he even remember any of it? I had no idea how hard this would be without you, Paul.

"It's strange with him gone," John confessed, revealing we both felt the weight of his absence. "This is usually the moment you presented a compromise and we'd agree."

"I was just thinking that too." I circled the last of my bacon in yolk and took it in, watching John read as he spoke. "To think I used to bargain trading chores to make you read."

"You once told me: 'The best way to see the world is through words of another.'" He flipped the page and took a bite, eyes on the pages. "I didn't understand what you meant until I had an entire library of words written by others. Different places, times, and history through the eyes of many and not just one."

"It can teach you a lot," I gathered my plate and began rinsing it in the small sink by the water barrel. "I once had a library within reach, and in some ways, I miss it."

"It must've been grand and hard to leave behind."

I froze, stiffening as I placed my bowl back on the shelf.

The weight of my braid, where it fell parallel to my spine, was a burning reminder of my past, and the secret I couldn't reveal, even if he knew. Muttering under my breath a million curses, I marveled at my own indecisiveness.

Why did I bother to grow the cursed thing back?

"Sixteen knots, right?"

Turning, I saw his gaze was on me and no longer the book as he bit into his bacon. I couldn't gauge the emotion, the look on his face, or even in those blue eyes.

When did he become so intimidating?

"Yes." I turned away, heading for the front door. "There's work to be done. Spring came late this year."

"Dante." His voice was loud and sharp as my hand reached the door. I refused to face him or to meet the burning gaze at my back. "I'll be out there to help you soon enough."

"It's my work, not yours," I muttered.

"It's my farm and I work for no one, and I will not have someone working for me." The book closed and the scraping of his last bite filled my ears. "Plus, you won."

"Won?" I turned back, confused, and he grinned to see he had my attention again.

"The longest braid." He stood and flopped his dirty dishes in the sink. "It means I take half the chores, doesn't it?"

I laughed, memories flooding me. "You're like a dog with a bone. You just never stop."

Pushing out the door, I was relieved to be free of his gaze, and the tension fell from my shoulders. The John that had left was still inside him, though part of me was scared to know who this new, more seasoned version would prove to be as time passed.

CHAPTER 8

Rite of Priesthood

Two months passed, and nothing new had been shared between us since the first week. John asked about Paul's last days, and I shared the bittersweet end. I didn't tell him how angry and broken I felt when he left me behind. As far as John knew, the scars on my knuckles were from working the field and not from the days I spent punching a tree to release the built-up rage and frustration. In return, he shared snippets of his life with *The Church,* and how Captiva City differed being a harbor town unlike the mountain villa feel of Glensdale. The stories of his studies along with his friends, Knight Valiente and Bishop Montgomery, added to a sense of jealousy growing deep within me. Closing my eyes, I imagined how it must have been to stand next to John with the screeching gulls, crashing waves, and salty breeze. He was busy poring over his books more often than venturing outside. Perhaps it would have been the same there as it was here, now that he was home.

I woke to the smell of breakfast, the same scent of the potato cakes Paul used to make me, and I hadn't been able to recreate on my own. John was finishing at the old wood stove and placed two plates at the table. We sat and started to eat, but it was horribly quiet. A surging river of unspoken questions raged between us, neither of us knowing when to voice them. The tension and awkwardness grew with how we shuffled around one another in the small cabin. I couldn't decide who was the greater stranger to the other; John toward me, or I to John. We had made friends so easily when we first met. It had seemed natural in how we talked to one another, unlike these past few weeks.

"When do you plan on going to Glensdale?" I broke the silence, staring at the last bite on my tin plate. "I assume you are preparing to take over the church there."

"There's still something I need to take care of before I'll be allowed to take over the church." John laid his fork down, folding his hands together and leaning his elbows on the table. "The Bishop of this region should be coming here any day now. Possibly even today some time."

"Bishop Marquis?" Scooping up the last bite, I glared at him. "Last I recalled, he doesn't think kindly about daemons."

"Yeah, you met him before?" An eyebrow lifted, John's curiosity piquing. "Or does his nastiness spread to every ear?"

"No, I met him when I was younger, a child in his eyes." Leaning back in my chair, I smirked. "He came to make sure we hadn't burned the church down while he was looking for a priest. I recall him calling me a 'wormy red-eyed heretic' and worse. Since Viceroy Falco was out on the battlefield, my father and I welcomed him. Anyhow, he's greasy, fat, and rude."

John laughed, shaking his head, "I can't say I disagree. Unfortunately, I met him a few times during my studies, and I don't care for what he'll be coming here to do."

Giving him a confused expression, I pressed for an answer, "What *will* he be doing here?"

"Finalizing my priesthood." His face reddened, and he looked off to the ground. "And if you are okay with it, I would like you to be my *Barrière de Force*."

"*Barrière de Force?*" I tilted my head, trying to call his eyes back to mine. "Why would I need to be your *Barrier of Strength?*"

Is it because I'm all that you have left? Wouldn't your knight friend be enough for this?

His eyes waned and locked with mine. "Every priest receives the branding of *The Church* across their backs. The person we choose to hold our arms should be someone who has helped us on our journey, and more importantly, will always aid us on our path."

My heart sped up and my face flushed. Opening my mouth, it took a moment before my words would come out. "Of course. I've got to go weed the field; if you need me, come get me."

The awkwardness had come rushing back between us, my chair screeching and out the door I went. I didn't want to look into those eyes anymore. My emotions tangled, my chest ached from the drumming of my heart. As my feet left the front porch, I heard the thud of John's chair hitting the floor.

Did we both jerk up from the tension building between us? Did he want to say more to me before I rushed out? Or did I turn away because I couldn't bear to talk further on the matter?

Shaking my head, I grabbed up the old bucket by the field and began to work my way through the rows. Most of the plants we seeded were tall enough to recognize, making it easier to pull weeds and unwanted plants. Crouched low, the dirt was warm and wet between my fingers as I pulled them up and dropped them in the bucket. With each one, my thoughts reeled with the fact I would *have to watch that fat pig brand John.* My stomach soured, and I no longer cared if Bishop Marquis would recognize me as the missing Prince of *The House.* Besides, I had seen the bribes passed from my father's hand to the Bishop's greedy fingers. My father was a clever man, not an under-the-table dealer and the whole meeting of the man had burned in my memory.

Despite the practice of bloodeating, I still admired King Traibon as both the King and my father. He had been able to persuade the Lord Knight Paul to lay down his sword. The notion of living on gifted land and immunity from *The House* left the old man to live his days out in peace. Unlike Viceroy Falco, my father would seek out every means to not shed unnecessary blood. Deep down, the King of *The Court* had a softer side, though easily mistaken as corrupt or turncoat by those who followed Falco's lead. He would bargain, and he always knew their answer before he even made the offer. Paul was getting old and he had a grandson, so he was given a secure place to be. Bishop Marquis wanted a life of luxury and therefore an easier prey to win over with gifts, money, and access to certain events.

Remember, Dante. The wake you leave can swing in your favor or bring about your destruction. You are the Prince of Bloodeaters, and no one will deny you anything, but your enemies will use everything you hold dear against you. He reminded me of this every time we were alone.

Sweat dripped off my chin, strands of my hair slipping out from under the hat and sticking to my face. Grunting, I lifted the filled bucket and marched out of the field and behind the old shed where the compost pile was located. It served as fertilizer for the fields, but I had to start building it back up once more after using so much of it to prep for the new seeds. Tossing the weeds on top of it, I dropped the bucket at my feet.

They'll burn the mark of the Church across his back, and he'll be sworn into their ranks forever. Celibate and unable to turn off his path. Breaking his vows after this would be a crime worthy of eternal imprisonment or death. I can't let this...

Leaning an arm on the shed, the weight of what would

unfold brought my nerves to an unbearable level. John would be Glensdale's next priest, where Viceroy Falco slaughtered his previous predecessors, where the crimes fell on the deaf ears of the corrupt Bishop, and where my past would be biting at my ankles.

Why can't I tell him? Am I really going to stay silent about it all, about how I watched Falco feed viciously on the last priest as I stood watching at his bedside? Am I worthy of the title of Barrière de Force? *Worthy to have you as my keeper, John? Am I man or a monster?*

My stomach twisted, and my breakfast slapped across the compost pile. Wiping my mouth, I shook it all off, the thoughts and the nausea. Grabbing the pitchfork, I turned the pile, hiding the weeds painted in my shame and guilt. Stabbing the pitchfork into it, I gripped the bucket and made my way back to the field. Noon was approaching, which meant it would become a greater burden to work under the sun. Squatting down, I went back to the hypnotic chore of weeding, desperate to lose the thoughts eating at my soul.

A horse's neigh broke me from my trance. Looking up, through the trees, the gaudy white and red robes adorned by gold embroidery was loud against the deep brown backdrop. *Bishop Marquis.* Another horse followed close behind, his thin and stringy servant with no braids carrying the branding iron. My eyes locked with the black symbol, a cross made of flourishes and a cardinal rose at the intersection. Muscles tightened in my body, and I slammed a weed into the bucket. I approached them, wiping my hands against one another, knocking them free of black dirt when I caused the Bishop's horse to pause.

"Good Lord, I don't think I've ever seen such a large one." His pumpkin-shaped head paled, and he yelled over his shoulder, "Jonas, look at'im! He's tanner than any farmer I've ever seen, even on the coast of Terahime where no snow reaches."

"Yes, Bishop Marquis, he is rather... large." The tiny man tightened his grip on his reigns. "But are we sure this one belongs to Father John?"

On that note, I dropped to a knee like so many servants had done for me. "Welcome, Bishop Marquis. Father John is inside working. Thank you for travelling out so far to bless John with the mark of priesthood and giving him your blessing to create a clergy in Glensdale."

I could feel his eyes glaring down at me. He snorted, wiping sweat from his face and flicked it across me, "Pretty words for a daemon. You're quite educated. Have we met before?"

I flinched, swallowing back my annoyance, "No sir, I have been here on the farm and never went to Captiva City with John."

"I know that much." His tone came forth in an irritated spatter. "You sound so familiar for a red-eyed heretic."

Flashes of me kicking his shin and calling him a "pumpkin-headed slime ball" rushed to mind. Smirking, I kept silent.

"Don't they all sound alike?" scoffed Jonas.

A great eruption of laughter came from the bishop. "So right you are, Jonas!"

"Bishop Marquis." John's voice cut through us all and I found him staring at me, his blue eyes bright with anger in the sunlight. "Stand up. You don't need to go that far."

"Now, now," the Bishop waved his hand. "He was showing proper respect for me. I appreciate a well-trained daemon, Father John."

"Last I checked, you only bow to royalty." John's tone brought me to my feet, my face red as I broke from his glare. "Now then, I have prepared a space inside. You'll find my grandfather was adamant to have a large hearth which should be more than enough to heat the cross with." I started for the field, but John grabbed my forearm, speaking in a hushed tone so only I could hear him. "I still have a few matters to discuss with the Bishop. Finish what you need to do, wash up, and bring a fresh pail of water. I will not go through with this without you there, Dante. Do you understand?"

"I understand." We locked eyes for a second and he let go, allowing me to leave.

"And don't ever bow to anyone like that again." The heat in John's stare sent chills across my spine.

Squatting down next to the bucket, I watched all three of them disappear into the house. I ripped out the next weed, crushing it in my fist. John put the final decision in my control; it wasn't just his decision anymore. Another crushed weed dropped into the bucket, and I turned to the adjacent row, my back to the cabin. With each pluck of a plant, I grew more frustrated. Never in my life had I felt so raw, so exposed as I did around him.

How could John put it on me whether he finishes the last rite to become a priest? Or is this his way to see if I really meant what I said all those years ago? Does he think I will back down from helping him achieve his dream?

I had run out of weeds, the bucket overflowing this time. Smashing them down, the bitter smell was a passive rebuttal to my harsh handling. Reaching the compost pile, I threw the bucket against it, anger erupting in anticipation of what waited for me on the other side of the cabin door.

Dammit!

Neglecting the scattered weeds and broken bucket, I stomped across the field and back to the water pump. Gripping the handle, I gritted my teeth and fangs, the typical result of a daemon losing his temper. The burning sensation was nothing compared to what the stone-faced John would endure soon enough. I held on and began pumping and filling the bucket. Scores of blisters painted my left palm, I ignored them until they started bleeding. Flustered, I washed up and grabbed the bucket of water, refusing to delay the inevitable any longer.

When I burst through the door, the room of clergymen fell silent. The muscles in my right arm flinched under the weight of the bucket of cool water. A piece of my shirt was ripped, and John's eyes fell to the exposed slither of the skin of my abdomen. Balling my left hand into a fist earned his attention as well. There, wrapped tight across my palm, was the other piece of my shirt. My fingers hid the blisters I had allowed when flesh met sun-scorched metal. Let this be a reminder of John's own endurance.

Never will I forget he became a priest worthy of carrying the symbol of The Church *burned into his back.*

"Did you hurt yourself?" John's brow furrowed, but behind him, the branding iron was glowing red hot. "Do you need–"

"No, I'm fine." Forcing my eyes back to his, I redirected him. "I made sure the water was cold."

John gave a half-hearted smile. "Then let's get this over quickly."

He had moved the table and chairs closer to the fire already. Standing, John began to unbutton the black over-coat only worn by priests. Tossing it over the back of his chair, he pushed it to the table. Next, he pulled the white blouse off. I held my breath, taking in his athletic build for the first time. Like my own skin, he had signs of sword practice which meant he befriended Valiente to learn what his grandfather hadn't been willing to teach him. John then unbuckled his belt, and I swallowed.

"It helps to bite on leather, I'm told." John's voice pulled my eyes off his hands and back to his face. "Some have bitten their tongues off. A farewell tip from Bishop Montgomery."

I paled, John handing his belt to me, "What am I to do for you?"

"Hold my arms." John straddled the chair, reaching his arms across the table, hands balled. "As long as you hold me firm and still, this should be over quickly."

"You won't feel the hot iron but smell the burning flesh first." Bishop Marquis carried a grave look; it wasn't his first time performing the rite. "The pain comes when air hits the mark as we lift the iron."

Jonas grimaced. "This is so barbaric. I cut my braid and devoted myself to the Bishop rather than endure the rite to be a priest. It's cruel."

"Enough," barked John, taking charge of the room. "It is my rite, and I am ready."

I stood, watching Jonas and the Bishop struggling to pull the cross from the hearth.

"Dante."

The old man had made it large enough to double as a black-smith's fire. *Never know when you'll have to go to war again.*

"Dante."

PING! Bishop Marquis' hand slipped, the corner of the cross hitting against the stone slap of the hearth. Jonas cursed under his breath, shoving it back into the flames to regain lost heat.

"Dante!" John's fingers gripped my shirt, tugging me closer. "Pay no mind to them."

"But, shouldn't I go help them?" Panic written all over my face, I protested, "If they can't lift the wretched thing, what point is there?"

"Look at me, not them." I did as he commanded, my eyes locking with his. "Gimme the belt and hold my arms. I don't even know how strong my will is for something like this."

I gave a disapproving tilt of my head, shoving the leather into his mouth. I grabbed his forearms; they were slick with a cold sweat. He was nervous, scared even despite the pow-erful composure he put on for the Bishop. My eyes began to wander back to the bumbling fools, but John flexed his arm muscles and furrowed as if saying, *Stop it.* The glow and heat of the cross approached. I refused to look, though they seemed to be holding it steady this time. Without any warning, red hot metal hit flesh. John's muscles stiffened, his teeth digging into the belt, but he kept silent.

Stubborn as a mule, that one... the old man would have laughed over it.

The cabin filled with the sound of sizzling flesh against metal like bacon on a frying pan. Beads of sweat popped and sputtered against the edges. Worse, the smell was unnatural, and I bit the inside of my cheek still watching John, and John watching me. The glow of the hot iron was starting to dissipate.

"We need to pull this off, Bishop," Jonas warned.

Shuffling back, they pulled away with speed. John lurched up, but my hands held him firm to the table. The wooden panels creaked under my weight. He tried jerking free, his head shaking like a wild animal as he screamed through the clenched belt. The cross clunked back into the fire, what little flesh stuck to it eaten away by the flames. John's chest heaved, sweat pouring over him as the skin on his back hissed until it fell silent. Jonas didn't look back once, just kept his focus on stoking the fire and glaring at the cross with disgust. Bishop Marquis held a sickening smile, glaring at his handiwork on John's back.

"I don't think anyone has ever held so still for one," Bishop Marquis complimented, John's muscles relaxing as he slumped forward on the table. "This will be the prize branding. Wear it proudly, Father John." He turned his stare to me. "The water. We need to cleanse the cross and cool it so we can leave this hovel."

My temper was pressing forward, "One moment."

John had given up the fight, panting from the pain echoing through him. I let go and turned to where I left the spring water. Ripping my shirt farther, I pulled it off and dumped it in the pail.

"We have no need of a dirty shirt!" I ignored the Bishop's outburst.

Satisfied it had soaked up all it could, I turned back to John. The wet blouse blanketed across his entire back. John opened his eyes, looking at me in wonder. I smiled, knowing he had gained some relief. Turning back, I handed over the rest of the water to the red-faced bishop. He shoved it into Jonas's arms and began poking my chest.

"What insolence!" Grunting, I took a step back and threw my hands up. "What do you think you're doing?"

"Serving my keeper," I declared, a coy grin sliding across my face. "Is that not my purpose?"

"Uh!" Bishop Marquis's cheeks ballooned out before he found something to say. "Who on earth trained this daemon?!"

John started to laugh, though wincing from his efforts. "The warhero, Lord Knight Paul Thompson."

"Wh-what?" The Bishop's face paled, looking jaundiced over the answer. "You can't be... there are no accounts of him training a daemon servant nor having family."

"Oh, he trained me, and with that sword leaning by the stove." I watched Bishop Marquis' eyes fall on the hilt and scabbard of the claymore and a shudder rattled through him. "Lord Knight Paul." His eyes fell to my bare chest and abdomen scattered with sword slashes. "He trained you to do what exactly?"

John sat up, pulling the corners of my broken blouse over his shoulders. "I suggest you and Jonas be at the horses by the time he finishes refilling the bucket with water. Otherwise, you'll get to see firsthand what my Grandfather taught him to do with the sword he gave to *him.*"

"Jonas." He was shaking in a mixture of rage and fear. "What's taking so long?"

The Bishop started for the door. Jonas fumbled with

the bucket before splashing it on the cross and firepit. He dragged it along, scoring the wooden floor and painting it with wet ash. They half-ran to their horses, the steam still rolling off the iron cross in a few places. I turned back to see John lean back on the table, closing his eyes. Walking to the hearth, I groaned.

"What's your problem?" John spoke without moving an eyelid.

Squatting, I nudged the puddle in the fire with the poker. "It looks like we're out of luck for having a fire tonight."

"I've had enough of fires." I walked back to him only to find he had fallen asleep.

Outside the two clergymen were arguing, horses squealing. Grabbing the bucket, I opened the cabin door. They froze, silent now as they climbed on the horses and galloped back the way they came. Smiling, I headed to get more water to soothe John's burns. Tomorrow I would dry out the hearth and see to it he kept the burns clean and free of infection.

Maybe the buzz buttons have started blooming, if he's lucky. They were always good for numbing a bad burn.

CHAPTER 9

Glensdale Cathedral

The walk to Glensdale took most of the morning. Not one word was spoken between us as I trailed close behind John. I tucked my hair up into my straw hat, wearing the brim low to cover everything but the tip of my nose and lips. This would be the first time I stepped foot inside the city walls since I left my title of Prince behind. I shifted the taut leather straps on my shoulders, the pack stuffed from the weight of John's books and clerical items. Staring at his back, all I could see was the brand hidden under his black coat and the occasional twitch of his jaw muscle. He was still fighting the pain. I imagined sweat was dripping into broken scabs like hot embers across his skin.

Where did he learn to hold so firm? He left an innocent boy and now is a man worthy of holding face in the worst of occasions. What happened in Captiva City, John?

City guards eyed us both, nodding a head in respect to John's status as priest and spitting at my feet as I followed.

Have they always treated servants this way?

John paused, taking in the two- and three-story shops

which made up the main street. It was setup for business owners to have their shops on the bottom, workshops on the floor above and even living space. I had frequented many of them at some point, relishing in luxury items and custom-made pieces of clothing and accessories. A grin crept forward; how silly it seemed now. At one point, I had spent late nights flirting with many of the daughters and sons of the aristocrats who insisted on showering their Prince with gifts. Strangely, I didn't miss it at all.

"Which way to the church?" John raised his brow. "I was never good at navigating Captiva City, and well, I've never been here. You're from here. You mind leading the way?"

"Y-yeah." I broke away from the hatter's sign and stood beside him. "You're lucky. In Glensdale, the main road dead ends at the cathedral. You should see the towers as the road curves to go uphill."

"That's good to know." John was glowing, excited to be so close to the next step of his life's dream. "Are you sure you can carry all of that, even uphill?"

I brushed my hand close to his back, and he jerked away. "We both know you can't help me, so stop asking."

"I hate when you do that." He scowled, following me as I marched forward. "You don't have to remind me it's there; I can feel it just fine."

I shook my head. "Be thankful I'm not the Old Farmer. I'm sure he would have given you a hearty slap across the back as payback for going through with it."

"Ha!" He sped up, walking beside me. "You're right. I should be thankful that you're far gentler with me."

I gave him a knowing side-glance, and I couldn't stop the smirk on my face.

The road was peaking, and before us, the gothic cathedral came into view. It was dark, looming with jagged spires stabbing into the sky. The stained-glass windows were narrow and tall, unlike the ones I grew up seeing in the manor. It was more castle than church from the outside, the walls black under the curtains of ivy trying to scale its walls. John approached the heavy double oak doors, iron hinges decorative and stretching out to hold their weight. His hand slid across it, a look of longing on his face. He had worked so hard for this moment.

"Well, the doors seem to be in working order." I gripped the large looping handle, tugging the door open. "A little stiff but some animal fat can fix that."

Taking a step back, John waited for me to open both doors wide. John took in everything the old relic had to offer. Cobwebs stretched across like skewed curtains of lace, dust covered pews with lack of use, while the podium laid on its side on the pulpit. Light sparkled in, colors painting the ancient interior with worn-out tapestries frayed and dirt-layered floors. John smiled. This was *his sanctuary.* I flopped the heavy pack to the floor, plumes of dust rolling outward as the clatter echoed through the vaulted ceiling and its decorative rafters. Pigeons cooed, far from welcoming us into their home. John lifted an eyebrow at me, and I shrugged. We walked down to the podium, and he stood it back up. A frown took hold on his face.

"Is... is this blood?" His eyes locked on the splatter across the wood his hands still gripped. "The black stains here, and across the floor?"

Falco never bothered to clean it up after...

Swallowing, I whispered, "Yes."

"Bishop Marquis said–" I placed my hand over the stain, catching his attention.

"The Bishop lied. Whatever that fat bastard says is a lie. He's paid off." A weight fell off my conscience. "Every priest who has come here has been met with death."

John searched my eyes. "You knew. This whole time, even

that day when I..."

Turning away, I couldn't bear to see the anger building in those blue eyes. I marched through the pews, flipping the fallen ones upright. His glare burned into my back, but I ignored him. He needed to know the reality of being the priest of Glensdale. Regardless, I had made a promise to him, and the Old Farmer knew the dangers of his grandson's dream. Neither I nor the old man had the heart to tell him back then, making me responsible for his life and the reason why I trained under the Lord Knight.

John, we couldn't tell you no. I wanted to see you succeed, and so here I am as your Sword and Shield. Let me cut you a path.

An old broom lay on the floor of one row, and I slid in to grab it. Turning to sidestep back out, John stood there, fists tight. I tightened my grip on the wooden handle, unsure of his expression. Muscles flinched on either side of his jaw before he spoke.

"Would it be too much to assume you were there when the last priest died?" It stung knowing he could see through me.

Was it always this easy for you to read me?

I shook my head, letting him know he wasn't wrong. "I saw. Not here, but what followed."

"Saw what, Dante?" I tried to step past him, but he pushed me down on the pew, leaning over me as his fingers dug into my shoulder. "Tell me. Who did it?"

We were nose to nose. "I think you know this part."

"Do I?" John leaned farther in, whispering into my ear. "*Le Chien Enragé.*"

I shoved him back into the aisle, pulling myself out of the row. Without another word or look, I swept the floors in silence. John marched to the bags, his frustration loud in each step. He was so bullheaded, but so was I. Lugging the pack over his shoulder, he hissed before carrying it to the back room and slamming the door. It echoed like a million shouts of anger beating against my soul. Again, as the farm taught me, I let myself fall into a state of nothing. Sweeping, shoveling the piles of dirt out the door, and straightening the rows of pews consumed me. Grabbing up the broken ones, I dragged them to the back, stacking them in a dark corner. Every action echoed and clattered within this cursed place.

I was never much of a carpenter, but you have a real knack for it. The Old Farmer's voice had a way of sneaking up on me, the past seeping into the present. *Glad one of us can fix a chair, or we'd have our asses in the dirt.*

I smiled, the memories a warm and fresh welcome. Pausing, I saw John hadn't left the back room; then again, it was where all the records were kept. He would be poring over them, something I am sure Bishop Marquis wouldn't bother to check for evidence of the Viceroy's crimes. There, in the handwriting of his predecessors, would be the unspoken truth and facts to back what I had let loose. I dragged the last broken pew to the back, dust rising and falling from the impact. Turning, I decided it would be best to shove the working ones to the front.

"Well now, this one came with a helper." Viceroy Falco's voice sent a chill across me. I had stopped two rows from the doorway, my back to him.

Not now, not when John's upset, vulnerable, and I'm...

"This ought to be double the fun." He was cooing in the same manner he did before taking a life on the battlefield.

"I can get my keeper, Father John, for you, sir." My voice was dry and cold.

His steps echoed, the heat of his body hovering behind me. "Do you not look your superiors in the eye when you speak to them, servant?"

Biting my lip, I feared he would recognize me, though we were now the same height. "No sir. I am forbidden to look anyone but my keeper in the eye."

Would he believe that or find it insulting?

Scoffing, he shoved me, "Summon the priest."

Marching down to the office, I pulled my brim low, shielding my face. *If he figures out who I am, John will be at a greater risk. It definitely insulted him to know I denied him a glance.*

Pausing in front of the door, I walked in without knocking. Shutting the door behind me, John gave me a bewildered look. Books lay open and haphazard across the dust and cobwebs of the desk and cot. Sitting up straight, he opened his mouth, but I spoke before he could.

"Viceroy Falco is here." He paled. In a matter of minutes, he found the reason and cause of the deaths. "He wants to see you."

Stiffly, he rose to his feet and gripped my arm, whispering, "Will you stay close?"

"Did I not promise to be your Sword and Shield?" I gave him an angry glance.

He bit his bottom lip, slapping books closed and shoving them under the cot.

"Are you ready?" We both felt the weight of uncertainty.

Brushing off dust from the front of his coat, he whispered, "Not really."

He nodded, and I opened the door to find Falco hovering by the pulpit. "John, I present the Viceroy of Glensdale, Falco, the great war hero who pushed back *The Court* over a hundred years ago."

Clapping came from Falco; he was leaning on the podium. "A servant who also knows daemon history. How impressive."

John bowed his head, his braid flopping forward like an elegant golden rope. "It is an honor to meet you, Viceroy Falco."

"Is it?" He was glaring at me, and I shuffled behind John. "Well, I must say none of the priests before you had a servant, or at least one who stayed so close with such a well-balanced head."

"Thank you, Viceroy." John put on a stone-faced demeanor; his fear gone. "I hope to be far more useful to Glensdale than my predecessors. I understand they didn't meet your satisfaction or abandoned their duties."

"You have been talking to Bishop Marquis, I see." A slimy grin stretched across Falco's mouth, his canines like fangs on a wolf. "I must admit, they didn't meet my *taste*, per se."

I gripped the back of John's shirt, an instinctive response to memories of watching Falco feed and drain the last priest dry. He didn't flinch but shifted his stance. "I'm not sure *taste* was on the request, but I can assure you the cathedral will be in working order soon."

Viceroy Falco hopped off the pulpit and motioned for the office. "Shall we talk in private, Father John? I can't help but notice I make your servant uneasy."

"Absolutely." My heart skipped; my muscles stiffened at his words. "Da–"

He spun in time to catch the fear in my eyes and the gaunt expression. *Don't say my name. Please don't say my name.*

"*Danseur*, take a break and watch the door of the office," John said. I swallowed, uneasy to leave him alone with Falco. "The Viceroy and I have matters to discuss, and I don't want to be interrupted."

I stepped to the side, feeling helpless as I muttered, "Yes sir."

"So obedient," cooed Falco as John led the Viceroy into the office. He took another glance at me. "But why on earth would you call him the *dancer?*"

John's words trailed in the air as the door clicked shut. "Because I found him dancing with a cherry tree."

It made me smile, soothing the anxiety building in my chest, but the peace didn't last long. Agonizing minutes passed by with nothing but garbled conversation and the cold stone wall digging into my back. I stared at the office door, watching the light crawl across the pews as time crept onward. The door opened; my eyes widened. I lifted off the wall, my nerves tightened around every joint. John walked out and gave me a nod to let me know all was well. Falco walked out with a fanged grin filling his face. He was still carrying on his conversation.

"Now, my dear priest, you need not to worry. We have never had a break out of the Madness here in the city." He paused, glancing at me as if something nagged at him. "Even with my reputation. I am sure *Monsieur Danseur* has shared with you."

Did he figure out who I am? Or is he assuming?

John stepped between us, obscuring his observant stare. "I would prefer to hear more of your reputation from you, Viceroy."

Falco squinted his eyes, and his lips tightened. "Another time, Father John. I have other matters to attend to before it gets any later."

"Ah, a shame." John led him down the aisle and out the door. "Let us continue our own work as well."

Pausing at the doorway, Falco gripped John's wrist. The move made me jolt, but then he dropped a heavy coin purse into John's palm. "Let this be an investment. You have convinced me you are nothing like the others. Buy yourself a horse to make sure you can travel with ease between home and church. I look forward to hearing your first sermon."

Blinking, John's face reddened. "Viceroy, this is quite a lot of coin."

Laughter filled the air, "See to it the church is in working order. I'm curious how different you and your *Danseur* are compared to the others."

With a careless wave over his shoulder, Viceroy Falco walked away, joined by his waiting attendants across the way. John turned, ballooning out his cheeks. We could breathe again. Rubbing my forehead, I waited for John to join me in front of the pews. He grabbed my hand and slammed the purse into my palm. Bewildered, I watch him continue toward the office.

"I'll entrust this to you." With nothing more, he slammed the door.

"J-John?" Gripping the door, I found it locked. "Exactly what do you want me to do with this?"

There was silence before he shouted through the door. "Whatever is needed to make repairs to get the church ready for the King to see it."

"The King?" My head banged against the door; things were becoming difficult. "How much time do I have?"

Another long pause, "A week." I heard a book slam against the desk; he was pissed off. "I couldn't convince him for any more time."

With the door locked, John would be safe without me standing guard. Marching out of the church, I pushed the main doors closed. Evening was creeping in, and I didn't have much time left to secure a horse or make an order with the local carpenter. I could fix the pews, but not in enough time to clean the blood stains and replace tapestries. There was also discussion needed tomorrow to replace the décor with something fitting for my father to see. At least I knew my father's taste and could gain John the approval Viceroy Falco hadn't planned on us achieving.

But did Falco recognize me? And why did John shut himself in?

CHAPTER 10

Basque

I put an order in with the carpenter to replace the broken pews. He agreed to salvage or trash what he couldn't reuse for the ones I placed in a pile. Furthermore, I earned a discount when I made a deal to bring him some old oak trees on the edge of our property. John left me in charge, but I wouldn't put the actual location of the cabin at risk or make the road less daunting to get through there. Instead, a large horse would be helpful around the farm, so the discount gave me leverage for haggling. If I could pull some strings, I would have more than enough to replace the broken tapestries with patterned cloth. It would be easy to hang fabric in soft dips to cover stained walls and the areas in need of repair.

Following the fence line, I watched a worker running a horse through his motions, canter to gallop to trot and back again. The nostalgic scent of hay and manure filled the air, the buzzing of flies as I passed the manure wagon, and the pings of horseshoes being made on the other side of where I walked in the wake of my memories.

"Can I help you?" I reached the stables at the bottom of the hill where the royal horse breeder kept his shop. The man who approached was a stout, muscular sort of the lower class with two knots. The dirt on his face, arms, and apron told me this was one of the many farriers who managed the horses' hooves and horseshoes. I hadn't seen this human in the years I frequented here as a Prince, and he wasn't the one I came to do business with. "Are you buying for your keeper?"

"Yes." I tightened my fist on the coin purse. There would be no hiding my identity with the owner. Being here was a great risk, and asking a favor would leave me exposed. "I was looking for Count Chapman. I have a private matter to discuss with him."

"Duke," the man corrected, eyeing me over. "When was the last time you came to town if you're calling him Count?"

"A little over ten years, sir." He nodded, a sign he could forgive me on the incorrect title. "Is Duke Chapman available?"

"And your name?" He lifted an eyebrow, suspicious of me.

"Danny." My face flushed. I couldn't give my real name and I wouldn't entertain John's nickname of *Danseur.* "But he may remember me as the kid who wanted golden horseshoes."

The man smirked. "That's absurd. They'd never hold up to the horse's weight."

"That was the first thing he told me. A year later, I broke an iron shoe on my favorite mare. He told me I shouldn't treat it like gold. Fussed at me for it, but I told him I already took a beating from the horse. She kicked me off for the first time since I broke her in."

A laugh erupted from the gruff-faced farrier. "You grew up with horses then?"

"Yes, but I haven't had one for some time." The tension in my shoulders relaxed, enjoying the moment. "I manage a farm these days, so I'm in need of a draft horse. Not the smoothest to ride on, but I'll need help plowing and moving a filled wagon."

"I see." He crossed his arms and hummed. "We have a few here, good stock, and rare stock, in fact."

"Duke Chapman always had the best." I could see the man growing less suspicious as the conversation continued. "I hear he is the royal horse breeder."

"Was." My baffled expression made him flinch. "I see. You've been on the farm too long. Let's see if he's up for a visitor. Might do his spirit some good."

He went through the door, and I waited in silence outside. I could hear the heavy footsteps on wooden stairs through the two-story shop. A knock echoed down, the door creaking, and then muffled sounds of a conversation. There was a long pause, and I could tell there was a repeat of information given. After another pause, the steps descended, and the door swung open. My eyes met the farrier's, his suspicion back.

"He said to send you up." I went through the doorway, but he grabbed my shoulder. "If you cause him any trouble, I'll take my smith's hammer to your skull."

"I'm not here to stir up flies." It was something I heard Duke Chapman say every day when I aided in breaking foals.

Nodding, he recognized the line and was reassured I knew the Duke, and his iron grip let go. My feet thudded against the creaking steps, eager to knock on the door and talk to a familiar face.

"Come in," Duke Chapman had a deep, rustic voice, and it hadn't changed.

Stepping into the lantern-lit room, I closed the door behind me. Leaning my back against it, I looked up from my feet to meet his eyes. There he stood, shorter than I was for a change, greeting me with respect even as a servant. He had gained silvery hairs in his beard and braid, but the notable crooked nose and piercing brown eyes were sharp as ever. He took me in with great caution, his brow folding unsure. I realized I was more of a scar-knuckled farmhand than the scrawny pale Prince he once knew.

Can he find the old me in this new facade I've built for myself?

Tugging off my hat, I let the sixteen-knot braid fall. I had taken the time to knot it with care in advance before leaving the cabin. That, and I feared John's reaction if I dare cut it a second time.

John's terrible at braid classification to begin with, even now.

If trouble erupted, if I had to, I would protect John from Falco or even my father by reclaiming my title as Prince. Part of me regretted knotting it in the way of royalty. The Dutch-style braid started at the crown of my skull, the knots large and prominent as it fell over my shoulder and dangled by my hands.

Duke Chapman sat down, his jaw gaping, "D-D-Dante."

"Yes sir." My voice sent a shudder across his shoulders. It was all coming together in his mind. "I'm sorry to intrude on you like this after… everything."

"You're alive." A shaking hand covered his mouth, Duke Chapman's eyes poring over every detail. "And you've grown. Where the fuck have you been? What happened to you?"

I shifted my stare back to the floor, shame biting at my soul. "I ran away, chose a new life. A life I wanted, something peaceful and free of bloodshed."

"They said an assassin killed you." Confusion was building on my face at the Duke's angry voice as his expression filled with disbelief. "I lost my position because I was one of the many people suspected in your death. The whole city shut down. Houses raided, barns burned, and blood spilled. It was as if the Madness had invaded, but in the end, your father stepped in and declared you dead, putting a stop to the investigations. Who knows how violent it would have become if he hadn't."

"Dead?" Chapman's face paled as rage seeped into my voice. "Who said I died? What proof was there of this?"

"Viceroy Falco."

Crushing my hat with my fists, I waited for what unfolded.

"They found blood all over the courtyard, a dead maid, and a broken mask guests had seen you wearing at the party. Viceroy Falco stripped many of us of our royal duties and access, though when we were proven innocent, he promoted our ranks as an apology."

"Son of a bitch." Grabbing my braid, I coiled it on my head and shoved my hat back on. "I'm sorry to put you all through this. It seems Falco saw me leap off the balcony and staged my death. He's been sliming his way closer to the royal family; he intends to take over."

"No kidding." Duke Chapman leaned forward, scowling. "He had no favor with me or anyone he stripped out from under your father. There's just the King in a house of wolves."

"I should have figured it out sooner. Should've asked myself why no one had come looking for me, but if I was assumed dead..." Crouching to the floor, I covered my face. *How could I not know how far Falco would go? I knew he was willing to do anything after he and I...* "Was Falco missing a servant after that?"

"Missing?" Scratching his jaw, Chapman nodded, "Now that you ask, two were missing."

"Two?" I peeked over my fingers. "A mistress and a slave."

"A slave, yes, but I didn't know Viceroy Falco had a mistress." An eyebrow lifted, prying into the matter. "I suppose it was the *maid*. A red-haired gem of a girl. I'd seen her in his household a few times, but I didn't think about the idea he would stage a murder and go as far as slaughtering folks to gain access to, shit, everything. Stirring up flies, my ass."

"I thought I'd live a simpler life," I mumbled, standing once more. *How selfish.* "It seems I still left one piece of unfinished business behind, and he's been making a mess."

"Like a hog digging for truffles," snorted Duke Chapman,

packing a pipe with tobacco. "You plan on letting anyone else know you're back?"

Every muscle in my body tightened.

How am I going to clean up the mess I set into motion? Make amends to those who paid with their lives for Falco's lies? And what about John? My keeper and I'm... I've sworn to be his Sword and Shield. If I go back...

My soul and mind were at war. *John* echoed through my head, making my chest ache. I had made a vow and a promise I intended to always keep. Duke Chapman glared at me, seeing the wavering emotions in my eyes. With great patience, striking a match on his boot, he lit his pipe in a great arrangement of puffs. The whole time his eyes dug deeper. He wouldn't let me leave here unless I gave him an answer. Duke Chapman may be human, and I could overpower him, but the farrier downstairs was another matter.

No one wins a fist fight with a blacksmith, whether he sharpens a blade or shoes a horse. The Old Farmer had chuckled, telling me of a time he'd weaseled out of a fight. *One hit from that arm, and you'll be taking a dirt nap. Don't care if you're a daemon or not, Dante.*

"I may still have my braid, but I have a keeper." Smoke blew out of the Duke's nose with a look of distaste. "It was my choice, my request, not his."

"His?" He lifted an eyebrow, taking in another puff of tobacco.

"The new priest, Father John." Swallowing back the last of my hesitation, I revealed why I'd come back. "We both know Viceroy Falco would eat him alive, literally. When he told me he had plans of coming back to be the priest of Glensdale, I vowed to be his servant. I suppose this all falls in place. As a Prince, I wouldn't be able to deal with Falco, not if I ended up having to kill him for coming after yet another priest."

He nodded, tapping the pipe on his bottom lip, "You're

right. As a Prince, you can't kill a Viceroy and the *Rabid Dog* enjoys eating up the clergymen like whores to a virgin. Then, what was it you came to see me about?"

"I came to you because I need a draft horse, preferably black. It's hard to follow one through the woods at sundown." Happy to be changing topics, I listed the jobs I had in store for the new horse: "It'll need to pull new pews in a wagon, uphill. Carpenter should finish those up in a few days after I bring trees. I have the coin. Not sure if there's enough for the stock I know you keep here."

Watching him gnaw on the pipe gave me a nostalgic sensation. "I've got a Nivernais gelding. He's still green behind the ears, but I know you've dealt with stubborn horses before. Normally, I'd charge a hundred-fifty coin, but no one I've shown the high-headed fool to wants to even try to work him. He's got energy, and he's from the best stock, known for handling mountainous terrain and surefooted."

Opening the coin purse, I pored over how much I had left. "I've got about two-hundred coin left, but I still need to see the textile merchant and a few other vendors. How much slack are you going to give me on this?"

Smiling, smoke bubbled from his lips. "Fifty coins. If you need a second horse to pull, I'll loan you one as a gift to the new priest in town."

Pouring coins from the purse, I pulled out seventy-five. Walking across the room, I placed the stack on his desk, and he laughed.

"I said fifty. Did the sun bake your brains?" He slid the stack closer, spreading coins across the table. "But I respect you for knowing the value of the horses I keep."

"You didn't have to cut me such a huge discount." Grinning, I shook his hand. "I appreciate that I was missed."

"Aye, you were." He lowered his voice, "Are you serious about taking down the Viceroy?"

"Someone has to." His hand tightened around mine, keeping me there. "No one else can get as close as I can."

"Then tell me this." With a yank, his tobacco-laden breath filled my nose as he brought my ear closer, his voice lower. "Is it true you and Falco were lovers?"

Sighing, I confessed, "For a very short while. His mistress let something slip and it ended. It's most likely why she ended up dead in the snow that night."

He let go, nodding. "So be it... NIKOLAS!"

I flinched at the unexpected shout. The door swung open, and the farrier from before stood red faced from launching his large body up the stairs. He eyed me, then the table littered with coins. Letting out a long exhale, he caught his breath. Duke Chapman chuckled. Nikolas had mistaken the Duke's shout as a sign of trouble.

"Danny bought the Nivernais." Nikolas covered his face, groaning at the news. "I'll let you lead him to his new horse."

"Duke Chapman, I didn't think anyone wanted the stubborn gelding." He turned, waving for me to follow. "Hope you know you bought the biggest asshole in Glensdale."

"We'll see if we can call a truce," I smirked.

"Dante." I froze as Chapman called me by my name. "Good luck and know we have your back here at the stables."

Face red, I nodded in acknowledgment. Nikolas remained silent, and I prayed he hadn't made the connection that I was the lost Prince. Shaking it off, I decided it was good to know I had allies in town. We turned the corner of the shop, heading down the second assortment of stables where a heavy-muscled, black giant was pacing in a corral. As the massive horse rounded the side where we stood, the beast curled his lips up and nipped at Nikolas before continuing his canter. The ground sank under his weight and repetition of his routine. He needed no lead to drive him to his chore. Leaning on the corral fence, Nikolas pulled me back off.

"Don't do that unless you want to lose a chunk of your face or a hoof to the jaw." He spat into the corral which brought the massive draft horse to an instant halt, ears flat as he glared at the blacksmith. "I've never seen a horse so high-headed. He sees everything, and he makes up his own mind. No one's had any luck putting a saddle on that one. We can get him haltered for a wagon. Though he gets too excited and needs to be worn down from a day's hard work. Problem is he might kill you before the sun sets."

The horse walked straight at them, pausing to paw at the spot where Nikolas spat. Those large equine eyes screamed, *Rebellion.* He stood over seventeen hands high, making the top of his shoulder a little above my eye level. Gazing over the build of his bone structure, I thought the thickness of the muscles under the pitch-black coat was beautiful. The way his hooves sank in the mud, he weighed over two-thousand pounds, a ton for sure. The mane was long and wavy and in need of a good brushing, but his aggression kept groomers at bay.

"You got any sugar cubes?" The horse flicked an ear at me.

"Why on earth would I have any of those?" Nikolas rubbed his nose, curious. "I suppose Duchess Chapman has some in the kitchen."

"Get me some."

Nikolas rolled his eyes and disappeared back into the house.

The horse nodded, as if to say, *Good riddance.*

I giggled, and he wrenched his head my way, ears tall and nostrils wide. "High-headed indeed."

"Here." Nikolas returned with a handful of cubes. "She said Dante used to spoil the stock with these. I imagine she meant you."

They haven't forgotten me.

"Yeah." I ventured to the fence, and the horse narrowed

his eyes. "What's his name?"

"He has no name." Nikolas spat again. "Any horse that kicks me doesn't deserve a name."

Glaring over my shoulder, I razzed him. "You took his balls and never gave him a name?"

"How'd you know I castrated him?" His face soured.

"Duke Chapman only lets his most trusted worker do that job." Laughing, I turned to the brooding Nivernais. "I'd be pissed too."

"No joke. You really did hang around here! I'll leave it to you. I got cleaning to do. The sun's getting too low to work shoes." With that, Nikolas disappeared.

A snort and neigh brought my attention back to the corral. The horse shook his head and took two steps, sniffing the air hoping to catch a clue of what I held in my hand. Lifting my eyebrows, I opened my hand flat and looking equally intrigued at what lay there. Another few steps and I could feel the huffs of his breath across my palm. I smiled, the aggression and tension easing out of his shoulders and neck.

"I think I shall call you Basque." His ears flattened but flicked forward again. "It's a good name, I swear. A poet and writer famous for his wit and outspoken nature."

As if content with the information, he lipped the sugar cubes from my hand. Basque rolled them around in his mouth, his eyes sparkling in delight. His massive head and neck leaned over the fence, searching my shirt and pockets for more. My hands slid across his cheek and down his neck. He was solid as a stone wall but warm and healthy. No signs of respiratory diseases as he snorted, and his teeth were clean, just the right age to be a gelding ready to work full time.

"You think I'll be able to strap a saddle on you?" Basque nodded his head, approving of his name, his treat, and accepting his new owner.

CHAPTER 11

Game On

It didn't take me long to discover Duke Chapman didn't have the heart to sell or discard any of my old tack. My saddles, chaps, stirrups, reins and bridles were piled up and stored in a forgotten corner of a shed. Nikolas mumbled something about how he swore that stuff was for the Prince, but when the Duchess agreed I could keep or sell whatever I wanted from the pile, he left me alone to dig through it all. By the time I picked out the large pads and saddle meant for the Percheron draft horse I had ridden in winter, a crowd had gathered. Duke and Duchess Chapman as well as four workers lined the corral to see how I would tame the newly-named *Basque.*

The Nivernais stood still as if a statue as I lugged the weight of the padding and saddle across his back. With another handful of sugar cubes, I had him haltered and bridled. Unsure of how tame he had been before me, I took my time rubbing down his shoulders and legs until I could pull up and check the hoof and horseshoes. Again, the group held its breath as I went to check the rear shoes. My hand glided with ease over his rump, his skin taut, hair smooth, and muscles like a solid clay mold. Basque flicked his tail, slapping my face and snorting. I gave him a look, and he relented, allowing me to check his back feet.

"Is this your work on the shoes, Nikolas?" I was glad to be walking away as I spoke; the horse's hooves were as big as my head. "If so, you did an amazing job. Best I've seen."

"Yeah, that's my handiwork. He's too big to let them go bad." Duke Chapman nudged Nikolas's arm, and he blushed with pride. "Be a shame to see him go lame over a bad shoe. Even if he's got a nasty temper."

Nodding, I tugged and checked the straps under and across his belly and chest. The stirrups were lowered, but it was still a long way off the ground. I inhaled, holding my breath as I nearly hit my knee to my chin placing a foot in the cradle. It took a few hops before the muscles in my leg pulled the rest of my body up. While I was swinging my leg over, Basque sidled. I shushed him, and he shook his head and huffed. I let myself sit fully in the saddle, thighs aching from how wide he was under me.

"We taught him how to carry a rider. He should know how to do this." Duke Chapman raised his pipe at me. "Congratulations! Normally he kicks us off a few times before letting us settle in the saddle."

Everyone burst into laughter, and I shot him a look. This wasn't the reassuring news I wanted. Squeezing my legs and clicking my tongue on my teeth, I trotted him around the corral. His head was high and his muscles twitched under me. He wanted to cut loose. I could feel the unsteady jerking of Basque's desire to break into a gallop and let his muscles stretch. I pulled the reins up, and he stumbled to a stop, snorting in disapproval with ears flicking back.

"Is it still legal to break into a gallop down the main road?" My cheeks were aching from my grin. *I haven't done this in over ten years, and I've missed it.*

"Yeah, but I wouldn't do it with–" Duke Chapman dropped his pipe as Basque leaped in response to my legs squeezing around him.

"HAH!" Slapping the reins on Basque's shoulder sent him into a longer stretch.

With little effort, the Nivernais launched himself over the corral railing. It took every muscle in my legs and arms to not fly off backward while keeping my hat in place. The ground thudded under his weight, a plume of dirt and dust trailing behind as I urged him to gallop down to the gates. The guards there startled at the approaching black tank, and one fell to the ground with terror on his face. With little signal from me, Basque came to a stop. Snorting and flicking his tail, Basque let his feet dance, muscles relishing in the burst of energy he had been allowed to release. I fought to turn him around, and we raced back to where the stables lay just before the uphill climb. Again, he followed my signals as if I had trained with him directly, paying attention to every shift, pull, and squeeze, whether it be my body or the reins. They had worked him harder than normal, perhaps hoping to make him a more appealing buy.

"I thought he'd come back without you like he's done a million times before," laughed Nikolas. "I bet the guard down there wet his pants seeing him galloping down the street again."

"That explains why he tripped over his feet." Laughing with everyone, I decided it was time we parted ways. "I have much to do, and the sky is turning already. I'll see you all around."

"Glad to have you back, Danny." This time Duchess Chapman spoke up. "This place doesn't feel right without its... without you."

I heaved a sigh, giving her a knowing glare. Tugging the

reins, I rode off to the market. The sun was setting fast, and I had little time to finish what I wanted to achieve with the money in my pocket. Passing the fabric stall, I had a more important task to address. John's back wasn't healing right, and medicine would be needed to stave off fever, or worse, infection. Tying Basque to the hitching post, I left him gulping water in the complimentary trough. My thighs ached from the ride, and the drop back to earth was farther than I expected, making me stumble. Leaning on his shoulder, I caught my balance. He flicked an ear as if to say, *Are you kidding me?*

Ignoring Basque, I pushed through the door of the old shop. Inside it was musky, dark, and the smell of herbs and medicines stung my eyes. Fighting through it all, I found the counter and the basket displaying heaps of dried herbs. There between them was a tiny bell, and I rang it. Something banged beyond where I stood, and I heard the woman cursing. Hobbling out, the woman took me in with cautious maroon eyes. She sat on her stool, her patchwork skirt falling to her ankles with tattered edges from dragging on the ground. Her bodice was patterned with stitching I hadn't seen since the paintings on the walls in the King's mansion. Her three-knot braid had a long, free-flowing tail of curls marking her lower-class, unusual for a shop owner in the city.

"What do you want?" Her voice was like a slap to the face. "It's almost closing time. Spit it out."

"Buzz buttons and recommendations for treating burns."

Her mouth twisted. "Buttons are up on that shelf you passed: good for numbing the tongue, tooth, or skin. I recommend chewing them up or spitting in the medicine bowl. Works best in a paste. Speeds up the effect." I made an unsavory face at the idea. "What sort of burn we talking about?"

Opening my mouth, I paused, grabbing a handful of buzz buttons and responded with, "Blacksmith burnt himself with iron—branded the shit out of his back."

"Happens." She shrugged, "Keep it moist. Use fresh water, keep it out of the sun, and if he's willing, out of the heat of a fire. I have something made up. Happens a lot with the war picking up again."

"The war," I echoed.

She hopped off her stool, sorting through the jars on the shelves behind her.

"Didn't know it was picking up pace again. Been working out in the fields too much."

"If you ask me, Viceroy Falco's been at it again." Reading the scribbles on a jar, she scoffed and placed it back, still searching. "Rumor has it, he's been dropping a lot of coin on new armor, swords, even assassinations aimed for King Regius and his daughter Sonja in Captiva City. Dangerous stuff. He's gone mad if he thinks *The House*'s army is strong enough to march on the capital of *The Tower*. Oh, here's what I was looking for!" She spun around and slid the jar across the counter.

Staring at the dusty jar, I pressed to know more. "He's funding the next wave, not King Traibon?"

Why is my father letting this go so far? He should have stepped in if she knows this much.

"You have been out with your head in the dirt." I reached for the jar, but she grabbed my wrist. Our eyes met, maroon reflecting maroon in a way that sent chills across my skin, and I knew she could see through me. "Your father's sick, Dante."

Closing my eyes, defeated, I asked, "Does everyone recognize me so easily?"

"How can we not know our Prince?" she hissed, letting me go. "Look, I have my suspicions, and as a lower class, I slide under Viceroy Falco's interests. Take this with you, too."

"How sick is he, my father?" She dug through unseen drawers. A pouch of tea and a small vile of strange liquid landed next to the ointment. "What is all of this?"

"Medicine for your father." She tossed a satchel at me. "Take it all. He's been poisoned, I'm sure of it. It's like watching your mother all over again, and the Rabid Dog has to be behind it all. I've only seen King Traibon's face from afar, but it won't be long before he's bed-bound. The sooner you get that antidote to him, the sooner we'll know for sure."

Swallowing hard, I felt my hatred for Falco building. *My mother... poisoned. No one bothered to say a word to me?* "How much do I owe you?"

"Nothing." She waved me on. "Know you have supporters, and we're damn glad to see you alive and well. If you need anything, just ask for me by name: it's Madame Plasket at your service, my Prince."

Reaching into the pouch, I dropped twenty gold coin on the counter. "Thank you, Madame Plasket."

Rolling her eyes, she grabbed her broom up. "Quick, before I have to beat you out of my shop. The sun's setting, and I'm exhausted. Out with you!"

The shop door slammed behind me. Basque stared, curious what I had done to anger her. I climbed back in the saddle with a grunt of discomfort, and we headed to the church. My thoughts were twisting into a sea of anger and despair. To humans and non-bloodeaters, Falco was a plague, but now he turned his decay on his own kind. Emotions tugged at one another: *my father is ill, but I promised to keep John safe. I can't have a keeper and be the Prince. This is my life now. I'll have to make a choice and stand by it.*

Basque neighed, signaling we had stopped in front of the church doors. The hitching post was intact, though, if Basque wanted to, he could snap it with a single tug. Looking on either side, I noted that the church had only a single hitch in the front. If we wanted this to be a proper church, I would need to make more, and add a trough or barrel for water. Nobility would take wagons and horses to come for the weekly service, but with nothing to cater to the horses, it would deter many from bothering to come.

Pushing inside the church, I found John on his hands and knees scrubbing the pulpit. *Stubborn.* It was the word the old man had used to describe John on the nights he spent comparing us. *You're bullheaded, but that boy, he is stubborn made into flesh. The priests and nuns are gonna think a mule came there to train. Ha!*

"I was going to do that tomorrow," I scowled down at him.

John rocked back, sitting on his knees and wiping sweat from his forehead. "It was bugging me. Couldn't look at it anymore. Didn't want it here disgracing this place any longer."

"And what about your back?" My eyes shifted to the black jacket still on and hiding what lay beneath. "Normally you would take that off for something like this."

He winced, "I outdid myself, if that's what you're asking."

"I managed to get us a workhorse and the carpenter..." My eyes shifted, noticing some of the pews from the junk pile were missing. "Did he come by already?"

"Yup." John leaned back down, scrubbing the last dark spot with contempt. "He said he'd be back tomorrow to toss the rest. Nice guy. Said he remembered when you were younger." He paused his scrubbing and every muscle in me locked tight. "Do you think *he* noticed who *you* were?"

How could he not, if so many who saw me today know who I am, who I once was? And John, John knows, but like Paul said, he wants me to say it, to make it clear from my words. I can't. It scares the shit out of me to dare say it to him of all people. Stubborn incarnate. Even then, is he really ready to hear me tell him?

The church fell dark, the last vestige of sunlight gone. John was on his hands and knees, frozen as he glared at the bloodstain. The expression on his face made my heart thud loudly in the space between us. I gathered my nerves and marched toward the pulpit. He started scrubbing again, his teeth clenched tight. I couldn't read if he was mad at me or still brooding about Falco, but it didn't matter. Leaning down, I gripped his hand, making him stop. He jerked twice before facing me again. His lips parted, but no words came out before his face reddened with frustration.

"I don't know if Falco noticed who I am." His shoulders slumped at my words. *I can't say it, not yet, not here in this moment.* "I do know I need to look at your back. I'll finish this. You go take off your jacket and shirt. Let me tend to your wounds." Patting the satchel, John released the brush. "Go cool down and steel yourself. We both know it will hurt like hell to pull off your shirt, let alone for me to clean the burns."

John launched to his feet and slammed the office door behind him. The stained glass windows glowed with the light of the street lamp flames outside. Grabbing the bucket and brush, I scrubbed away the last of the blood. The podium was gone. I imagine he had the carpenter take it to be refinished. Dropping the brush into the dirty water, I marched back outside to slosh it across the street.

Basque snorted, curling his lips. Circling back to the doors, I froze. Viceroy Falco stood between me and the church. His thin lips stretched into a grin. Neighing, Basque pawed the ground as if to declare his own disdain for the visitor.

Did he figure it out? Does he know?

I aimed to step around him. He gripped my throat, slamming me against the wall next to the door. My shoulder blades ached against the cold stone. His fingers dug deeper into my neck, limiting my air. His eyes glowed red in the darkness, his fanged grin wild and feral. With his free hand, Falco tore away my hat. I struggled, my braid falling between us. He leaned in, forcing his lips on mine. I twisted away, but he pressed harder, forcing his tongue passed my lips only to be bitten, and he moaned with delight. His weight against me was infuriating. *Why am I letting him overpower me so easily?* The smell of the cologne and blood flooded me, and my stomach turned. *Nothing about him has changed. It's like our last night together all over again.*

"Oh, how I've missed you, Dante." Gripping his arm, I ripped it away. "So tall, broad... stronger."

Wheezing for air, my neck stung. *Dammit! Does he still want me that way?*

"I suppose digging in the dirt for ten years did you some good." He tossed my hat at me, and I caught it, crushing it in my fist and throwing it to the ground in defeat. "The rare tone of your skin, the muscles in those arms and torso... my! What wonderful improvements. At first glance, I wondered if I was dreaming, the Prince, back in Glensdale?"

He knew it from the start. Taking in a staggering breath, I croaked, "Why stage my death–"

Before my words could finish, his hand gripped my mouth. He shoved me back, my skull connecting with the stone wall. The world shook. My head rang from the impact. A warm trickle slid down the back of my neck. I had to fight to keep my eyes straight as they attempted to crisscross again and again. His breath hit the side of my neck. Memories of our last night together shook through me. My fright brought back my focus, eyes straight again. Jerking me forward against him, he pressed harder and his lips found my ear. With his arm over my mouth, digging into my jaw, I couldn't push him back. My anger was eating me alive. We were of the same build now, and still I couldn't dominate him.

Does he plan on inflicting the madness on me? Biting me for old time's sake, like when we... when he...

"How in love are you with your precious priest, I wonder?" He nuzzled my neck. I shuddered as he kissed my skin, inhaling my scent like a predator to its freshly caught prey. "Does he know you were in my bed? Does he know you watched with curious eyes as I took the last priest of Glensdale?" He ran his tongue across the vein he once pierced in the throes of passion. "Does he know how I once fed on you and took your Madness away for the sheer intimacy of the act? How jealous he must be, no?"

Dammit! My legs are shaking. You'd think I was ten years younger and smaller than him all over again.

The heat of my rage rose, and letting go of his arm, I aimed for his neck. My fingers grazed his skin and he let go, laughing. I growled in frustration, eyes falling on the hilt of his sword. He could slice me in half if I tried to fight him with no weapon or shield. The knife on my thigh was only good for utility purposes and would snap under the weight and precision of Falco's sword.

Next time, I'll have a sword and be able to fight back. My fists balled up, holding back my desire to beat his face in. *I can't let myself fall prey to my past self.*

"I do indeed like this new version of you, Dante. Handsome and a fighting spirit." Viceroy Falco's eyes were filled with excitement, his shoulders shuddering as it rattled through him. "Don't worry, my little Prince. I will keep your secret safe from your lovely priest as long as you play along with me."

"What do you want, Falco?" Rubbing the warm slick line on the back of my neck, my fingers returned covered in blood. "You're always after something."

"*La Dame d'Croc.*" The smile fell away, Falco's jaw twitching. "I want it back."

"It was never yours to have." His fist slammed into my cheek bone, sending me spiraling to my knees.

The taste of blood danced on my tongue, the inside of my cheek bleeding where my teeth dug into flesh. Glaring up at Falco, I spit across his feet. A bright flash filled my vision as his boot struck the side of my face. My back thudded against the wall, my spine lit on fire with pain. Basque fussed and snorted, unsure what to do. Another kick to the ribs left me desperate for air.

The old man would have my hide for letting this asshole beat me down like this. A smile crept across my bloodied lips. I could hear words from the Lord Knight. *If you're still bleeding, you ain't dead yet; suck it up, Buttercup.*

"Where is it? Tell me, or I'll march in there and put the stains back across the pulpit where I prefer them to be!" He sounded like a child throwing a tantrum. "ANSWER ME!"

Hugging my ribs, my cheek throbbing, I growled, "I don't know. Threw it in the woods over ten years ago."

Reaching down, he gripped my jaw, and I flinched, expecting another onslaught of punches.

"Then I suggest," he hissed, forcing me to look at him, "you fucking find it before I make you watch me drain every last drop from him after he's seen you bent over my bed like a whore."

"What's going on out here?" John's voice sent me into a panic.

Falco let go.

No, you idiot. Go back inside, where it's safe! Gripping Falco's wrist, I refused to let him go anywhere. "We were finishing up our conversation." I came to my feet, ignoring the aches and throbs.

Falco's eyes narrowed and I let go. "It's finished, for now."

Rubbing his wrist, he looked to the bare-chested priest at the doorway. Lifting an eyebrow, he smirked. He returned his stare to me, his lips moving, *I want him.* I caught my breath; we were still within arm's length. I spat at Falco, the blood hitting the ground between us from my broken bottom lip, blood dripping from my chin. John took a step farther out of the door and stopped, seeing my body stiffen in alarm. I could feel my cheek swelling, but I refused to take my eyes from the Viceroy. Falco licked his lips as if wishing he could have a taste of me or even John. John shifted again, making Viceroy

Falco lean toward me. I held my breath, fists ready to react.

I've seen that look. Anytime he looked at something he wanted or intended to take by force. He wouldn't...

With a sparkle in his eye, Falco whispered, "Game on, and John's the prize."

"Viceroy Falco." John's expression filled with rage. "Never lay a hand on him again. As his keeper, it's my duty to protect..."

"Keeper?" Laughter poured out of Falco. "I see why you like him. He's got some fight in him, too."

"Falco," I wobbled forward, ribs stinging and hissed, "Game on."

I should have thrown my weight. After ten long years I thought seeing him again wouldn't matter. Dammit! And now he's going to use John against me at every turn.

CHAPTER 12

Falling

Neither John nor I moved until Falco disappeared from view. Basque settled down with one last snort and flicked his ears at me. I could breathe again, but my ribs throbbed, making me wince. John wanted to say something, and I shot him a look: *Don't.* He opened the doors wider and nodded for me to come inside. Swallowing down the pain, I waited for him to close the church doors, and I followed his lead. It was dark, the cathedral looming over us with the weight of its foreboding nature. We slid inside the office, and I closed the door, watching John sit in the chair.

I can't let him know how much of a beating I took, or I'll have to deal with trying to keep his temper from goading him to kick in the Viceroy's door.

He had a bucket of water and a clean cloth beside him. "I can take care of this, you rest..."

"Nonsense. I promised and you can't possibly reach it all." Sitting in a chair behind him, I dipped and squeezed out the rag. *It's not the first time I've dealt with broken ribs. The old man landed a few good cracks on me in training. Heaven help me if John ever found that much out.*

My hand paused, hovering over the angry burns of the cross I helped make. Sections were raw as if no scab would form or bother to cover the flesh underneath. A pungent smell threatened of building infection. Sighing, John tensed his shoulders. I jerked to move and stopped again, unsure if he would be ready for the pain to come. Leaning harder against the chair, John prepared himself and I began cleaning the markings.

"I don't know which of us is the bigger moron." Hissing from the wet cloth touching his charred skin, John broke the silence. "Do you have to scrub so hard?"

"It wouldn't be this bad if you hadn't been so careless today." My eyes fell to the blood-soaked shirt and spots on the inside of his black coat. "You should have told me. When did it start bleeding again?"

The muscles in his back tensed, "On the walk here—we weren't even halfway—when it started to ooze and sting like hell. You would have wanted to stop, or worse, convinced me to turn around and wait another week. It should be healing better than this, don't you think?"

"I think Bishop Marquis enjoyed pressing it too deep. You ruffled his feathers." Ringing out the cloth, I placed it over the cross. "It'll be less of a nuisance if we can keep it clean."

"So, is that our horse out front?" John placed his chin on his forearms, leaning forward on the back of the chair. "Does it have a name?"

"*He* has a name: Basque." Digging into the satchel, I grabbed a few of the buzz buttons and dropped them in the stone mortar.

"Basque," he echoed. "I take it he's got wit to him then."

"Without a doubt." Spitting into the bowl, I used the back of my knife to smash and work the ingredients together. *I lost the pestle already. Great.*

"Did you just spit into that?" John turned, glaring at me. "Are you going to rub buzz button spit on my back?"

Pausing, I looked to him and the bowl again. "Yes."

"Ugh, it's like living with Grandpa all over again." John covered his face. "Got an infection? Let me chew on this root and spit it on there. Got a bee sting? Let me chew–"

"–on some tobacco and spit it on there," I finished for him. Laughing, I kept working the ball-shaped buds into a mash, spitting again. "I got my share of that one after I made the mistake of not checking the tree before hitting it with the axe."

"Ha! That's exactly what I did!" We were both laughing now.

Shaking my head, I managed to make a paste. "Not sure how well this will work. Going to hit the worst areas first and work it in."

"How did you find out about the buzz buttons?" John's back muscles twitched as I pulled away the wet cloth and dabbed the paste on the first angry spot. "Was that Grandpa as well?"

"Actually, no." Each flourish and line of the branded cross felt rough and agonizing under my fingers, but I pushed on, working the paste in and around. "I remember a maid had a toothache and carried some in her pocket. She would chew on them, and she thought it would be funny to let me try one and see what was so grand about it."

"What did it taste like?" With each returning touch, his muscles would tighten and release. "Though, I imagine your mouth went numb as hell. It's working better than I expected."

"You might as well chew on hay if you ask me." Digging out the last of the paste, I worked over the cross one last time, cursing Bishop Marquis. *You'll never touch John again.* "My mouth was numb for hours, but the taste was still there. Everything was salty. I don't see how she could chew on them all day, but her tooth had to be pulled by the blacksmith in the end. She ended up not needing them anymore and gave them to him for burns. It all just stuck with me, I guess. Never knew if I might need to know that information."

"I see." His shoulders were relaxing, but my work was far from being done. "And what's in that jar? I imagine it's next."

"A special blend by the herbalist, Madame Plasket." Cracking open the jar, I cringed. "And it smells like horse piss."

John covered his mouth and nose, looking desperate. "It might have horse piss in it."

Another wave of laughter erupted between us.

We soon fell silent, the lantern flickering across his back. The numbness made spreading the ointment easier on us both. It brought little reaction as I worked his back over, my fingers diving in and out of open flesh, desperate to heal and relieve John's pain. The curves of his muscles, the way his spine dipped inward and back out were well-made from training. He hadn't sat at a desk studying in Captiva City but done his own share of sword practice and hard labor. Lost in the task before me, I worked my thumbs downward to the end of the cross at the top of his hip just above his pants. Pausing, I noticed the small cuts here and there but said nothing. I dipped my fingers into the vile-smelling concoction and worked my way across his shoulders. The top of the cross rested just below the nape of his neck. John leaned into the pressure of my fingers, enjoying the way I massaged the ointment into his tense muscles. Heat rose in my cheeks and I froze.

Shit, I'm falling for him all over again. I pulled my fingers away, wide-eyed. *I love him, but he's a priest and I'm a... I was... I was over him. When he didn't come back, I swore...*

"Why'd you stop?" One blue eye looked over his shoulder, and I spun away. "What's wrong?"

"I'm finished." Closing the jar, I was shoving stuff back into the satchel, a sad attempt to hide my flushed face. "It's dark. We need to go. I still have things to do around the farm."

"Oh." He stood, stretching, "That feels much better. I can

move easier." His hand grabbed my shoulder and my heart sped up. "Dante, thank you. So, are you going to do something about... this?" He motioned to my face with a twirl of a finger. "I can help."

My eyes caught a fresh shirt on the desk. "I'll deal with it later." Grabbing it, I threw it in his face. "Get dressed. I'll get the horse ready."

By the time he pulled the cloth off his face, I slipped out of the office door. Rubbing my jaw, I paced down the aisle in disbelief. Ribs throbbing, my face swollen, I was too overwhelmed by my revelation to care anymore. When I started this path, I hadn't expected to feel so worked up around John. The way he carried himself, the confidence he displayed in the most pivotal of moments, was exciting and dangerous. He had been in pain all day, I knew it to some degree, but the stained shirt still hanging on the back of the other chair spoke volumes. The strength and willpower he held was breathtaking, and I loved seeing it, being part of it, and *I want more of it*.

Basque lifted his head, snorting at me when I slipped out of the front doors. He shuffled his feet, showing he was ready to go, bored with standing there staring at a stone wall. Much to my surprise, the church doors banged shut and John locked them. Slung over one arm was the blood-soaked priest's jacket, leaving nothing but the white blouse. The cotton was thin, spotting from the ointment and oozing burns, the cross visible even in the faint moonlight.

"Here, shove this in the satchel." He bumped past me while shoving the jacket into my chest, eager to greet Basque. "Good grief. He's huge."

"He's a pain to saddle up but well trained." Basque nuzzled John's hand. *Instant acceptance.* "I'm jealous. I had to use sugar cubes before he would give me the time of day."

"I make friends easily, I suppose." He rubbed down the

horse's neck and shoulder. "Tight muscled. He's hungry for work, huh?"

"Yeah." Sighing, I realized we had one horse and two men. "I can walk back while you ride him."

John turned with a frightened expression, eyebrows high. "I've never ridden a horse."

"I find that hard to believe." The jacket was sticky with blood, but I shoved it on top of everything inside the satchel. "Well, I guess you can sit up front and–"

His face twisted, "Did you forget about my back so quickly?"

Heat rose in my cheeks, making them throb from Falco's hits. I was thankful it would hide the blushing for now. "Are you going to be okay riding behind me?"

"As long as you don't mind me holding onto you." Scratching his jaw, John confessed, "I'd hate to fall off a horse this tall."

Swallowing back my nerves, I placed a foot in the stirrup and launched myself onto the saddle. John's eyes were wide, the feat intimidating. Sliding forward in the saddle, I slid my foot out of the stirrup. It took him some effort to get his foot into it. John gripped my arm, and I pulled him up. He landed heavily on the saddle and Basque neighed, nipping at my leg in complaint. John looked pale and dizzy at seeing how far off the ground we sat. Shuffling closer, he slid his arms under mine, gripping my shoulders with both hands.

"I find it hard to believe you've never been on a horse." Chills waved over my skin, his body pressed against mine and the strength in his arms stirring emotions. *I'm going to die of a heart attack if my heartbeat doesn't slow down. I feel like a young girl fawning over her crush.*

"I never said I haven't been on one," he corrected. "I was a small child, and the horse wasn't this big. How can you relax? My legs hurt because he's so wide."

"Who said I was relaxed?" My heart was pounding, and Basque's heavy trot made John press firmer against my back.

He's so warm; I can't say I'm not happy about this circumstance.

"You were meant to ride a horse," John mumbled, his forehead resting between my shoulder blades. "You belong up high. You deserve to be seen."

"I think I'm definitely above everyone in this saddle, John." I was dodging what I knew he meant. *He means as a Prince; how much did the carpenter tell him?*

I nodded to the guards, and they gave us more than enough space to ride through the gate. It was hard to gauge if Basque intimidated them, or if they had been informed of the former identity of the priest's servant: the lost Prince of Glensdale.

The carpenter remembered me, the same with the herbalist and even Duke Chapman. Then, the way John addressed and shielded me from Falco. Our conversations filled with carefully chosen words. No one was fooled by my new appearance, but I'm too afraid to ask John how much he has figured out. He must know by now who I am, but does he know of my past? That Falco and I were lovers long before I entered his life on the farm?

Fingers gripped my shoulders tighter, the city fading behind us on the road. John nuzzled my back, his cheekbone pressing against my spine. My entire body was on fire from the spinning thoughts of desire.

This is torture. If I could, I would give him all of me, but being his Sword and Shield will have to be enough. I can't be the reason he strays from his path. The way he looks at me just reminds me of the day he left.

It didn't take long before we were deep in the woods. John pressed his weight ever harder onto me. His hands slid off my shoulders and gripped my shirt. Knuckles dug into my chest and abdomen while the muscles in his arms tensed to keep hold. The pain made it hard to breathe as the ribs throbbed. Shifting in the saddle, I tried to coax him to move them elsewhere, my ribs tender from Falco. Basque high-stepped over a fallen tree and John's hands landed heavily onto my upper thighs. My back straightened, face hot, and his hands gripped me. A moan escaped my lips before I uttered words.

"J-john?" His head was sliding across my back. *Shit, he's falling!*

Dropping the reins, I gripped his wrists and lugged him forward. His face smashed between my shoulders and startled him. John's arms jerked upward, returning to their first position of gripping my shoulders. Fingers dug in, leaving my muscles aching under the strength they carried, and I swallowed back the arousal building against my will.

"Did I fall asleep?" The tension in his body made him feel like a brick wall behind me.

"You started to fall," I inhaled, unable to voice my feelings or reveal the new discomfort building, sparked by the moment. "We're almost home."

"Are you feeling okay?" John relaxed again, his grip softening. "You're burning up and sweaty."

At least he can't see my face or the front of my pants. "I'll be okay. Ribs are tender, and I still need to take care of Basque."

"I can help y–"

"You need rest." I shifted in the saddle, agonized as I rolled my shoulders. "You've never cared for a horse. I have. Leave it to me. There will be plenty of time to teach you later."

John let out a heavy sigh. His hands slid away from my shoulders, gliding across my body like hot silk, and I cursed under my breath. John's hands rested on my hips, and a million jaded thoughts longed to have his hands fall and grip me once more. To explore more of what my body had to offer. *This is nothing like when I was with Falco. The way I want him to touch me, kiss me, lay with me.*

We broke through the trees, and Basque halted hard. John slid forward, and we both stiffened. I hadn't been alone in my agony. In an instant, John dismounted and was into the cabin before I could react further. I covered my face. The heat of my desire should have been steaming into the cool night air. Basque flicked an ear and nuzzled my leg, ready to be unsaddled.

"I'm so glad it's dark out." After the throbbing subsided, I hopped off Basque and tied him to one of the porch posts. "I don't have much grass, but we'll bring the wagon tomorrow and bring back hay and feed."

Walking over to the water pump, I filled the larger bucket with water for him. He slurped it down, swatting his tail with glee. Making it inside the cabin, I found John passed out, laying diagonally across his bed. He was on his belly, the door still open to his room. Closing it, I went to the far corner of the main room, passed the fireplace, and slid a chest off to the side to reveal the cellar door. It creaked as I tilted it up and climbed down the ladder into the dark abyss below. Every time I went down there, I marveled over how long it must have taken the old man to build and dig it all out. It was large and long, not entirely under the house.

The Old Farmer had prepped it so he could hide. In the farthest section was an assortment of weaponry and armor that I wasn't sure John knew about. Regardless, I was after some old sweet potatoes in a basket by the ladder. I couldn't see the entirety from there, even with a lantern. The shelves obscured and shrank the initial impression. If I slid between a few rows of jars and dried goods, I could see that the room was wide and open.

Prepare yourself to fight anywhere. Echoes of the past nipped at me as I left. *Go nowhere without a sword.*

I had made that mistake. If I'd had a sword, I could have taken Falco down and freed everyone of his stigma. Outside, I pulled out my knife and cubed the two sweet potatoes out on a tin plate. It wasn't much, but Basque was enamored with the new treat I provided. Content he would be fine until morning, I ventured back inside. Bringing a lantern into my room, I dropped the satchel on the floor and pulled off my shirt. Purple and blue splotches painted one side of my body. Falco had an inhuman–no, indaemon—amount of strength. Cursing under my breath, I pressed to gauge the extent of my injury. *I'm lucky. None seem to be broken.* It hurt like hell with each hard jar of Basque's canter, but all I could think about was how John held his own pain and where he placed his hands.

Lying back, I covered my face. Thoughts of hands gripping my thighs rushed back. I held my breath. Falco had seen through me before I allowed myself to consider the fact that the tension between us was simple: *I love John.* To make matters worse, Falco wanted me and John. To him, I was the Prince he could dominate, and John was the plaything he could use to punish me at every turn.

I can't let him do this; I won't *let him do this. If he thinks I will submit to him like I did so long ago, he's wrong. I'm not that person anymore.*

CHAPTER 13

Bruised Ribs

It was high noon by the time John and I rode back into Glensdale. We had taken the time to cut down some trees for the carpenter, and I did everything I could to work through the pain of bruised ribs. We needed room to make a stable for Basque, so it worked in everyone's favor. The Nivernais was beside himself to pull not only a wagon with two men on it, but a load of heavy trees. When we reached the city gateway, the guards seemed relieved to see the giant horse put to work and tame. The carpenter refused to take any more money for his services. He took off his hat and bowed to me and I threw up my hands, making it clear it wasn't necessary.

Dammit, he knows who I am, too!

The church had been left alone, for once. The last time a priest came, Falco hired vandals to destroy it, and my father had to replace the stained-glass windows. He was furious with the Viceroy over the matter when his spies told him who funded the rampage. Three days later, Falco marched into the church late one night when the priest would be there. I imagine Falco lunged at him like a feral dog, ripping into the priest's neck at the podium and dragging him back to his bedroom where I was still asleep in his bed. It was the first time we bedded, and the wounds where he drank from me were still fresh.

"Look, Dante." He woke me, and I turned to see a half-dead man shoved to his knees in the space between us. "I brought us a plaything."

I had no words. There in spilled white sheets dotted red with my own blood, I watched him grow excited to have me bear witness to this sin. *That could have been me; it was me.* My stomach twisted. I then realized what the mistress said was true. *He only beds you, so he can be closer to his true love, La Dame d'Croc. Other than that, he's a glutton for human blood and torturing his playthings like a dog chewing on a bone.*

"Are you watching, Dante?" Falco dug his fangs deep into the priest's neck where blood was still pulsing from the original wound. His eyes locked with mine as he sucked. The man's face wrenched in pain, and my heart leaped to my throat. Falco pressed harder, ripping open the priest's jacket. *Plaything.* His hand slid down the man's chest, smudging blood across it. Pulling away from his neck, Falco let him drop to the floor as blood dripped down his chin. He drank until the priest's heart ceased, devouring his life without any regret, any compassion. "Did that not excite you, my dear Prince?"

Shuddering, I shook the sour memories from my mind. *No way in hell he's getting his hands on John.*

Dragging the shattered remains of unwanted pews to the wagon, I urged myself to come back to the present. Basque became the talk of the town after how calm he had returned. He needed no guidance, no attendant to keep him standing still despite the bouncing and loud bangs coming from the wagon. The local merchants all took turns to meet the new priest and mutter under their breaths. Jealous of Basque, they all wished they bought the blasted beast when Duke

Chapman was pushing him onto them.

My ribs stung, my breathing labored, but the work had to be done. John was taking it easy, wiping and cleaning the pews. By the time I returned with the first round of new pews, he had mopped the entire cathedral floor. Besides the webs lingering in the vaulted ceilings and rafters, the rest of the place had changed into a place of light. For the first time in ages, it looked like a thriving place of worship.

"I take it from the look on your face I do good work." John was lugging out a bucket of dirty water, tossing it across the ground. "Did you get Basque some hay yet?"

"Yeah. The carpenter was spoiling him while we loaded the pews." I lugged the first pew into the church and set it into place. "How's your back doing? If the buzz buttons seem to be working, I can get more."

"Did we use them all this morning?" He motioned to help me carry in the second pew.

"Yeah. I wasn't sure if they would help, so I bought only a few." Grunting, I grabbed the far side, and we hobbled into the church, lining it up with the existing rows. The whole way, my ribs lit up with a sharp pain. I sucked in air, holding it in a failed attempt to lessen the searing pain. My teeth clinched, leaving my jaw aching as we shuffled to place the pew on the floor.

"See if the herbalist has anything for your face, first." John flopped on the pew, flinching when his back hit the wood and forced him to lean on his knees. "It looks like it hurts."

"It's more swollen than painful." I sat down, my ribs stabbing painfully with each breath. "It's my side that's killing me."

John's eyes widened. "Let me see."

Glaring at him, I caved and lifted up my shirt to expose the angry shades of red and purple painting the muscles across my ribs. "They're bruised; it'll just need a week or two."

He puffed out his cheeks, the look in his eyes angry. "Falco."

I started to push my shirt down, but he gripped my arm, still glaring at the marks as if to sear them into his memory.

"John, it's fine." His fingers tightened on my arm before releasing me.

"Don't go anywhere without a sword." He pulled himself off the pew, his back to me. "I'm glad you chose to carry Grandpa's broadsword today; you earned the right to do so. I don't care if he's the Viceroy of Glensdale. You fucking run him through next time."

He walked off and disappeared into the office. The bang of the door echoed through the church; it was the shout of anger John couldn't scream out loud. He was upset with Falco but also at himself. None of this would have happened if he hadn't insisted on coming here. If he only knew I blamed myself for not being prepared, for hesitating to fight back and letting him get dragged into my own past. Leaning back, I steeled myself to rise to my feet. It was time to see Madame Plasket again. The office door still shut tight; the authoritative solidity of it was like seeing John's back seconds before. *He will be fine for now*, and I slipped out of the church.

Petting Basque on the shoulder, I snuck him another handful of sweet potatoes. Snorting with satisfaction, I left him there, confident he wouldn't wander off. I couldn't bear riding him just yet. I took the long walk to the line of apothecary and item shops. It wasn't far from the church and far gentler to the aching and throbbing in my side.

Inside the pungent shop, Madame Plasket sat on her stool, shaking a jar of mysterious liquid. Her eyes watched me, an expectant look on her face making me feel as if I were late. I grabbed the basket of buzz buttons from the shelf, dropping it on the counter. She lifted an eyebrow at me. Placing her jar down, she reached across the counter, grabbing my shirt before I could step away. Lifting my shirt, she gauged the marks and let go.

"I heard rumors." Scoffing, she slid the jar to me. "Figured they were true, so I made you something special. More buzz buttons for the priest, then?"

"Where do you get your information from, Madame Plasket?" Picking up the jar, I opened it to smell it: *menthol and peppers?* "It seems you know more about me than I know about myself."

"I may own and run an herbalist shop," she smiled, sweet and menacing, "but you should know I am also in charge of making exchanges for the dark arts."

Freezing, I closed the jar. I gauged her expression, weighing what I knew of Glensdale's dark underbelly. With a smirk on my face, I replied, "And why would the Assassin's Guild want to help a runaway Prince?"

"I already told you." She grabbed an empty jar and filled it with buzz buttons. "Falco's bad for business, worse for Glensdale and its King, and has royally screwed us over more than once."

"Why should I trust you?" I put the jar back on the counter, wary of its contents and purpose. "Don't you have the means to take care of him yourself? Why ask me?"

A loud cackle burst from her, "If we kill a client because of disfavor, we'd go out of business. Besides, there's no crime in being charitable to the new priest in town and winning favor with him and his servant, no? Or better yet, aiding our Prince who's in need? You need training? Supplies? We can aid you in many ways without breaking contracts."

"You haven't answered me." Palms flat on the counter, I lowered my voice, "Should I trust you?"

Sighing, she patted my shoulder. "If I wanted you dead, Dante, I would have gotten you and the priest with poisoned buzz buttons."

"R-right." My blood ran cold. "Or even the ointment."

"Now you're using your head." She slid the two jars back to

my side of the counter. "Rumor has it, if the priest impresses your father, he will allow *The Church* to bring nuns into the city for the first time in ages. I want you two to re-establish a sanctuary for *The Church*. We need that support if we are to bounce back from the damage Falco's done while you were playing farmhand in the woods."

"Then I suppose I need to get back to work." Placing the jars in my satchel, I started for the door.

"Dante." I halted. "Don't let him get the dagger or we're all good as dead."

There was no need to answer. I had done my part once before. Pushing into the street, I paced down the road. It was so quiet now compared to over a decade ago. The merchants used to shout and call out to passing crowds from decorated stalls. The street was bare and silent despite the pleasant weather, and it made my skin crawl. Viceroy Falco had broken the citizens, fear filling the atmosphere. Instead, customers dove in and out of shops, rushing to stay inside rather than outside. No one wanted to be on the streets; it wasn't safe with Falco back in town.

A flash of midnight blue and golden embroidery flapped in the wind, calling me into a textile shop. Inside, I found a round man sleeping in a chair. Rolls of fabrics and rugs piled around him as he snored with his mouth gaping open. Clearing my throat, I woke him, and he sat up, alarmed. Crushing the bottom of his palms into his eyes, he blinked to see who entered his store. Using the sleeve of his shirt, he wiped the drool from his chin and his face flushed in embarrassment.

"E-excuse me, sir." He wobbled to his feet, shorter than I expected him to be. "It's been slow today."

"It's okay. I'm here to buy some fabric for the church." Scanning the room, I saw a few options, but not the ones I had come to get. "I was wondering if you had any *La Nuit Dorée du Roi?*"

He eyed me from head to toe. "There's only one family who knows we carry that pattern." Again, he picked apart my looks and clothes, and his eyes paused on my scarred knuckles before declaring his thoughts out loud to me. "And you don't look like anyone from King Traibon's court or service."

"I didn't think King Traibon banned you from selling it to commoners." Rubbing my forehead, I took another glance of the merchandise. "If that's the case, I suppose anything close to it or similar color and pattern should suffice."

"Papa!" The merchant billowed, his eyes still holding firm on me. "Are we allowed to sell *The Golden Night of the King* pattern to any who ask for it by name?"

A door creaked open from the back and a bent over old man shuffled in, his cane thudding against the wooden floor. He squinted at the merchant. Scratching his chin, he hobbled closer to me. My cheeks flushed. I knew him even though his eyes were milky with cataracts and old age filled his features with more wrinkles. His brows lifted; a shaking hand covered his mouth. He seemed unsure, his thoughts visible on his face: *Are my eyes really going or is it my mind?*

It's not a grand secret, but I can't let this poor old man wonder if he's lost his mind.

"I would have thought you'd been long gone by now, Lord Harrison." My voice triggered for him to reach out, and I shook his hand.

"My God, where have you been, my dear Prince?" The merchant bowed down and Lord Harrison cackled. "Ignore my grandson. He was a young boy in the days you visited my shop."

"Please, no formalities." Sighing left an ache in my chest. *He was older than the Old Farmer, but he hadn't faced what the Lord Knight survived.* "I'm here on behalf of the new priest. My fath– the King is coming for the first service and the tapestries are worn out."

Nodding, Lord Harrison turned to the merchant. "King

Traibon never put a hold on that pattern. We just keep it hidden. He asked for it by name; he shall get it. I suppose you will be draping the walls and possibly need runners for the aisleway as well?"

Flinching, I had neglected to think of a runner. "It seems you know more about my needs than I do." Pulling open the coin purse, I drew a few coins out and handed the coin purse to him. "Falco's buying apparently."

"Ha!" Lord Harrison weighed the bag in his palm, a sign of years of habit and practice being a tradesman. "This is more than enough. We'll even do the decorating in that case and Marcus here will take a look and see how else we can make this first service one the King will enjoy."

"Indeed, it would be an honor to aid you. I heard stories of you, though I wish you'd come back and take– OUCH!" Marcus fumbled over a rug to shake my hand.

The cane dug into his toes, "It's an honor to help get the church running again."

"Thank you." Nodding my head, I left without wasting any more time.

The entire city knew who I was, including Falco, *but does my father know I'm back and alive?*

Swallowing down the rising fear, I focused on getting back to the church. I left John alone far longer than I had intended. Panic forced me to pick up pace, my side stinging in reply. My heart thudded in my ears. Basque swiveled his head and curled his lips as I came around the corner. He pawed the ground with his hoof: *What took you so long? Give me sweets!* Shushing him, I pushed into the church and paled. Viceroy Falco stood midway in the aisle.

"My goodness, you have done wonders in such little time." Falco's voice bounced off the walls and ceiling. "Perhaps it's good that I put faith in you, Father John."

John and the carpenter were on the pulpit, fastening the

new podium to the floor.

"There is much work to do still." John stole a look at me but returned his eyes to Falco. "It would be going far better if you hadn't beaten my servant in the streets last night."

The carpenter paled, looking to me then to Falco.

"He needed to learn some manners." He took one step closer to the pulpit and my blood boiled as I gripped the hilt of the sword on my hip.

"Viceroy Falco." My voice filled the cathedral, making him spin to face me. "Let me walk you out. As you can see, my keeper is in the middle of business with the carpenter."

I could feel the carpenter staring at my bruised cheek and John relented, "Thank you, *Danseur.*"

"As you wish." Falco's eyes narrowed, and I escorted him out as he whispered, "You shouldn't leave your precious items unattended. Someone might come along and break them."

I stopped at the doors watching him walk away, "And spoiled brats don't get prizes for their tantrums." Slamming the doors shut, I could breathe again.

The laughter muffled by the door made my shoulders visibly shudder. Behind me, the carpenter was whispering with John. If there had been any respect left for Falco, it was gone after John let it be known he'd laid a hand on the Prince. Looking for the *La Dame d'Croc* would have to wait until after King Traibon came to John's first sermon. Turning, I saw they had finished lining up the pews while I'd been away. John's blue glare never left me. Letting go of my sword, I motioned for John to follow me into the office, and he wasted no time to follow.

"What took you so long?" John hissed, slamming the door behind us.

"My ribs." Pulling out a jar of buzz buttons and the new jar, I sighed. "And I managed to strike a favor with the textile merchant. He'll be sending his grandson Marcus over to decorate."

Picking up the jar of new medicine, he opened it. "Well, this is a more pleasant smell. What is this for?"

"Me." I pulled my shirt off and lifted my arm, the pain agonizing. "Do you think you can return the favor?"

"How much of this crap do I rub on there?" Scooping a gob onto his fingers, he dabbed the icy medicine sparingly.

"What are you doing?" Scoffing, I grabbed his wrist and pressed his palm flat across my ribs. "Rub it in. Helps to use your whole hand and not the tips of your fingers. I can't reach, and it hurts like hell to do anything at this rate."

His cheeks reddened, "I didn't want to hurt you."

"It already hurts." I was flustered. "I just hope this helps."

Inhaling deeply, John took another gob, rubbed it between both palms, and applied it across the purple-stained skin. "I'm not afraid of him, you know."

Sighing, I whispered, "I know, but you should be."

"Are you going to be here when the King comes?" He paused his rubbing a few seconds before continuing again. "Or do you plan to stay in the background?"

"It's not like I can stand on the pulpit and preach with you." I eyed him, gauging the focused expression on his face. "I'll be here, not because of Falco, but to support you. Was that not the pact we made ten years ago? Was that not the reason why your back is on fire day in and day out?"

John's cheeks reddened. "You're right. It was a stupid question." He pulled away, grabbing my shirt to wipe his hand. "I've got work to do, so this should suffice. Take a break. I'll need you back to full health as soon as possible. I was just wondering if you wanted... never mind."

"What is it?" Creasing my brow, I watched him shake his head. *What unfolds inside that mind?*

He left, leaving me wondering what it was he wanted to say. I knew something unspoken lingered between us. That moment where his lips would part, stay open for a few seconds before he would slam them shut again in silence. His cheeks were red and twitched with frustration while a mixture of dread and unspoken questions filled his eyes. I could never guess what was going through his head. Unlike me, he was unpredictable, and he reminded me of the old man.

Always think ten steps ahead, Dante. The birds had eaten the seed, and the Lord Knight gnawed on his pipe, scowling at me from the porch. *And if you can't think that far ahead, let John do it. That boy's far cleverer than he lets on, but worthless if you ask him someone's rank. He could never grasp that, but don't let it fool you. John's got survival instincts like no other in this world. I swear he'll outlive us both.*

CHAPTER 14

King Traibon

Between Lord Harrison, his grandson Marcus, and the carpenter, we managed to finish the final touches a day before John's first service. Nostalgia bit at my heart and soul seeing the fabric from my childhood hanging from the walls, competing for attention with the stained glass windows. I smiled, knowing both had been picked by my father and would catch his attention. As for the complication of keeping myself hidden from him, I consulted Madame Plasket. She gave me some attire fit for an assassin and a jeweled masquerade mask. It reminded me of the one I dropped when I left Glensdale.

The black leather armor and heavy hooded cloak over my large frame made me a menacing figure. I didn't care for the limited view through the mask, but it didn't matter since I was putting on airs as John's personal bodyguard. No one would question it, not with the unspoken past involving Glensdale's missing priests. Combined with the Lord Knight's broadsword and sheath at my hip, there was an ambience building, making me a higher rank than John. I stalked his heel like an obedient hound as the doors opened. The building rumbled with chatter and resonated the whispers filled with garbled compliments on how gorgeous the remodel had been with such short notice.

Wagons were pouring in, and I was thankful John heeded my advice to reserve the first two pews for high ranking individuals of thirteen-knots or higher. The first to claim these seats were Duke and Duchess Chapman, both eager to shake our hands and satisfy their curiosity to see the new priest, *their Prince's keeper.* The rows of pews were filling fast, many of them with nobility looking for an excuse to dress in lavish attire outside of the usual ball. The crowd coming through the door started to thin, and I rolled my shoulders, growing bored of the honeyed words each person offered John at the pulpit. In the past, it had been me shaking those same hands and receiving empty words of praise.

The banter came to a hair-raising silence as Viceroy Falco walked through the open doors. A woman shaking John's hand hurried away to sit, making the air grow cold around us. The sunlight pouring in did nothing to break the dark aura Falco carried into the church and down the aisle. Eyes avoided looking his way, afraid to draw his attention. He started with a wide grin, but with each step, each glance, his grin fell further into a scowl. We had managed to do more work, with more materials than he had given us money for, and he was losing his first round of the game he set in motion. John was beaming to see Falco falter.

"I'm so happy to see you made it, Viceroy Falco." John bowed his head, his blue stare unafraid of the disdain dripping from Falco's glare. "Is King Traibon still attending?"

"Where did you find the extra coin for this?" Falco wasted no time as he waved an arm around the church. He was aiming to crucify John publicly in front of his potential flock. "This pattern is pricey, the new pews, the runners, all of this and the horse are more than what I gave you. Are you stealing from my people or swindling folks for charitable donations already, Father John?"

John stood tall, back straight with a sheepish expression. "My dear Viceroy, you must know I have my own means of making money and trades. I started my life as an honest farmer, you know. Right here in this city, in fact. Not to mention, it wasn't just you who wanted to donate to the church." Duke Chapman paled overhearing this, letting John know he may have said too much if he intended to reveal who aided him. "*The Church* wants to pour forth all the funding it can to make things right in Glensdale. It takes money, and your charity wasn't wasted, I assure you. My superiors in Captiva City sent me here with a generous amount, surely Bishop Marquis told you? Or could it be he didn't know this either? Strange. I'm sorry I didn't share this with you in our previous discussions."

A hand on my sheath, I shifted in silence. Duke Chapman sighed; John redirected Falco's rage toward *The Church* and not those who traded and worked with us. For the first time, Falco's face was red with anger, and I wished he could see the smile on my face. I bit my lip, resisting the urge to laugh, and my eyebrows raised high.

Wow, I'm rather jealous. I don't think I've ever seen anyone but my own father spin him around in a game of words.

"And this...hired help?" He lifted an eyebrow, his chin pointing behind John and at me. "Or a *dancer* in costume?"

"No offense, but not many priests have survived their first sermon, or so the rumor goes." I pulled my hand to the hilt and tightened my grip at John's words, biting my tongue. "Besides, I'm sad to see Bishop Marquis isn't here. I thought he would attend and come with you. He spoke so fondly of you."

"Yes, perhaps he didn't realize you would be hosting a sermon so soon. Was he not here a week ago to scorch *The*

Church's mark into your flesh?" Sneering, Falco parried John's words, trying to regain control of the conversation. "I'm sure he had more important matters to attend to at this time."

"I see. The Marquis and you must be really close." John lifted both eyebrows, his hands motioning an invisible offering between them. "He must have forgotten it's forbidden to speak of the ritual to anyone, but I suppose I can let this one slide."

Falco flinched, his face becoming red once more before he growled, "I look forward to seeing how today's service goes."

Trumpets were blaring outside, causing everyone to turn to the doors. A lustrous blue and gold carriage pulled to a stop outside. Everyone sat, lowering their heads and awaiting the new visitor. They did this with precision, as if something they had all been trained to do in the presence of certain company. I tugged John's coat, and he followed my lead as we both knelt on the pulpit. He gave me a quick look, confused and unsure what was unfolding. Men and women in bright knight's regalia poured in, a menacing yet beautiful display of guards blooming before us and filling the aisle all the way to where we knelt.

Whispering over John's shoulder, I answered, "King Traibon is here."

I glanced over to Viceroy Falco, and his expression told me my father wasn't supposed to be here. Grimacing, I could only wonder if news had reached the King that his son was alive or even the fact that I was a servant to a priest. My heart beat loudly, my palms sweaty. *I'm not ready for my time with John to end here like this*. The carriage door opened and out came my father. I remembered him being taller, but I had been shorter the last we stood facing each other. His eyes were sunken and dark, and leaning on an elegant cane, his frame seemed so frail. He had rotted away in my absence, and a sharp pain stabbed at my chest. His once snow-white complexion looked jaundiced even in the bright sunlight. An attendant held his free arm as he took his time walking down the aisle.

Eyes wide, King Traibon took in the fabric and gave it a toothy grin, his fangs still large and sharp. He recognized it and giggled, whispering into the attendant's ear, who nodded and smiled with him. I could hear him mumbling, his voice still deep as ever like a lion's roar. *Madame Plasket didn't lie.* He looked like he was dying, and that was unnatural for any daemon unless he was being poisoned. Again, I bit my tongue, thankful my grimace was hidden behind the mask I wore. King Traibon had made it to the front of the pulpit where he inhaled deeply and took one last look around before speaking.

"Thank you, Father John." He motioned, giving John permission to stand. "I found your letter refreshing, and I couldn't resist the invitation."

Viceroy Falco and I both paled. My mind spun into a panic. *When did John send a letter? How did he get it to my father without Falco snatching it up? What on earth had he written to my father to bring him from his bed, sickly as he seemed, to come here today for a sermon? Oh no! He wouldn't dare tell him about me, would he?*

"It's a great honor to see you in person, King Traibon." John bowed once more, smiling. "I was so afraid your health would keep you. Please, sit and rest well. I pray you enjoy my sermon."

My father gestured for John to take control of his church. The priest bowed again to the King, and I stood at his heel where I stiffened, unsure of where to go and what to do. Every fiber wanted to hide, to be out of sight. My father was staring at me, making me shift. There was a familiar sparkle to his eye, one that made me feel like a kid again as I shuddered.

You always knew what I'd done before I could confess. What do you know about me? About John? Are you here to take me back?

"Thank you all for joining me today." John's eyes sparkled as he scanned his audience, and the next step in his dream came to life. "*The Church* has always wanted to spread its warmth to Glensdale, and I am blessed that Glensdale, alongside its King and Viceroy, have been great supporters in helping me regain this lost treasure on their behalf." He motioned to the span of the church and many murmured in agreement. "I hope this is the start of a long-standing friendship between us in a time where war is slowing, and lives are so precious."

As the sermon started, I scanned the room but always came back to hopping between Falco and my father. I was grinning, watching Viceroy Falco grow sicker by the second. Then I would falter, a swell rolling in my chest as I returned to King Traibon. As much as I wanted to bring my father the cure in my satchel, the guards would run me through.

"Let me start by introducing myself." John's voice filled the room, and all eyes locked on him. "I am Father John Thompson. Like so many here, I lost my family to the war, and moreover, to the Madness. Priests of *The Church* are sworn to preach peace, to encourage a cure, to fight back this plague. I was fortunate to have a surviving family member who took me in and gave my childhood and my life a second chance. It was in this moment that I wanted to make a difference in the world, to stop others from being devoured by this plague, and here I am before you to fulfill this dream, this passion." He didn't just stand behind the pew but paced back and forth on the pulpit. At times, he raised his voice, making the bodies jolt in unison. "Glensdale! The world doesn't know how kind and beautiful you truly are. I know different. I've always known different. Yet, we also know it is here that the birth and creation of the Madness comes from those who are bloodeaters. It is not my intention to condemn those who live this way.

Nowhere do you see this rampant in your streets or ravaging your lands. So, I am here to plead for you to not be hateful, to not use your curse to ravage those who may stand against you. The Madness doesn't discriminate. It kills daemon and human alike: fathers, mothers, children, *The Church, The Court, The Tower, The House.* It doesn't choose sides once let loose. Like a rabid dog, it will turn and bite its owner if not put down swiftly."

Many shifted in their seats and I swallowed. *How brave you are at times, John. Do you intend to piss the entire city off? Or worse, every bloodeater here who sees you as an* hors d'oeuvre? *Why not flat out scream FALCO IS TO BLAME and save us the shenanigans? Granted, the old man would have been howling in the back, slapping his knee over this one.*

"Bless you! Bless those who are willing to do anything to protect those they love, even drink from the blood of their enemies. *The Church's*—no, *my* wish is to see you take heed, take great care in your practices so that we can cure the Madness. I pray-tell that we can make amends, and have this war come to a close. Humans, daemons and bloodeaters alike can join forces in order to cure, to teach, and to mend what the past has ripped apart. WE CAN BRING GRANDEMERE TO ITS FORMER GLORY!" If anyone dozed off, they were awake now in his roar for unity. He held a book high with a golden title of *Histoire de Grandemere*, slamming it to the ground suddenly. The sound made several yelp in response as it echoed into the rafters. "We were once united as one! There was no *Tower, Court* or *House* battling against one another at our borders, but a unified people who traded without fear and came together in times of need. Our country is sick. *Grandemere,* the *Grandmother* needs us to right our wrongs, repent and heal. Most importantly, care for one another again."

Many nodded to themselves and whispered to their fellow attendees, as if joining in his cause as the words spilled forth.

So, this was the purpose of coming here and being a priest. You want peace in the world, unity, and a way to combat the Madness. Sighing, he was still rambling, telling stories of old from his book. *And now you share fairytales to lighten the mood. Perhaps you'll actually be good at this after all.*

I was sweating to death, ribs aching from the weight of the leather garments I wore. *This old man out-winded a daemon doing farm chores,* always the prodding of the past. I would have to endure. If Falco tried anything, I might have a chance to scathe by without a scratch if I blocked properly in this gear. Lord Knight Paul had discussed armor in great detail with me, the purpose of the gear and styling, how I should change my offense and defense accordingly based on what I wore versus what they wore. How insightful he was on observing and misleading the opponent.

You never know when you can't replace your gear. You should always know the weak points in your opponent's own. He had pointed out gaps in the various garments he hid in the cellar. *Note, they are all in a different spot. You keep them out of your holes, and be sure to fill theirs with your sword.*

I found myself staring at John again. Sweat dripped down his face, and he leaned on the podium. He abandoned his pacing, winding down. His hands gripped the podium white-knuckled, his breathing labored. I marveled over the physical drain his performance brought on. *A powerful sermon designed to impress a King.* My father had a stern expression on his face, but he wasn't watching John. Each time I peeked his way, the King had been glaring at me. I couldn't stop myself from shuddering, looking away, afraid if our eyes connected, he would shout, *Caught you! Now come home, Dante. Forget this ruse!*

"Glensdale and King Traibon, thank you for such a warm reception." John called my father's stare to him. "And let's not overlook Viceroy Falco's generous donation to aid in prepping the building for today's service."

My father lifted an eyebrow and shot Falco a suspicious look. A slurry of whispers erupted throughout the congregation at the news as they clapped in confusion. Standing, Viceroy Falco sent the gossiping to a dead silence before taking a bow. He was playing the charitable part and not one soul in the church believed it. He never intended to have the King's favor and protection on this place, yet here it was uninvited by the way his body language played out.

"I'm glad to have such a wonderful priest here in Glensdale." Falco's words were hollow. "Please do take good care of Father John while he makes this place his new home."

Confused, the claps started slowly and botched. King Traibon leaned to his servant, whispering. They nodded and glanced at me. Again, I was thankful for the mask hiding my panicked face. *And if my father saw the bruise on my cheek, he'd lose his temper knowing Falco put it there.* The attendant nodded and rose to her feet, walking in my direction. Meeting my gaze, she motioned for me to come closer. Swallowing back my fear, I crouched at the edge of the pulpit.

Just my luck. It's my cousin Ruth dressed as an attendant. I can't say a word, or she'll know. I used to read bedtime stories to her, and she used to throw a fit if anyone else tried. If anyone could peg me by my voice, it'd be her.

"King Traibon would like a word with Father John before he leaves. We will wait for the church to empty and speak privately in his office." I nodded, agreeing to it on John's behalf. "Thank you," Ruth said.

"Thank you all!" John was saying. "Know that my doors are always open, and I hope to see you return for next week's service." I leaned in to whisper in John's ear, and he smirked at the request. "Please," he continued, "if you don't mind, King Traibon has requested a private audience. Once he is done, feel free to stop by or even tomorrow."

The room filled with the echoes and noises of the mass of attendees leaving. Many took one last look at the décor or fussed over how impressive the priest must be meeting with the King so early in his career. John made waves, and Glensdale was filled with the excitement he brought in after openly challenging the Viceroy. Falco would have his hands tied, unable to make a rash move like he'd done all week.

"King Traibon, I'm more than happy to stay..." My father lifted a hand, making the kneeling Viceroy stop.

"You're not needed." My father turned to his guards. "See to it that the Viceroy and everyone leaves the building. I wish to speak with Father John in private, with only my attendant."

I watched as Falco was nearly shoved down the aisle and out the door. Turning back, the attendant was aiding my father to his feet. It took all I had not to rush over to help. Blinking, I realized Ruth wore a traditional butler's attire made for men with pants, waistcoat, and a long-sleeved shirt. Her hair was braided in such a way it wrapped around her head, hiding her rank at first glance. Fifteen knots made her one of the Royal Guardians, a branch family, but her features would make her a cousin on my mother's side unmistakable. At one point, we could pass as siblings, dark brown hair, fleshy lipped, and tall.

Wait, could it be she's taken her father's place already as Captain?

Flashes of the youthful daemon who tugged me by my ears rushed forward. Ruth had tagged along with either my Aunt or Uncle, or worse, unsupervised with her eldest brother. Later in her early adolescence, she had been quite demanding, though I was one of the few who would brave defying her orders. A smirk crept across my face at the memories it brought seeing her again.

"Father John, may we use your office?" King Traibon motioned for him to lead the way.

"Absolutely, your Majesty." John nudged my shoulder,

lipping, *Wake up.* "I can have my bodyguard watch the door for us."

"I want both him and Ruth to be in there." King Traibon leaned heavily on his cane. "I think it's important that they hear this as well."

John opened the door, and I stood beside him, gawking at Ruth.

When did she get hips and grow a foot higher? I see even my cousin grew up during the time I was away. How foolish of me. Out of everyone, I'm glad she's the one aiding my father. She always bested me and even Falco in parrying with a sword. Her intuition and agility was hard to match or defend against.

Closing the door behind me, I stood there, unsure what to do with myself in the tiny room. My father took a seat on a chair, and John sat beside him, a stern look on his face. Ruth was staring at me and leaned down to whisper something. It brought a smile on King Traibon's face and he nodded. Clearing his throat, he took in a deep breath, something he did when he had heavy news to report on.

"First off, the allegations you wrote regarding the back-door dealings between Bishop Marquis and Viceroy Falco wasn't something new. I wasn't completely unaware of their exchanges." King Traibon leaned back, settling into conversation as if he were talking with family or even me. *Why the informality with John?* "In fact, I paid off the Bishop in hopes to tone down the deaths of the priest, but I hadn't realized his backhanded deals with Falco were becoming more malicious."

"I can show you the journal entries and slips." John motioned to some books on the desk. "But, before we continue, may I ask who this young lady next to you is?"

"Ah, forgive me." My father looked to her, and Ruth straightened her stance.

"I am Captain of the Royal Guard: Ruth Burns." She gave an elegant nod, giving John a sincere smile. "Nice to meet you,

John. I was a little startled when the guards gave me a letter with my name on it. Could I ask how you knew to reach out to me and not the King directly?"

"I once got advice from a knight in Captiva City. He said it's best to reach out to those the King trusts in hard times. Those working against a King can be narrow-sighted in actions and interceptions. Roundabout ways of achieving the same goal can prove to be... less dangerous." John scratched his jaw. "In short, I was afraid the Viceroy would make sure my letters never reached the King, but you on the other hand, he could not care less about."

She laughed, covering her mouth. "It threw me, receiving a letter from a secret suitor. They indeed rushed that letter to me. Rumors are still going around about it."

Under the mask, my face went red. Part of me was jealous and the other half scared.

John laughed, "I apologize if that came off brass. My grandfather was a clever man, and he used to tell me *gossip will reach further than fact.* I took that to heart when solving the matter of how to reach you directly, my King."

"I respect a clever man." King Traibon nodded, his eyes sparkling as he enjoyed the events unfolding. "Lord Knight Paul and I became unlikely friends, so I couldn't help but see who his grandson had become. I see you're just as sly as he was. Perhaps more so."

I shifted, leaning against the door and rubbing my side, ribs throbbing again. *He faked the letter to Ruth knowing it would be carried to my father when she realized what was there. Still, I wonder what he said to bring them both here? Ugh, and to think the old man and my father were friends. Neither of those assholes hinted as much. Fate and destiny are strange things.*

"Is this...," Captain Ruth paused, bringing my attention back to her. "Is this the man who you said has sworn to protect you?"

"He's well built for a daemon." My father looked me over from head to toe and I wondered, *Is that all you have to say to a daemon like me? Well built? What would you think knowing it was me under this façade, I wonder?* "Silent, but he's been injured?"

John flushed, a mixture of anger and guilt written on his face. "You can thank Viceroy Falco for that. If it had been me to take that same beating, I wouldn't be sitting in this chair, but six feet under."

"I see." Tilting her head, Captain Ruth's eyes fell to my hand resting on the pommel. "Isn't that a Lord Knight's sword?"

"It was a gift from my grandfather." John stared at me, gauging my eyes. "He trained under him for a long time while I was away becoming a priest. Granted, I'm not sure if he wants to take on the title he deserves just yet."

Title? I narrowed my eyes at John. *As a Lord Knight? Or are you implying Prince?*

"I see." My father's stare made my blood run cold. It was the same look he had given me when I made a bullheaded decision he was against. "He's gotten this far. Does he not wish to speak for himself?"

The eyes in the room weighed heavily on me. A mask lay between my father and my true identity, but somehow it felt paper thin. I gripped the pommel for moral support, my teeth holding my tongue. *My father will recognize my voice.* His maroon glare hadn't changed, burning into me, and I agonized over how weak his body looked. The passing time was excruciating, but I refused to say a single word. *John, don't you understand that revealing myself will rip us apart? I can't be your Sword and Shield if I let the King know his son is alive and well. Not even Ruth would let me walk out of this room without reclaiming my title and leaving you to Falco's fangs.* I shook my head and shifted my stance. *No, I won't say a word.*

"He'll speak when he's ready." John ripped their attention

back. "After all the conspiracies and rumors, it may be best this way to protect him from further onslaught."

My shoulders slumped, the tension cutting lose. An audible sigh hit my mask and Captain Ruth raised her eyebrow at me.

"If you say so." She twisted her lips in doubt, "But that is the posture of a man who doesn't want people to know who he is and knows his voice is a dead giveaway."

The tension returned. *Why does she have to be so damn insightful?*

Laughing, the King tugged on her sleeve. "Leave him alone. He'll tell me when the time comes. He's made a decision. Now respect it."

Oh, for heaven's sake... he knows it's me! Damn him and his spies! Who could have told him? Chapman? The carpenter? Would Madame Plasket try to sell this information in the underbelly? Or could it be something John wrote?

"Back to the matter at hand." Clearing his throat, John changed topics as if he could see the distraught expression under my mask. "If I end up dead, I assure you it will be due to the Viceroy or his hired help. Is there any means for me to counter him without stepping on too many toes? I simply want to keep myself and my... friend here alive."

"I see." Again, Captain Ruth put her fingers to her mouth. "Seeing the King here in the church has helped you gain some time. I'll increase the guard's patrols here, make it clear that his majesty would like to come visit from time to time as a cover."

My father stole a glance at me as if pondering how to phrase something. "I've been sick. The cause of it is unknown, but I'm not dead, yet. Falco might see it as a desperate move to make peace with my life and let him think it."

"Everyone knows I up the security anywhere the King frequents, so no one will question this... not after... after seeing..."

Ruth burst into laughter, startling us all for a moment. "I'm sorry. I just can't. I can't get over the whole thing. I have to say it. No one is going to question anything you do John after seeing how you hung his majesty's bedroom fabric on your walls. Ha!"

Shit. I covered my face, thankful to have the mask. *I didn't think this through at all... I just knew it was his favorite.*

John looked at me, "Really?"

I shrugged at last, throwing my hands into the air in reply.

"He has great taste." King Traibon was pulling himself to his feet, giggling. "We will meet again, I hope. Know that if I fall too ill, you are to come to me, John and..." My father creased his forehead, his face red with annoyance.

The room of glares aimed in my direction once more. *They want me to talk, and I won't do it.*

"Danseur." John wasn't going to give up my pet name so easily.

He knows I hate being called that.

I opened the door, eager for the encounter to end. Captain Ruth led the way, and as the King started to pass me, he stopped. I turned to see why, and he gripped my shoulder, sending my heart racing. I froze, waiting for him to snatch the mask from my face, to shake me and demand I speak, to embrace me as if he couldn't bear to play along anymore.

Leaning in, he whispered, "If I am bed-ridden, you are to come with John, and you are not allowed to refuse me this last request, Dante."

I opened my mouth, my voice failing me. *Dammit, say something to him!* Clenching my teeth, I didn't know where I would start. I glared into those red eyes, the reflection of my mask mocking my silence. At last, I managed to croak, "I promise. If it comes to that, I'll come home."

Letting go of me, he chatted with John all the way to the door, leaving me there by the office. The muscles in my shoulder stung where my father's fingers had dug in. It was something he had always done to me, always with those same words, *You are not allowed to refuse me. I am your father, Dante.* My chest ached, both happy and pained by the past and present waging war in my heart.

Why aren't you dragging me back now? What else are you not telling me, Father? And John... what in the world did you write in that letter to bring this out in him?

CHAPTER 15

The Wall We Built

When John returned to the office, I was sitting in his chair drumming my fingers on the desk. I glared at the mask, matte white with an apathetic expression. Dark blue brush strokes made the expression dark, mournful even. Gold dotted flourishes framed it, as if a golden crown melted down and dribbled out of the bottom lip and down off the chin. I had abandoned it there as my thoughts raced one way then the other. Unlike the half mask I once favored, this one was made to be heavy and take a hit in battle. The Assassin's Guild was known for wearing these, but often used red and gold or red and black décor to mark them as part of the guild.

My first mistake was hoping I had been forgotten, that no one would recognize the man I've grown into during the last decade. The other was realizing John would reach out for help the moment he knew my life would be at risk. What a fool I can be. How selfish of me to want to keep all of this on my shoulders and deny the fact there would be an effect for every action and choice I've made. I hurt my entire city and kingdom, and yet here I sit. Not one person has blamed me or dragged me back. Not one person in this city has forsaken me or called me a traitor, or even said my dream is too ridiculous.

John slowly pulled the door closed, our eyes meeting. His brow furrowed, a silent apology, but neither of us knew where to start. He leaned back on the door as if afraid I would lash out at him like a caged tiger. My fingers halted, and I picked up the mask staring at it. Deep down, I wasn't sure whether I was mad or relieved. My frustration escalated in a matter of seconds just hearing my father say my name so easily, so coolly.

Breaking away from the mask, I locked eyes once more with John. "Exactly what did you write in that letter, John?"

His face turned red. "Nothing that I didn't mean."

Leaning back into the chair, I glared up at the ceiling, staring at the cobwebs quivering in the breeze. "I didn't want anyone to know. Especially not my father."

"I know," he whispered, his eyes falling to the floor.

"It was risky, letting him find out about me." I glanced at him for a second, the candlelight shimmering off his golden hair and shadows crossing his face. *Oh, how attractive he could be.* "I don't understand why they haven't announced it. Haven't dragged me back. What we have here could have been torn apart."

"What do we have?" The blue gaze shot up, a scowl on his face. "This thing, between us, Dante. What is it exactly?"

My heart leaped to my throat, the question startling me, and my blood ran cold. I opened my mouth, but there was nothing. No words to describe it, no feelings I wanted to make known, and the murmuring of desire laughed at me as I pursed my lips in contempt.

I can't confess my love. We both know if I dare say it, dare to break down the wall I've kept between us, that you'll march across this room and kiss me. If you do that, I will shatter into a million piece—or worse, ruin you.

"I know where I want it to go."

John's voice ripped through my soul. Fear gripped my heart, squeezing it. Eyes wide, the look in those blue eyes was fierce, as if he could see through the wall with the hole he had made. There would be no going back. *Don't say it.* I had no words, just dread pressing down on me despite how much I longed to hear him say it, to tell me, *I love you, Dante.*

"But I'm unsure..." John caught the terrified expression on my face, and he lost the fire in his eyes, guilt replacing it. "Dante, the day I left I..."

"I don't want to talk about it." I grabbed the mask, placing it over my face to hide the emotions tearing me apart. "You're back, and that's all that matters."

"Did you miss me like I missed you?" he asked. I cursed the silence in the room that allowed his words to reach me. "Did you think of me often? I want to know."

Jerking from the chair, I remained silent. *We're both fools!* John still had his back against the door. I reached for the knob, but his hand covered it before I could. *Childish! Selfish!*

"I don't have time for this." *I can't go there, not when I love you. Not when I see that you feel this way about me. Please, don't make today hurt anymore than it has, John.* "Move!"

"I want to know, Dante." His gaze made my body burn with desire. "I want to know everything."

That look sent chills through me, sparking the caged arousal at my core to rake across the breaking walls. *It's so easy to see myself with you, see that face in the throes of passion. My soul is breaking, and you know it.* My fingers slid over his hand, and he gripped the knob tighter, threatening to defend it. The heat of our hands was provocative and John visibly held his breath a moment before trying again.

"Everything, Dante," he repeated. "I deserve to know."

"Do you?" Something bitter woke inside me, and I was no longer willing to remain silent in the surge of emotions he had shaken loose. "You took ten years to come home, John. What more of an answer do you need?"

Gripping my hand over his, I twisted the knob. I slid my mask on, afraid for him to see my own expression. He was biting his lip, and I left the moment the door opened wide enough. I expected to hear him call out, to chase after me and swing me around on my heels. Pushing through the front doors, I passed the guards placed to watch over the church and stomped down the street. Aimless, I found myself in front of the herbalist shop and barged in, still riding on my anger. Madame Plasket raised an eyebrow. She was leaned over her counter flipping through a tome filled with sketches of plants. She straightened herself as I continued my march, slamming both palms on the counter.

"Well, aren't we in a bitter mood despite how well the sermon went?" She shut the book and pushed it off to the side. "What has crawled up your drawers today?"

"Who told my father?" I growled through the mask.

"He already knew by the time I got to his doorstep, if that's what you wanted to know," she laughed. "But you aren't wrong to think I would pass the word onto him. Anything to gain favor with the King is worth an attempt on our part."

"Do you know who told him?" I pulled away, pacing the aisle as I rubbed my aching side. "And does Falco know that my father is aware? I need to know exactly where I stand."

"Now you're asking the right questions." She folded her hands together, a coy smile on her lips, and a sparkle in her maroon eyes. "Rumor says a letter made its way to your father, and shortly after that, he was looking for information on your whereabouts. As for the other, the whole city and your father are keeping our lips tight and heads down. None of us want Falco to be aware we know you're back. Instead, you have us backing you at every turn when it's safe for us to do so."

"Safe?" I halted, looking over my shoulder at her. "Exactly

what's going on in Glensdale? How did Falco get this much control to put the Assassin's Guild at a disadvantage?"

"It's the same thing that's been going on since before our first Prince left." I gave her a stern stare, and Madame Plasket rolled her eyes. "It's not all about you, Dante. To be honest, your father's been battling this hidden war since *The House* was established. Your leaving, or possibly being dead, was just the tip of a sword's edge we've been cut by since before your brother's conception."

"What brother? And what hidden war? I want to know more. Tell me my family history through the eyes of the guild."

"As my Prince commands. Mind you—you don't become the ruling family to a new kingdom without keeping enemies close. Falco has been doing everything in his power to chisel down the royal family for a few centuries now." Searching my eyes a moment, she asked, "Have you ever once wondered what happened to your older siblings, boy?"

My frown deepened. I pulled off the mask and set it on the counter between us. "I've always wondered," I whispered. "But I'd have to know about my brother in order to question anything. Even the day when I found myself on the frontlines with Falco and nearly took an arrow to the head; it made it clear what had really happened to my sister. Fallen in battle is simply a cover up."

"You got your answer then," she snorted.

"Yeah, but Father didn't discuss it after that. Nor has he talked about Mother much with me. He never spoke of his first wife and all the pictures of her, and my brother apparently, were removed." Searching the air for questions, I pushed forward in hopes of filling the gaps. "I had an older sister, and we had an elder brother. Both are half-siblings, yes?"

"Yes. The eldest was your brother Ashton, though he fought in the wars that created this nation we now call *The House*, then disappeared. He'd held the title of Grandemere's

Champion for years before this. Ashton's prowess with any blade and hand-to-hand combat was unmatched. The legends say he became a bloodeater without the *Fanged Lady*, but that would mean the forgotten black arts were practiced more freely in his youth. He once took out an entire legion with only a shield as a weapon during the war."

"Disappeared, not dead?" I seared my brother's name to memory. "What happened to the first Prince? I want to know more about Ashton."

"I imagine he's dead by now. No one's heard anything from him since he left here nearly two hundred years ago with his lover, Francesca. You have to understand; it was different times." Madame Plasket gave a look of pity, my expression clinging on all the information. "Champions used to be daemon warriors who battled in arenas for the leading human families. These families would eventually turn against one another and..."

"Daemons would be used like weapons for a time before fighting for freedom. Thus, humans unified under one ruler and became the nation known as *The Tower*, we *The House*, and later *The Court* would develop with parties from both kingdoms." She twisted her lips at me. "I know this part of the history well, so back to Ashton."

"Your brother and Francesca were both gladiators. Those two took to war like ducks to water when the war started. Ashton fought for his family, but after he won us our freedom, they both wanted their freedom and fell off the map. I imagine if he or Francesca are still alive, they go where the fighting is best, hit every tavern where the beer flows freely, and there's plenty of tail to be had."

"I see." I smirked, but then I lost the humor in it. "Then no one knows much beyond that about Ashton. Is he the one the stories are about? The legend of the immortal and the seventh night?"

"No, in fact, that's the legend that's all scrambled in my own records. Whoever that daemon was is still around, but who and how, no one knows." She shuffled on her stool and straightened her back. "Your sister, Lillian, well…"

"She went to battle in my father's place." *This story I do know, I think.*

"Yes, well, he was recovering at the time from a near mortal wound." *And there's the detail I didn't know. Father must've blamed himself and still does.* "So, she went with Falco, and when he returned, he announced Lillian fell in battle. The people of Glensdale were angry, demanding he bring back her body. Instead, any who dared to come close were met with a horde of battleworn humans and daemons all suffering from the Madness. Folks were lucky to come back alive and in one piece trying to find evidence. *The Court* retreated into the Perevina Mountains after that and no one could get word in or out."

"But she was only there because my father was wounded?" I could see the puzzle pieces coming together. See where Falco plucked one feather at a time, making my father flight-less as he went. "How did that happen? I have a tough time believing anyone managed to do that to him."

"Your mother, Evelyn. She was supposed to assassinate your father." Madame Plasket patted my arm, smiling over the secret details.

"Wait, my mother was an assassin?" The room spun with the information unfolding. "Who hired her?"

"Falco," she cooed. "But her thoughts were if the King fell by her hand, he didn't need to lead us anymore. After losing Ashton and Lillian, your father's first wife died soon after, but we suspect foul play even with her death. I thought Evelyn would have a fighting chance, but she couldn't figure out where the poison was coming from and turned her focus on giving birth to you in those last moments of her life."

"Mother was one of your assassins then?"

Laughing, Madame Plasket shook her head. "Oh no, we entered the sisterhood here at the same time, dear. I stayed in for the long game, but she fell in love that night. Your father was so brave, he let her land that stab intentionally so he could steal a kiss from her. The two of them had crossed paths, and he'd pegged her as a hired assassin months ago. It infuriated her that he was so quick-witted to even best her. It became a game to them, like an estranged dance with daggers and backdoor dealings. They were in a battle of wits for years, and he'd bested her at last. That night she snuck into his bedroom to get back at him, and he knew she'd come, madder than a wet hen."

Raising my brow high, I digested it all. "Why does it not shock me that my father enjoys testing his fate so loosely? But what about now? Falco's got the whole city scared."

"Aye, he does." Sighing, Madame Plasket propped her chin up and flipped open her book again. "He's got us in such a bind, we can't get in and out of the city so easily. Worse, he's hired mercenaries and aligned with Bishop Marquis. All the towns outside of Glensdale have patrols looking for us, and they've got orders to erase anyone who stands against him. A lot of people don't come home or make it to a proper grave when they travel outside these walls. Inside, we do what we can to watch and protect the innocent."

"Bishop Marquis doesn't seem all that threatening. Why drop his name into this?" A knot turned tight and hard in my gut.

"That's where you're wrong, Dante." She stole a glance, then flipped to a page with Nightshade on it. "He keeps dark company, *Arbre Tombé* or the Brotherhood of the *Fallen Tree*. Men we've never seen in Grandemere before. Rumor has it these men know the dark arts, and Marquis is gathering information in the church's catacombs. We think he's looking for a lost artifact and keeping the civil war boiling so the Reapers can lay grounds for taking over *The House* and *The Tower*. They even aim to dismantle *The Church*. It's rumored *The Court* isn't so much passive but aiming to combat the Brotherhood. With what, I haven't any idea."

"Who are they?" Books and reports from the royal archives had spoken of the Assassin's Guild, the factions of royal families prior to the war. This was a new threat.

"We need to get Falco off our heels before we can find anything out. For now, keep your priest safe and know the city will keep your secret. Let Falco think you're hiding and have something to lose, other than your life and John's."

"Right," I huffed. The day had chiseled away all that I could handle. "Thank you for being so generous with your information."

I started to leave, but she called out, "Dante, nothing in this world comes without a price."

Nodding, I pushed down the nerves her words rattled.

They are all giving me this information, this freedom, in exchange for taking out Falco. Everyone in this wretched city, my father included, is betting on me, and I don't know if I'm strong enough to take him down as a normal daemon.

My throat tingled from where he had gripped me almost a week ago, and I could still taste him on my tongue.

I vowed that I would never become a bloodeater. Without the Fanged Lady, *no one has been able to become one since I left, yet not one soul has said a word to me of it. Only Falco. We all want the Madness and unrest to end. I'll have to end this, even if it costs me my life in order to keep Glensdale, my father, and John safe.*

CHAPTER 16

Vows are Breaking

The streets were darker now, the day gone, yet the weight of everything still stung. I paused downhill from the church as my gut twisted. The ride home would be tense, possibly unpleasant if John aimed his questions at me once more. Huffing, I turned and ducked down an alleyway, meandering through the streets. I missed Glensdale, and it felt broken as I turned down one dark passageway and the next. Trash, rats, and forgotten souls would rise and fall at every turn. At last, I came out of the labyrinth of despair, and I halted.

"You!" hissed Falco, abandoning his soldiers under the lit streetlamp. "You and your fucking priest."

I back-peddled into the alley, but he was faster. Gripping the front of my leather tunic, he slammed me into the wall. My bruised ribs throbbed as he knocked the air from me. His eyes were wild, his face twitching with rage. It was all unravelling again; I was letting him gain the upper hand, and I hated myself for it. He reached up, ripping the mask from my face, and sent it clattering across the ground. Scowling,

I kept my eyes on his, my cheek still bruised from our last encounter.

"Did I not warn you I would kill him if you dare defy me!" He lifted me off the wall only to slam me against it again. "You're not the Prince anymore; you're not even a full-blooded royal!"

"Why the sour face and insults, Viceroy?" I smirked, delighting in how much his ire had risen. "You did say the King was coming to the sermon, after all."

"Shut your whore mouth, cur!" His fingers wrapped around my neck, and my heart stopped. "We both know that was a lie. So how'd you do it? How'd you get word to him and convince him to come? Did your father miss his own flesh and blood so much to drag his corpse to the church?"

Anger rose in me, and much to my surprise, I wrenched his hand from my neck. In a pure display of brute strength, I pushed back with all my weight. I wasn't the scrawny Prince he once dealt with, but a warhorse now. Falco's back slammed against the opposite wall. Roaring in a rage, I had turned the tables. Viceroy Falco reached for his sword. My hand slammed down on the pommel, shoving his blade back into its sheath. He tried once more, and I gripped his hand over the hilt and rammed it back in place. My forearm came crushing down on his throat, silencing him. It was my turn to throw threats.

"You fucking touch him, and I'll rip you in two." My arm shifted off his throat, and he rasped for air. I ran my hand across his chest, over his ribs and hip; his breath caught knowing I traced the purple scar so few ever knew or saw. Leaning into Falco's ears, I hissed, "Touch John, and I'll finish what the old man started."

Falco's grip tightened on the hilt, and he attempted to jerk the blade free. The muscles in my arm and shoulder tightened, pinning his hand there. Fingers dug into my forearm; Falco was failing to pry my grasp free, and I snorted. *He's afraid; he's panicking.* For the first time, I realized what the old Lord Knight had given me: *freedom from my past.* I pulled my knife free and placed it against his neck. *This is it. This will be the last string to cut.* He froze, a smug look crossing his face. I blinked.

"It's forbidden for a Prince to kill anyone outside the battlefield."

"I'm not a Prince," I smirked, pressing deeper and breaking the skin ever so slightly. "I'm dead, thanks to your efforts ten years ago. Phantoms can haunt and kill as they wish, can they not?"

His confidence melted away. "You got me. Now what do you want?"

"Your life."

"Afraid not." His eyebrows lifted high, and he glared back to the entrance of the alley where guards had gathered. "Kill me now, and you won't make it out of the trash heap."

I weighed the odds: I hadn't memorized the way I came, and no one knew I had ventured here. "Consider yourself lucky." Retracting my knife, I pulled away from him and leaned down for my mask. "Next time, I won't hesitate, Falco. I'd rather take my last breath before I let you harm anyone ever again."

He spat at the ground beside where I stood as I replaced my mask, scowling at his hesitant bodyguards. "I preferred you better when I could bend you over with one hand."

Nausea flowed through me, the flavor bitter on my tongue. *I wish I had a silvered tongue like John, to twist Falco's words against him.* "Watch your back. I aim to put down Glensdale's rabid dog."

I marched down and around the corner, relief washing over me. Leaning on the wall, I gripped my throbbing ribs, cursed, and punched the wall. My knuckles bled down the cobblestones as I overheard the rushed whispers around me. With a twist of my stomach, I launched into a full run through the labyrinth of alleyways. A homeless slave pointed, and I turned, only for an assassin to point down another way. I obeyed, gritting my fangs. *I am a fool. I could have killed him, and they would have been there to aid me.*

Taking one last turn, I broke out of the shadows of the buildings. Somehow, they led me up the street somewhere between Falco and his arguing men and the church. Pivoting, I ran full steam uphill. City guards looked baffled as I slammed into the doors, yanking one side open. The noise echoed through the church, the candles fluttering in the emptiness. Everyone had left. It was far too late to still be here. As I exploded into the office, John paled. On his hip was a rapier and he had started putting on a brown coat. Furrowing my brow, I slammed the office door shut and spied the priest's collar on the desk.

Is he preparing to come find me?

"Dante, your mask. It's cracked! Is everything..." John's words failed him as his eyes fell to the blood dripping from my fingertips. "You're bleeding!"

"It's my fault." Absent-minded, I lifted my hand to show where I had busted my knuckles open as John rushed over. "It's nothing."

"Did Falco..." Again, his words halted, and he pulled my mask off, relieved to see nothing but a healing bruise on my cheek. "Where did you go?"

"I went to look for information." I searched his eyes, curious now as to what he intended to do with a sword on his hip as he abandoned his post as priest. "John, what were you planning to do?"

"Come find you." The heat of his palm on my jaw combined with the caress of his thumb over my bruise sent a torrent of desire through me.

"John, I..."

John's lips locked with mine, and I found myself unable to

resist kissing him back. I spun him around, pushing his back against the door. My tongue licked inside his mouth, and he let me enter, only to chase me back into my own mouth.

How long I have waited for a chance to taste you, my priest!

As if he could hear my thoughts, he pressed harder, his hands gripping my tunic.

Falco.

Cold fear cut through the fire of desire, and I pulled away, ripping his hands free. Turning, I cold-shouldered him as dread filled me.

"We can't," I muttered, my stomach tightening with the weight of the crumbling wall between us. "You're a priest. Breaking celibacy is punishable by..."

"Death," he finished my words, making it clear he had stolen a kiss fully aware. "I know, but how can I deny..."

"Not another word!" I roared, fear shifting to rage. "My only purpose is to help you achieve your dream to be a priest. I'm a tool, John, a fucking tool! I can't be anything else for you without putting your life in further danger!"

"You think I don't know that!" He gripped my shoulder and spun me around, his face red with anger. "What good is a dream if you have no one to share it with!"

"Find someone else," I spat.

"I don't want anyone else." His tone softened, the rage shattered by heartbreak. "I want you, Dante. Only you."

I let myself stumble back and sit on the cot, holding my head.

How did we end up like this? Why does he still care even after ten years? When did I lose control of the situation?

"Dante..." John didn't dare move any closer as he stood towering over me.

"Not another word," I seethed. *I hate myself. Why didn't I snuff this out?*

John sat in the chair, glaring at me. His lips were drawn tight. Pain waved through my entire being. Self-loathing clawed inside me while my bruised ribs and throbbing knuckles reminded me this wasn't some dream. I could still feel the heat of his hand on my jaw, the silken stroke of his tongue against mine, and the rapture of releasing lust for only a minute.

What do you plan on doing with him? The old man knew; he knew John would be too stubborn to let go even after spending years away. *He warned me, but I kissed him back, and he knows now. John knows I want him, that I love him as much as he...*

Looking up, I met his eyes. "We can't."

"Can't." He furrowed his brow.

"It's dangerous; it's forbidden." A muscle twitched in his face. "You had to make that choice, John. Love or the Rite of Priesthood. Your answer is on your back. There's no going back on that vow."

"Look, when I was in the catacombs..."

"Enough!" I commanded and his jaw closed. "No more arguing with me on the matter." Pulling myself off the cot, I marched for the door and picked up my mask. "This can't happen again." My chest ached and wrenched in a horrible way. "Promise me."

John looked to the ceiling for a moment before reaching for his collar on the desk, putting it back in place. "Let's go home."

Chapter 17

Assassin's Guild

Viceroy Falco disappeared into the shadows after that day. John and I had come and gone from Glensdale without further encounters or complications. Silence took hold between us, a soundless war. We were at odds with one another and the feelings stirring within us. The presence of city guards and visits from King Traibon made it impossible for Falco to hire someone brave enough to intervene. Each visit resulted in private talks in John's office about what was happening in the city and ways we could work together. It seemed odd, not having these talks in the royal mansion or the war room. Falco's absence should have made me feel better, but we all knew from the twisting of our guts that he was planning something big.

Chills rattled my core. *Is the distrust seeded that deeply in my childhood home?*

I stood at the door, not willing to talk or interrupt their many discussions and theories. Besides, John and my father didn't need help planning solutions now that they put their heads together. At times, I would doze off, watching as John blushed when my father complimented him or jolt my eyes away when I realized my father caught me swooning. He'd snicker, humming, stroking his beard. Still, it was strange. Never had I seen my father work with anyone from *The Church* so willingly and openly. What killed me was watching each visit pass by, and with it, his health slipping further away. A great weight pressed on my soul. I could offer the medicine, but it was still a matter of trusting Madame Plasket.

Father, why haven't you brought up the poisoning or figured it out? Unless you're at the point of exhausting every resource within your reach, where is the authoritative demeanor we all once stood in awe of when I called this place home? I want to shake your shoulders and demand why you've handed so much control to Falco, but in the end, I'm afraid of the answer you have for me.

Every visit, he'd leave in the same manner; grabbing my shoulder and whispering some obscure line to remind me he'd never forgotten about me or the things I'd done. Today, he decided to rattle me. I knew he would; a familiar sparkle of mischief in his eyes made me tense as he approached, his grip a little firmer.

"Dressed like this, you remind me of your mother who once wore a mask like that one, Dante."

"I heard you took a dagger to the gut just to steal a kiss." I couldn't hold my tongue this time, still digesting it all. "I've learned a lot of interesting things about our family as of late."

He blinked, and a grin spread slowly on his face. "He speaks."

Circling around, he pushed me back into the office and slammed the door shut, leaving Ruth and John outside.

"What is it?" I watched him pace the floor. "Was I not supposed to ever know?"

"It's not that. Does this mean you know of Ashton then?" Hearing him drop the name so easily stung.

"Y-yes." I hated how he made me stutter in his presence. "He's the first Prince, a bloodeater, a champion, and he disappeared."

He sat down, stroking his beard again. "That's the short story, I suppose."

"Is he dead?" If anyone knew this, it would be him. *If you're the man I thought you were, you'll know exactly the whereabouts of Ashton.*

"Yes and no." He paled, looking me in the eye. "Last I heard, he had crossed paths with the *Arbre Tombé,* and no one knows what happened or where they took him. Rumors say he was last seen in Captiva City, but that was over a hundred years ago. He might be dead or he might be imprisoned. The first would be more forgiving since he's… well, let's pray for dead."

"What about Francesca?" His brow lifted; I had impressed him.

"I don't know. She cut ties with her family and ours. At least Ashton would respond with a letter on occasion." Coughing, he wheezed for a moment. "Dante, I'm sorry I kept all of this secret, but I was hoping if you knew nothing, then maybe…"

"I'd be safe. I see that now." Sighing, I straddled a chair and leaned on the back, thankful for the mask shielding my hurt expression. "I just wasn't sure how much was true, but I see it wasn't lies."

"Who gave you the mask?" He reached for it and I jerked out of range.

"Assassin's Guild."

"So they're helping you, after all. I attempted to contract them many times, but they refused my requests. Falco noticed, and I lost contact with them shortly after." Nodding, he chuckled. "At least they should serve you in the shadows while the city guard can serve you in the light. You indeed are your mother's son. Maybe I was fretting over nothing these past few weeks."

I opened my mouth to say more, but he lifted his hand. He pulled himself up and went through the door. I didn't dare follow. This was his cryptic way of keeping me at arm's length because he couldn't promise my safety. I saw how his eyes wavered and the twitch in his jaw. Never did I imagine the day I'd see my own father unable to move within his own city. I stood, anger pulsing through me. Kicking the chair across the room, I started pacing the office.

I have the cure, don't I? Is he hinting I can trust the guild, or is he just being sulky about Mother again? Dammit!

Ruth came to the doorway, baffled. I froze, embarrassed to have her catch me brooding. *I'd rather it be John.* The look in her eyes and the twist of a smirk made me wonder what thoughts were in her mind when she glared at me.

Do you see me as your cousin in assassin's attire and mask? The Prince of Glensdale playing pretend, perhaps?

"Brooding as usual, I see," she chuckled. "John is taking him out, wanted to make sure you were okay, but I see you defeated the chair."

"I'm in no mood to be mocked." I reached down and sat the chair upright.

In her armored regale, she looked worthy of a goddess, her braid coiled on her head and walled with the armored tiara of golden lions clawing at one another. The body panels and shoulder pads were no different than the former Captain's own, symbols of rank clear and concise. Golden lion heads roared at any who dared face them against the silver sparkle of polished metal.

"*Dante.*" I turned to her with a crossed look in my eyes. "Have you seen any signs of Viceroy Falco?"

Shrugging, I shook my head. "No." I rolled my shoulders; my muscles ached to be on the farm working. "No signs anywhere of him or his men."

Ruth scoffed, frustration building in her voice. "I've had

no reports of him for two months now. Granted, he kept his activities low for a solid six weeks before that, but he's not at home or his usual places." She leaned in, gripping my shoulder and whispering, "In short, be on guard. He's on the move and hiding from King Traibon's reach."

Sighing, I nodded in thanks.

"I really wish you'd just say something."

"There's nothing I want to say," I huffed, unwilling to fold.

Tugging a strap on her gauntlet a notch tighter, she flustered, "Stay on guard, please. Both of you, stay safe."

She disappeared, and I lost her in the flooding daylight of the open church doors. The citizens of Glensdale had started coming to the church to pray, to escape, and to feel safe from Falco. A cold breeze was blowing through, the first signs of fall and winter fast approaching. My mind wandered, fading into thoughts of the farm. Basque had proven useful, his stable built, his muscles speeding up much of my own work. He was the reason I was able to be here, still guarding John and watching his back. The old woman praying finished and left the back pew. The church was empty again. One more glance and I found myself alone with John, the church doors closing to keep the leaves and dust from sweeping into the building.

"Yes?" John blinked as I removed my mask. "What's wrong?"

"Falco's missing."

He lifted an eyebrow, brushing by me, "Good riddance."

The door to the office started to close, and I landed my palm against it. "I'm locking the front doors. I think I know someone who can tell me what he's up to, but..."

Staring at my hand, he replied, "But you need money?"

"Yeah." I watched as he circled to his desk and opened a hidden drawer. "It shouldn't take much."

"I imagine you wouldn't have asked if you didn't think he was up to no good." He dropped a small stack in my hand but held onto it. "What happened that night?"

My frown deepened. "I missed my chance to kill him."

Letting go, he furrowed his brow. "Be careful, Dante."

"Lock your office door," I warned over my shoulder.

"Remember to remind everyone the church will be closed between services next week. We have a crop to tend to..." John started laughing and added, "Never mind, I forgot you're supposedd to be a mute outside of the church."

Smiling, I placed my mask back on and left. There was one person in all of Glensdale who knew everything there was about the backdoor deals and dark secrets: *Madame Plasket*. The residents had started to roam the streets again with Falco's men at bay. Despite my assassin-like attire, no one rushed back in their shops like they had done in the first weeks I had been here. Pushing into the apothecary shop, I saw that Madame Plasket's stool and counter were empty.

"Hello?" My voice didn't carry far through the crowded shelves of herbs and ointments. "Madame Plasket?"

"Go behind the desk and follow the path," she crowed from somewhere out of sight.

Swallowing, I did as she wished. It took some effort to climb past the barrels and stool she kept just behind the counter. I sidled between the shelves, wondering how she managed to walk through all of this without half the items falling on top of her. My efforts were far from silent and I reached a dead end. The thought that I would have to turn around filled me with dread.

"Where are you?" I shouted at the shelves. "It's a dead end."

The shelf in front of me groaned and swung inward, revealing a hidden passageway.

Madame Plasket grinned, and with a wink, retorted, "There is no such thing as a dead end, Prince Dante. You'll need to learn that if you aim to be an assassin."

"Please spare me the honorifics." Leaning forward on my toes, I peered over her shoulder, curious. "Is this the place where you conduct your other business?"

"Maybe." She waved me in, and I sighed in relief to see the corridor was much larger. "It's best if we talk in my office. In here, we are among trusted ears and eyes."

"You really are in charge of the Assassin's Guild." Torches cast deep shadows between each placement, and at the core of the shadowed florets stood silent masked figures whose eyes glowed for an instant with the torchlight. "I almost didn't see half of the guards coming in. Standing in the shadows is a smart tactic. The torches are meant to disrupt the eye, right?"

She paused, looking back with a sense of pride. "You could have been an assassin in another life. Then again, I like knowing you are the next in line for *The House.*"

"Was," I corrected, following her through a heavy wooden door.

"Last I checked, your father hasn't disowned you nor declared you dead." Slamming the door, she slid the iron lock and motioned for me to sit down. "It's all in the details, Dante. Your father has always been good with words and being clever."

"He never declared me dead?" I took my mask off, setting it on the table filled with coins, a large bag, and a smattering of manuscripts. "Is it safe to assume Falco announced me dead despite my father?"

"Of course it was Falco. His inquisition was spiraling out of control, so he had to put a stop to it before your father lost his temper." She hobbled around the large oak table and flopped in a golden chair with thick crimson cushions, wiggling into it like a hen roosting. "Ah, which brings me to the next problem." She motioned to the large bag. "You know what that is?"

"Why is it you ask me things instead of telling me?" She snorted, and I relented, "Considering the leather and golden twine, I'd say it was a bag from Falco's own treasury."

"See, this is why I have respect for you. You like to come

off slow, but you're far from it. Unlike your priest, you're not quick to act. Which is also your downfall." Rubbing her forehead, she continued. "This was the money he shoved on me to massacre a flock of nuns scheduled to leave Captiva City and travel via the Blackwood Road. He thought it convenient to wait until it was on the edge of the Forbidden Wood, where Lord Knight Paul lives."

"Lived." Glaring at the bag, my blood boiled. "Where is Falco?"

Never underestimate the bite and bark of the Rapid Dog, the Old Farmer had warned one night, his eyes lost in the fireplace flames. *The madness leaves him thirsty, the blood leaves him stained, and his heart will be forever dark to all things that matter in this world.*

"He left about three weeks ago. Part of the payment was to escort him out of the city." From her skirt, she pulled something from a hidden pocket. Lighting a match in the lantern on the table, she lit the rolled cigarette in her lips. Its pungent smell invaded the room before she continued. "I believe he went to meet with his informant in Captiva City."

"Bishop Marquis," I hissed, my fists tightening.

"Ah, now I have a name and target." Chuckling, smoke boiled from her lips. "Lager." Despite the door being locked, a man showed from the shadows. Every hair on my body stood on end. I hadn't heard him, I hadn't seen him, and he knelt beside me now. "Put the word out to take down Bishop Marquis. He's meddled with our affairs and will pay with his life."

The assassin, nothing more than a black figure in a painted mask, slid out of view. Still, no sounds of the lock sliding nor where he had vanished. "I'm truly among the elite here. I thought we were alone."

"I'm never alone." Another inhale of smoke, and she gave me a wide grin. "Not many see this office and live."

"Why invite me here? Why this deep into your sanctuary and so openly?" My back stiffened. I couldn't keep my eyes from darting into the deep shadows in the room. "I assume I'm not here to be killed or interrogated."

"As I said, Falco has fucked with our guild one time too many. He treats us like his personal army or worse, blubbering mercenaries who don't know when he intends to screw us over." Glaring at the red bud burning at the end of her cigarette, she frowned. "So we are cutting off his hands and feet, such as his precious Bishop. Captain Ruth is adding the right amount of pressure, but King Traibon is growing weak, and we need you to know how far we are willing to trust and aid you. We need you to trust us and give your old man that cure in your satchel."

She gave a dangerous stare across the table, the smoke hovering all around her like a bad omen. "What would you have me do for you?" I asked, her purpose clear; *she needs a favor.*

"Keep your course. Falco is agitated, he's making mistakes, and it's because he has his eyes set on you and the priest like a horse with blinders on." A final drag of her cigarette and she snuffed it out on a tin plate on the desk. "I want to know why. He's not usually this rattled, even after a knife to the throat or gut. Why the obsession with you?"

Gauging her expression, I leaned forward on my knees. "He wants *La Dame d'Croc.*"

"Everyone knows that, but why toy with you?" She laughed, seeing through my weak attempt to dodge answering what I didn't want to acknowledge. "Why hasn't he slaughtered you both? Why hasn't he moved on, like he prefers to do?"

I searched the air, gathering my thoughts and emotions before I spoke. "Because we were lovers."

"Are you kidding me?" Scoffing, she gave me a distasteful look. "Who'd willingly fuck such a vile man?"

My face turned red, confessing. "I didn't. I wasn't the one doing the fucking."

Silence fell between us before she asked, "I see. Do you think he still wants you?"

"Yes." My chest ached. "He's smitten and enraged over it. For a man who desires power, dominance over all others, it is driving him raving mad to have me unwilling to bend over like I did before."

"What ended it? Was he the reason you left over ten years ago?" She leaned back into her chair, a new curiosity building in her eyes.

"Part of it, I suppose." I covered my face, ashamed to look back. *Selfish.* "His mistress let me know he was fucking me to get closer to the throne and the dagger. He wanted to bring in the next wave of bloodeaters himself. She was pissed and jealous he indulged in drinking my blood over hers, but it made me realize something more important. My role as the heir, my responsibility to make the next generation of bloodeaters, which we all know is the core source of the plague. How could I face myself each day knowing I was keeping something so destructive alive in this world?"

"I see." Her face twisted as she thought about the new information. "Do you know where the dagger is?"

"Yes, but finding where that place is will take time." I sat up, my mind racing. "We'll be tending to our harvest and prepping for winter next week instead of here at the church. I hope I can figure out where I left it."

"You don't think he found it already?" She dug her fingers into the large bag, the sound of clinking coins ringing in my ears. "He's been keeping tabs on your location for some time, Dante, and has paid well to do so."

"No." It was my turn to give her a dangerous look. "He would have used it to rip John apart in front of me if he had."

Scooping some of Falco's blood money into a smaller pouch,

she tossed it to me. "Here, for you and yours. Bait never has to pay for information. You're already putting your necks out to give us an advantage. Hope you beat the first snow before the ground freezes. Ale, lead our guest out, please."

Again, an assassin appeared from the shadows of the room. This time the figure was female, short but nimble. The masked assassin bowed, motioning for the door, and I stood. Taking a step, a wry smile crept up my lips, and I couldn't help but ask.

"Are all your assassins named after drinks?"

She gauged my face. "Yes, they are." Madame Plasket was holding back her own smile now.

"In that case, what is your favorite drink?" I lifted an eyebrow, knowing well this was a double-edged answer. "I'm curious, Madame Plasket."

She gave a toothy grin, her fangs hinting she was a bloodeater. "Red Wine."

There was an assassin who loved red wine, and I loved her. It was the old man talking to me, there next to the fire. *She's an ornery thing, but if you ever find her, don't piss her off.* He pointed to the ragged scar across his neck. *Stay in her good graces, and she might let you live.*

Chills crept across my skin, and I nodded in acknowledgment. Nothing more was said, and I followed Ale through the tunnels. We turned to travel farther away from the shop, then twisted in many directions. After a while, the hidden guards in the shadows were gone, and she grabbed the last torch in the row. Another turn and the smell turned sour. We were indeed in the underbelly of the city. Doors and stairs to nowhere seemed to fade in and out of existence, and before long, she stopped and motioned for me to use a door.

"Go through here?" I asked.

She nodded, opening the door and motioning me inside.

"Uh, thank you?" I stepped forward and slammed into a

shelf. Behind me, I heard her snicker. Tapping my shoulder, I turned with a frown on my face.

Grabbing my wrist, she handed the torch over.

"Don't you need this?" I asked.

She patted my shoulder. "No." Her elegant voice was muffled by her mask. "But you need it. Good luck, Prince Dante."

I covered my face with my free hand, "Does everyone know who I am? And again, the honorifics."

She pulled my hand down and placed my mask in it, "You forgot this."

Flustered, I slid it on, and by the time I looked up, she was gone. The torchlight stretched beyond the cobweb-covered shelves between me and the room. From what I could make out, I was in a cellar or basement of some kind. I closed the door behind me, leaving the humidity of the sewers behind in exchange for the dry dust-covered room. Making my way out from behind the shelf, I didn't recognize the broken vases and bent metal idols scattered on the floor. Shaking off the curiosity, I launched myself up the stairs, relieved the double cellar doors weren't locked from the outside.

Sunlight greeted me, and after several blinks, I found myself in the back alleyway of the church. A cold breeze bit at my cheeks and nose, flurries on the wind. Winter was here. Another wave of shivers ran through me, my spine tingling. At any given point, an assassin could slip in and out of the church to kill me or John. No one would find them, no one would see or know to look in the cellar, to look behind an old filled shelf for a hidden door leading to the city's underbelly. Coming around the corner of the building, I doused the torch in the trough. Basque gave me a disapproving snort.

Ignoring him, I brushed off the cobwebs and marched down to the office. I knocked once and before my knuckles could connect for the second, it swung open. Pulling my mask off, I stared at John's face as it filled with relief.

"Did something happen while I was away?" I shifted to look behind him and saw nothing and turned to look through the church. *Did I miss signs of a confrontation?*

"N-no," he stuttered, opening the door wider. "It seemed like you were gone for some time... again."

"Oh, I guess it took a little longer than expected." I paused, my cheeks red as I realized he had taken off his coat and shirt. My eyes fell across the angles of his collarbone, the taut muscles of his chest and the ripples of his abdomen spilling downward. "Uh, here." Shaking my head, I managed to hand over the pouch of gold coins.

"You have some weird luck," he mumbled, his eyes searching my face, and John smiled. "This is far more gold than what I gave you. How did that happen?"

"A gift." Out of another pocket, I handed him what he had given up. "Here's your money back."

John laughed, the drawer popping open as he hid it away once more. "Let's get home."

"Yes. Sadly, it's snowing already."

John pulled his shirt over his head before groaning up at the ceiling.

"I know, I know... nothing worse than losing crop to the cold."

"Not that." Picking up his jacket, he pulled it on and snuffed out his lantern. "I hate digging in frozen ground. It hurts."

I made a cringing expression. "I didn't even think that far."

"You wouldn't." He shoved me out the door, locking his office. "But then again, you have this immunity to cold. Only person in the world who would sit on a wet boulder in the night of winter to think."

I laughed. "I can do the digging."

"It's not fair." Again, his hand pushed against my lower back, and my face flushed. "We'll take turns. It's not right to make you do it all."

Why does my body light up like fire and my heart race when he touches me? How badly I want to be with you! How badly I fear to let myself indulge. It kills me to know you feel the same when I touch you, John.

CHAPTER 18

Truth in Harvesting

A chill rolled across the field, turning the sweat on my back icy. The ground had iced overnight, and we were scrambling to save what we could. My shoulders and back burned with my efforts as I broke up the ground. Behind me, John had a basket strapped across his back, hands digging through the frosty dirt to pull out potatoes, carrots, and salvage what we could of cabbage and corn. Glancing back, I would watch him pump his fists, blowing his hot breath in his palms, trying to relieve the numbness the cold brought. Mud was smudged across his face, and I smirked. All we had left to pull was the last of the sweet potatoes.

"Let's switch up." I stood straight, stretching my back. "I'm tired of being hunched over. Your hands have got to be killing you."

John rocked back on his heels, cheeks red. "You're much faster at breaking the ground."

"It's not a race." Leaning on the hoe, I jabbed, "What good is a priest with frostbite on his fingers? You won't be able to flip a page if you keep this up."

He pumped his fists once more. "Fine. Let's switch up."

Pulling the basket off his shoulder, he traded me the hoe for it. I wasted no time digging out the last of the sweet potatoes when John struck the dirt.

Ka-thud!

John halted, the vibration of the impact pulsing through the ground into my hands and up the muscles in my arms. He had landed it deeper than I had moments ago, and I watched as he broke up the ice on the top layer and left the soil soft and ready to reveal what lie beneath.

Ka-thud!

The way his arms and hands held the hoe told me he had endured extensive sword training. Each movement was concise, not in the sense of an experienced farmer, but of someone who understood the importance of finesse and the weight of the weapon.

"Tell me more about your friend—Valiente, was it?" He looked to me, but I dropped my gaze to the dirt, pulling out another potato. "You said he was a knight, but never said what his rank was."

"You know I'm terrible at counting knots and knowing someone's class, right?" He side-stepped, breaking and chopping, rolling the dirt.

"Still?" He flinched, but I gave him no chance to respond, "I take it she's a good swordsman?"

"*He.* He was an excellent swordsman. Perhaps one day you can meet him." Sweat was starting to build on his temple. *Ka-thud!* "He was charged to watch a flock of nuns. *The Church* is very aware of the dangers we face as clergymen opposing the Madness and bloodeaters. Seven nuns to a knight. I don't see what good one knight can do with that many bodies to protect. It seemed only appropriate I train and learn a thing or two. Never knew if it would be me needing to protect my own flock."

Ka-thud!

"I figured you asked him to teach you because of the old man." John froze. "Sorry, I didn't mean..."

"You're right." *Ka-thud!* The muscles in his face were tight. "I asked Valiente to teach me because I was jealous. I often imagined what my grandpa was teaching you and whether you'd even be alive in order to see me come home. He wasn't one to favor a daemon."

"He was a tough old man, but he knew what he was talking about." My hands dove into the cold ground. "I don't understand why you were so worried about me–"

Ka-thud!

"You're important to me. I found you, and I'm responsible for bringing you here." *Ka-thud!* He was working faster than before. "Valiente's a good friend. He made me realize many things, though I still haven't taken all of his advice. Not just yet, anyhow."

"Oh?" I lifted an eyebrow, bringing up two more potatoes. "What sort of advice are you still ignoring?"

John's face flushed. Panting, he leaned on the hoe. "I think we're done. This is all of it, right?"

"Y-yeah." He spun, putting his back to me, dropping the hoe, and marching out of the field back into the cabin.

What happened in Captiva City, John? I should have gone with you; I should have been part of your life during your struggles...

Sighing, I finished pulling up what was left. Basque curled his lips at me, snorting as I walked by with a basket of sweet potatoes. Pausing, I pulled out my knife and diced one up for him. His tail swished, and he perked up his ears. The black giant couldn't get enough of sweets no matter what form they came in. I continued to the porch and grabbed the handle of the cabin door. John's voice echoed in my head: *I found you.*

My thoughts flashed to the boulder, and I turned to face

the woods at my back. Closing my eyes, I scrambled to recall my steps in reverse. *That's right!*

Opening my eyes, I remembered which way it had been. I walked across the field, passed the shed, and slipped through the trees. It was harder to distinguish where I was going. Back then, it had been night and a landscape painted in white with trees made of black. Red and orange leaves rained down with each pulse of wind rattling the canopy overhead. With each turn, my chest tightened. I knew I was coming close. I paused, heart beating hard. There, through the trunks, I recognized the boulder I had perched on over ten years ago.

It took all my willpower not to rush over to it. Stopping at the base, I placed my hand on the cold stone. I had no idea what to do with myself by the time I had wandered this far from the city that night. Kneeling, I stared at a decade of debris between me and my past. Reluctantly, I reached down and started pulling away the layers.

Curiosity was building. *How magical is the dagger? Will I find it aged and rusted or will it look as if nothing ever happened?*

My fingers raked across something soft. I held my breath, my heart leaping into my throat. Reaching down, I yanked it out of the mud and decay. It was as if time had been frozen: my princely braid was dirty and still holding true to its knots. This was where I thought I had left my past behind, but Glensdale taught me otherwise. It was more about the memories I had left behind in the hearts of those I encountered. One didn't have to be immortal to live beyond one's means.

Setting the braid off to the side, I ravaged through the mud, exposing it to the world for the first time in ten years. *Where is it? Shouldn't it be here?* I scooted backward, pulling up the padded layer of leaves and sticks. *Nothing.*

Standing, I leaned against the boulder. My hands were painted in black soil; nausea waved over me. *La Dame d'Croc* was gone. It had been taken, but *by whom? Falco doesn't have it. Why would he need to string me along, beat me, and demand I give it to him? I imagine Lord Knight Paul would have asked about it, or rather, he would have been pissed to see it here. He would have tossed it in the fire and had me prime the hearth for good measure.*

A hand gripped my shoulder, forcibly turning me around. My back pressed against the boulder, and John glared at me. I froze, my blood running cold. *Did John take it?* One arm stretched out, a firm palm beside my head to trap me. The corners of his mouth curved downward in a deep scowl, and I searched his eyes. He had followed me, watched me dig around like a child dawdling in the mud. I could feel the heat rising in my cheeks, waiting for the words he was gathering.

There's nothing I could possibly say without knowing what he thinks I'm out here doing.

"You're looking for the dagger." It wasn't a question; it was a declaration. "Worse, you were considering giving it to the Viceroy."

He does know. He understands the full weight of what is happening.

I looked away in shame, but John leaned into my view. I could see my own maroon eyes flash in his and confessed, "To protect you. He's planning something big, I know it, and I have nothing to bargain your safety with unless..."

He inhaled deep, holding it there before he let it go. "How about you tell me why I found you here all those years ago? Who are you really, Dante?"

Don't make me say it. I don't want to let those words loose in fear you'll send me away.

I leaned forward to brush him off. His palm pulled from the boulder and shoved me back. The anger seethed through him with his palm hot against my chest. My stare broke from his face, afraid he could read my thoughts. I glared at his hand, my chest rising and falling with its calculated strength effortlessly. He too had scarred knuckles, the aftermath of sword training. My own anger was starting to run through my veins. *He wasn't supposed to shed blood. That was my job. That's why I sacrificed myself for him.*

"I think you already know." I narrowed my eyes, weighing the man before me. He winced and his brow lowered with annoyance. "You can't possibly be that naïve not to put it all together by now. You've heard how me and the King talk to one another, how the people of Glensdale act around me."

"Dante, I want you to tell me." The blue in his eyes was still as bright as the first time I'd seen him. His hand fell away, but part of me ached to have it still there, burning into me. "I can spout what I discovered, what I figured out, but I'm trusting you with my life. The least you can do is trust me with yours."

A sweltering ache erupted at my core, and it was my turn to flinch. "You're right."

"Right about what?" He was searching my face, waiting for some signs of surprise. "Stop being so cryptic all the time and just fucking say it."

"I need to trust you," I relented, sliding to the ground at his feet. *Never have I felt so raw, so defeated, and so shattered...*

We were where we started, the boulder, the sacred bond all visible in the glares being exchanged between us. Yet, neither of us knew who the other was besides the assumptions and speculations. We weren't daft; we weren't making blind decisions for one another, but the unspoken wall had to be addressed. How many bricks we would knock out in this moment would be dependent on John, and he knew that. This was why he had followed me.

I can never tell him that I love him, that I adore him, that I long to lay with him. He has sworn celibacy, he has become a priest, and I will not impede his path.

"By now, I'm sure you've figured out I'm the next heir to *The House.*" His mouth twisted and eyes narrowed. "I am

Dante, as in, the Runaway Prince Dante or the one thought dead thanks to rumors spread by Falco."

John crossed his arms, towering over me, "I figured that out some time ago." He was seething. I didn't use the confessional tone he had hoped for. "Why the dagger that night?"

"That dagger is called *La Dame d'Croc,* and it was my duty to use it to become the next King of Bloodeaters." I forced myself to look up at him. I refused to feel shame for the decision I made so long ago and rose back to my feet to face him. "You found me here because I had made a vow. I'll never become a bloodeater. That damned chunk of metal started the plague, and I intended to end it."

"So, you ran away with it," he concluded, covering his mouth. "Did Grandpa know?"

"He knew who I was." Huffing, I shook my head. "I don't think he realized I brought the dagger with me. I dropped it here in the snow." I gave him a dangerous glare, curious now.

John's eyebrows lifted high, "So why did the Prince of Bloodeaters decide to be the servant of a human? It seems so radical and obscure. It's the one thing I don't understand about us, about you."

"I didn't come out here to die, John." Smirking, he was dancing around the real questions he wanted answers to such as *what was I supposed to do with the dagger that night* or *why did I never go back even after he left.* "I just wanted a new life. You had a dream to fulfill, and it so happened to be the same one I had: to end the reign of bloodeaters. I wanted you to succeed, and I was willing to fight and defend you from my own people to see it happen."

I started to walk away, but he grabbed my forearm. "Why did you ask about Valiente today?"

My cheeks reddened. *I am jealous.* "I noticed the way you were throwing your weight into the hoe. It was something the old man had told me to note in an opponent. You only met one other knight in your time away, so I could only assume. You wanted my trust; do I really have all of yours? I asked you a simple question, and you stomped off like I had spit on your grave."

John let go, a sense of shock flashing across his face. "Dante, there's more..."

I gave him a stern stare. "I already know there's a lot of secrets you've made in your time away. Worse, it seems you have managed to keep me in the dark on several matters in Glensdale. The letter and deals you've made with my father were quite jolting for me. If you knew I was the Prince, why not ask me?"

"I'm afraid, afraid you'll get hurt." He covered his face. "You fret over me, you take beatings in the streets at night, and you go as far as making an alliance with the Assassin's Guild. I had to do something. I had to try..."

The words failed him, and a wave of anger rattled me. "I didn't hide any of that from you! You give me a task, and I fulfill it. It's not like you ever asked what happened or why!" My voice caught in my throat, and I grabbed him by the collar and pushed him against the rock. "If you think I will spill all that I am without a single question asked, forget it. I ask, and all I get is a view of your back as you march away angry!"

"It's hard! It's hard to talk to you!" John blurted, his fists rising to grip my own collar. We were inches from one another, shouting like spoiled children. "I watch how you laugh and smile with people in Glensdale, and all I can think is WHY! Why can't you smile at me that way?"

My heart stopped, my rage swept away by the butterflies in my stomach. *Don't say it, John.*

"You want to know what it was Valiente said to me?" His temper was taking hold; he couldn't stop himself. *This is why you walk away: your temper.* "You want to know what happened in Captiva City?"

No, not another word... I tried to pull away, but he tugged me forward. My feet tripping over one another, I slammed against him. I whispered, "Don't say it..."

John's lips tickled at my ear, his breath like hot oil across my neck. "He kissed me." My heart broke into a million pieces, my mouth running dry, but another whisper lingered unspoken before spilling forth, "And I realized I was in love with someone else, someone I can never have."

He can't end his dream here. I can't be the reason he breaks his vow for priesthood. I was meant to be his Sword and Shield. I was meant to be his Barrier d'Force.

The hot iron cross and burning flesh filled my mind. My resolve burned at my core, and an uncanny calm armored me. My fingers pulled his fists away, and I caught my balance. He wore a dreadful expression, and I wondered if I reflected it back to him. The world around us was silent, the wind between us cold. Strands of John's poorly-braided hair flickered like golden threads. My eyes hovered on those lips, so soft and warm where they had caressed my ear. Someone had stolen them from me, and my jealousy clawed at my soul. Snow flurries were starting to fall; winter had returned sooner than I wanted.

Against my better judgment, my lips met his. He accepted them; the silken heat exchanged between us breaking the wall further. My jealousy, my obsession, let loose momentarily. I pulled away, and his hands let go. His blue eyes pleaded for forgiveness.

"Was this the kiss you were hoping for?" I whispered.

John leaned forward for another taste, and I shoved him harshly against the boulder, glaring back. *We can't!* "I won't," I choked, turning away. "They'll kill you for it." It was my turn to leave him feeling lost and broken with nothing but the comfort of the view of my back.

I won't be the reason you break your vows... I can't be the reason they'll aim to kill you.

CHAPTER 19

Weight of One's Heart

Flurries fell in a never-ending waterfall. The forest around me was a painting made of horizontal white strokes with an equal measure of vertical black lines. We had left the wagon behind, knowing it would be too much of a risk with the weather. Once more I found myself gripping the reins as John rode behind me. Feeling his body heat against my back was a lingering curse of desire. My breath rolled out of my nostrils in heaps, and the snow pattered all around us, a hushed sound matching the silence we continued to endure. John's hands cupped my shoulders, unlike the embracing of under my arms from so many times before. John had unveiled his feelings, yet even now, he was unsure of how I felt about him, about his feelings, or even about Valiente.

Every minute of the ride I spent cursing him. *Why are you always putting it on me to make the final call for us both, John?* I couldn't decide which of my emotions should be shown. My soul was in a tug-o-war of elation, anger, and dread. *He meant me. And in that wretched bitterness of hearing, he kissed another.* Jealousy twisted its sharp point into my heart yet again. *It should have been me; he wanted it to be me. If I ever see that knight...*

Passing through the city gates, the guards nodded hello. John was a cornerstone in the community, and the locals wanted him to be around. They were showing support, offering aid and supplies without ever needing to be asked. Some of this was thanks to the attention of my father, but with each sermon, they grew more willing to truly help John of their own accord. He wouldn't leave here because of Glensdale's citizens.

The cobblestones making up the main street were thick with ice and fresh snow. Under me, I could feel the Nivernais' muscles tense with each step. We approached the last stretch and paused. I urged Basque forward, earning a curled lip before the horse relented. Basque's size made him fickle; so much weight on unsure footing would make anyone nervous. His hooves slipped on the uphill climb; I would have to lead him to the church. If his footing didn't catch, or he slid in the wrong direction, he could break a leg or go lame. Dismounting, I grabbed Basque's halter, shushing him with sweet potato cubes. Snorting, he gobbled them up. His hooves were still dancing, anxious as he slid uneven across the ground.

John was clinging to the saddle, his face paling. "What's wrong with him?"

My eyes fell to John's white-knuckled fists on the rim of the saddle. These were the first words he had said to me since I walked away from him over three days ago. It pained me to hear his voice only out of necessity.

"Get off," I demanded.

John wasted no time in doing so, losing his footing on the ice. My hand flashed out, gripping his bicep. Fingers dug into hardened muscle. Steadying his feet, he looked up at me red-faced. I broke my stare. Retrieving my hand, I closed my fist, savoring the warmth still lingering on my skin. It was torture, knowing he had feelings for me, and some part of me wondered if he felt the same desire every time we touched.

"Thank you," John mumbled, marching up the hill.

Turning back to the horse, Basque was happy to be able to focus on his weight alone. John's coded confession still echoed in my mind: *in love with someone else, someone I can never have.* I hadn't returned the gesture, nor could I tell him how much my heart raced with every lock of our eyes or the heat of our bodies coming close. *They'll kill him for loving me.* Sunday had come, and we could focus our minds elsewhere. Still, he was very aware how impossible of a thing he spoke of, and it seemed like he would be content leaving it. This unpassable wall of taboos where braided knots and celibacy lay a higher priority than matters of the heart.

By the time the service started, I was breaking ice in the water troughs outside. I didn't want to be in there; to hear his voice echoing across the rafters and the eyes of patrons who didn't see him in the same light as I did made me ill. The handle of the broom broke the last chunk of ice free. Basque slurped up the water, ice chunks clacking against the side. He finished, snorting and sneezing at me with self-satisfaction. Rolling my eyes, all I could do was sigh. He seemed content with the drink and shuddered, checking his footing once more. Duke Chapman had delivered enough hay for the horses to eat, and we scattered the rest across the area. It wasn't the best way to melt the snow, but it gave the horses a reprieve from iron horseshoes gliding across frozen cobblestones.

Rubbing Basque's nose, I muttered, "I find myself trapped between my heart and my head. You wouldn't happen to have any advice for a lost soul?"

He flicked his ears back as if saying, *It's difficult to free fools from the chains they make for themselves.* Basque gave me a short expression of pity before snorting about my pockets in hopes of finding the rest of his sweets.

The church doors opened, the service done for the day. Reaching to my side, I gripped the mask from where it clipped into my belt. Staring down at the eyeless expression, I decided not to place it on.

They all know it's me. Why should I hide behind an expressionless mask? Falco's gone, but how much does it matter that he's thinks no one knows it's me? I'm tired of hiding from my past. I need to make things right. My time with John will need to end soon before we go too far, and I find myself at war with The Church *in order to keep him safe.*

Many of the patrons had paused to look at me and gossip. Those who recognized me, like Duke and Duchess Chapman, nodded in acknowledgment. My identity had been held as a bargaining chip by Falco, but the citizens had taken it from him in order to protect their lost Prince. For that, I was thankful. Thumbing the mask, I saw it was nothing more than an empty sense of security for myself.

Always so selfish, aren't I? Thinking I had something more to lose than everyone else. How naive I can be at times. Wouldn't you say so, old man?

A smile came to my lips. Lord Knight Paul would have never let it go I that I went to church dressed like a yearling assassin. *He spoke of them with high regard. I wonder, could the lady he still had feelings for be a daemon? How was it that he described her? Ah, 'she was a spitfire, but she would be tamed by no man, taking the lives of any who tried, and leaving even me thirsty for her affection.'*

Sliding through the church doors, I saw it had emptied out quickly today. No one wanted to sit in a cold church, and until further repairs, the hearths and braziers were unsafe to use. We had burned through the money to provide necessities, pews, and ordering books from *The Church* to replace what had been stolen, burned, or simply decayed. Closing the doors, I turned to see no sign of John. He had left the pulpit, his tome still laid open. An ache rippled through my body, nerves twisting. Marching down the aisle, I caught the fluttering of the lantern in his open office door. Two shadows trembled in and out of view. I pushed the door open, my body tight with anticipation.

Is Falco back? Did he corner him?

"Dante." Ruth's voice struck me like a blade.

I froze. My heart was the ticking of a clock, my eyes too afraid to look at what expression might await me on her face. Her voice was clear, not a stutter, and in a wretched tone I hadn't anticipated hearing this soon. Crossing her arms, she shifted her hips, and her gauntlet's fingers tinged against the armor as she drummed them in her impatience. Still, I couldn't bring myself to look her in the eye.

"It's good to see you've given up the mask." She cleared her throat, "I was telling John that Viceroy Falco and two of his personal guards were seen heading south a few days ago, toward Captiva City. We've suspected he's had someone in his pocket for some time."

"Bishop Marquis," John dropped the information without hesitation. "I wasn't sure at first, but we can assume it's him. I have some written accounts, and when you line them up with him and the Viceroy, it becomes clear there is an undeniable exchange. I'm sure if we go to the whore house, we'd discover where most of the Bishop's funding was spent."

"R-really?" She pondered the answer. "That means he's getting padded pockets from several sources. He's playing a dangerous game: King Traibon, Viceroy Falco, *The Church*, who else?"

I forced myself to speak at last, "Falco may not be able to meet with him any longer. He'll be going in hiding; he knows he's royally fucked now. In fact, he may have gone into hiding, which is why Falco has come out. He's lost his dog."

Ruth smirked. "And he speaks!"

I rolled my eyes, but John interjected, "What makes you say that? Is he afraid of the Viceroy?"

"He's always been afraid of Falco." I shut the door. This had to be said where no other ears could hear. Whispering, I answered, "The Assassin's Guild has a bounty on his head."

Ruth's eyes widened. "And how on earth did you get that information?"

I could feel the weight of their stares crushing into me. If I let it slip Madame Plasket *was* the Assassin's Guild, I'd find my throat slit by Lager or Ale. They looked at one another, and I shifted my stance.

Crossing my arms, I lifted my eyebrows at them. "I can't say. Just know the Assassin's Guild wants Falco taken down as well, but have their hands tied due to... policies and reputation." Silence fell across the room. I hadn't escaped the curious glares of my cousin. "Trust me. I didn't join the guild nor hire anyone. I just happened to receive some support from them, and I'm not going to turn away a valuable resource."

"By no means," scoffed Ruth, cracking her knuckles. "They've stayed out of my way and even have the courtesy to do their business outside my city walls. Granted, I haven't a clue who any of the members are. All I know is that they are based out of Glensdale and have been here long before the bloodeaters moved in and claimed the town and territory for themselves."

"I had no idea they were that deeply rooted." I gave a nervous laugh. "The only other thing I know is they're all named after alcoholic drinks. It's a clever way to protect their real namesakes. Perhaps the reason no one ever discovers their identity."

"Sometimes they leave notes on the bodies out in the woods and on the roads." Ruth nodded. "All of them say, *laissez le sang coule comme du vin.*"

"*Let the blood flow like wine,*" John mumbled, "How poetic.

You really think he'll even get a chance to go into hiding before they catch up to him? I don't think he's that clever."

"He's been backdoor dealing several fronts for this long. He's cunning at best. I have a feeling he has connections in places beyond Grandemere. I suspect he might even be connected to *Arbre Tombé*, but I don't know much about who they are. He frequents port towns, so I suspect he may even be into some illegal trading."

"I think you're on to something." Walking to the door, Ruth nudged my shoulder. "It was good seeing your face and hearing your voice, cousin. Know that no one is angry at you. We knew you weren't planning to follow in your father's footsteps. Honestly, he would have been disappointed in you if you had."

She shoved out the door and closed it behind her, leaving John and me alone. Taking in a deep breath, I stared at the blue eyes piercing me. There was no smile, just a cold scowl on his face. I opened my mouth, but I had nothing I could say. He had done his sermon, and I had nosed into his office uninvited. Exhaling, I sank to the floor, my back against the door and the floor icy under me. We couldn't keep this up. I had to break the silence and stagnant bitterness growing between us.

"I'm sorry." I wasn't sure what I was apologizing for: walking away without saying anything, never taking the time to tell him who I was, or not speaking up about Glensdale's corrupted past involving Falco. Regardless, I was sorry for it all.

John sighed, leaning on his knees from where he sat in the chair. The muscles in his cheeks twitched, and I knew he wasn't sure what to say either. We were at a stalemate.

"No more hiding my past, no more invisible walls between us." The lantern wavered, casting deep shadows across the tiny room. "You ask me anything and I'll answer it."

"Do you really mean that?" His words stung; he knew there was something I wouldn't confess.

"It's not like I intend on leaving. I made a promise and I meant it, John." There was one answer I couldn't give: *I love someone I can't have, too.*

His lips tightened. We were ripping into one another with our glares. He was angry, brooding. I walked away after had stripped himself down to nothing and even had the audacity to bait him with a jealous kiss. He had every right to be pissed off, to hate me for my cowardice. If only he realized how much strength it took for me to hold my tongue, to not kiss him for a second time when he leaned forward that day.

"Why are you giving me the evil eye?" I wasn't going to let John stay silent any longer. "Is there something you want to ask me?" *He won't ask me for a reply. It's something else; I can feel it.*

"Falco." His brow furrowed. "Is it true?"

"Is what true?" My chest tightened. *I pressured him about Valiente. Now it is his turn to push me about Falco. It is fair, is it not?*

"That you were his lover." To hear it from John hurt, dropping like a vase from a balcony.

I had promised. "It's true." The answer came out flat and raw.

He digested it, the taste visibly sour on his face. "Do you still–"

"No." I stood, the idea of it making my shoulders shudder. "He might still have feelings for me, but he made me realize I could never be the monster the bloodeaters wanted me to become. I could never become the monster he wanted to keep by his side either."

John's cheeks were red. "I didn't realize..."

"How could you?" Covering my face, I let it off my soul, confessing to my dear priest all that I regretted in the time before he filled my life. "To be surrounded by people who are willing to fuck you physically and mentally for their own gain? That's something I hope you never have to endure. Not to the extent I have, fangs in my skin, arms of a heartless lover fucking me from behind."

John winced.

"That's my past. That's a time before I knew what I even wanted in life for myself, let alone for someone I truly cared for." I waited for him to soak it in, his face softening and a flair of regret written in his eyes. *It is more than he intended to hear from me.* "So yes, Falco and I were in a relationship for some time, but I ended it. And, not long after that, I left Glensdale."

"I had to deal with corruption and greed in Captiva City, but you're right. Being a Prince, the next heir, it makes me sick to my stomach to know how far they would go..." His words buckled, and there was a flash of anger. "How far the Viceroy would go. The way he beat you that first night, to think someone..."

I reached for the door, unable to bear anymore, but froze. "Know that I don't walk away to avoid the conversation. I leave because nothing good will come of what I'm feeling, to let those raw emotions fly without understanding what they are first. It still hurts, my past with him, now that I've found..."

"Dante, I didn't–"

Slamming the office door behind me, I could feel my body boil with sour memories. It made my head swim, the rush of feeling Falco's fangs at my throat and the sliding of his hand down my stomach or even his fingers digging into my hips. Back in those days, it had been exciting. Now, it was the sexual exploitations of a power-hungry man who hated seeing my face. I had stolen his dagger, his ability to make an army of bloodeaters, and he had made the mistake of falling in love with me. He would surely find a way to pay me back for these travesties.

On the other side, here I stood, in love with the man who now belonged to *The Church*.

What a cruel fate I have chosen for myself...

CHAPTER 20

Ruth's Message

Winter was reaching its peak, the days growing short and the nights ever-longer. I took some old stones and crafted a mini hearth for Basque. The first storm was rolling in, and the last thing I wanted was a frozen Nivernais. John bundled himself up, aiding me with haystacks I had bought from Duke Chapman and building it around to keep the wind out. He struggled to grip anything, cursing his fingers when they were numb and again for being limited in movement under thick rabbit fur mittens.

"Aren't you freezing?" Teeth chattering, John glared at me with a sense of jealousy. "Are all daemons immune to the cold?"

"It's hard to say." I was packing the dirt up and around the sides of the hearth, hoping it would keep the wind and melting snow from seeping into the tiny hearth. "It's that I don't mind the cold. I can still freeze to death, but my body doesn't ache or shut down like a human's."

"It's unnatural," he retorted, petting Basque on the nose. "Then what about heat? Does it work the same?"

Pausing, my mind flashed to the time John's hands gripped my thighs and how the warmth of his touch lingered. "No. I have to admit, I react to heat differently." Another memory surfaced, the searing of my flesh on the water pump handle. "Perhaps it depends on where the heat is coming from."

"Oh?" Basque started searching John's coat and pulled a mitten off looking for sweets. "What kind of heat?" he asked.

"I sweat under the sun, as you do," I started, packing more rocks on top of the dirt-covered walls of the hearth. "My flesh sears on hot metal, but..."

"But?" Picking up his mitten from the ground, he came and squatted next to me.

I could feel his blue eyes staring at me, but I kept my own on the fire dancing in the little igloo of rocks and dirt. "When..." He raised his eyebrows at me, and all I could focus on was the feel of his lips at my ear. *He's teasing me.* John knew how I felt and reacted, so I confessed, "The flame of a touch never goes away. Especially from a certain someone."

Breaking away from John, I stood and shuffled hay between Basque and the hearth. I didn't want the horse to get too close and burn himself. John didn't say a word. He shed his mittens and warmed his hands at the fire with a mischievous smirk on his face. When I finished, I tapped his shoulder with my fingers. A violent wind whistled through the trees and everywhere frozen limbs snapped and cracked. The weight of ice and the pressure of the storm would leave the forest in shreds. Tomorrow was John's next service, but until the storm broke and sun rose, we wouldn't know if we could even get past the debris. Satisfied Basque would be warm and safe, we retreated to the cabin.

Throwing a few more logs in the hearth, I opened the cellar door. The ladder creaked under my weight, and I held firm to the lantern in my hand. Weaving between the shelves, I weaseled my way to the open area where I had trained with the old man during the winter. The brazier still had fresh logs, so I used the flame of the lantern to bring it to life once more. A large dummy was placed in the one corner, its burlap flesh battered, and wooden bones nicked. Near the table was a heavy wooden training sword. It was the old man's personal design, iron weights added to force muscles to build up faster and to make slicing through a body ten times easier in battle when using the real weapon.

I picked up the sword and held it aloft, outstretched in one hand. I smiled. In the beginning, I couldn't hold it one-handed, and he'd given me hell for using two hands. It took months before I could even hold it one-handed, and more months to swing it properly. In fact, it was after plowing the field alone that first time when the muscles in my back had strengthened enough to support the added weight on my arm. John had been long gone, no one had come searching, and I had been left with the ramblings of a retired Lord Knight.

I'm not out here farming because I want to, but because I must in order to keep sharp, Dante. The old man always had purpose to everything he said and every action he took. *You can't swing a sword without the muscle, and you can't build the muscle without the work.*

"HA!" I swung, stepping forward to add my weight into the downstroke.

CLACK! The sound of wood against wood rang in my ears. The exertion was revitalizing. I swung again, striking down from the other direction. *CLACK!* I shuffled back and stepped forward, the upswing making my muscles ache. *CLACK!* Another step back and a lunge, followed by an upswing from the other side, *CLACK!* I yanked off my sweaty shirt, and pausing, eyed the claymore. *Sorry old man. I'm not worthy of wielding that weapon just yet; for now the broad sword will have to do.* I repeated the movement over and over, breaking through the stale sensation in my body. Since John's return,

I hadn't kept up with my training.

Let your muscles go stale, and you're good as dead. It amazed me how much Lord Knight Paul still echoed in my head, pushing me to become the person I wanted to be.

"I knew this was here, but I didn't realize he was using it when I was out in the field." John's voice stopped my swing, and I spun around. "Then again, I suppose you have to train somewhere in winter."

"Yeah, he stashed everything from his past in here." I pointed the sword at a huge wooden chest, some armor on display, and a shelf full of books and trinkets. "If you want, it's all here. I didn't go through it or even touch it. It wasn't mine to sort through."

John strolled closer, a hand sliding over the chest as he towered over the armor. "Was this what he wore in battle?"

"I think so." Wiping sweat from my forehead and chin, I walked over and turned the armor on its peg to reveal the deep dent across the back left shoulder. "He always bitched how his shoulder hurt in winter. I imagine this would be the reason."

"What on earth would make a dent in metal like that?" John's finger pushed in and out of the crevice, shuddering. "It can't be an axe, could it?"

"Knowing him, he stepped into a swing from an axe, pole arm, hell, even a club. If it was a bloodeater, they would leave a dent like that on impact." I turned back to the dummy, and switching hands from right to left, I repeated the movements. *Don't let them know you're left handed. Let them think they are already fighting the main hand.*

"Bloodeaters are stronger than a normal daemon." John pulled off his shirt, picking up the other training sword leaning on the chest. "But a daemon is stronger than a human, right?"

"R-right." I watched John grip the iron-laden sword with

one hand and gave it a practice swing. *Indeed, you trained hard in Captiva City.*

"Why did he make these things so heavy?" He swapped it from one hand then back again. "I was going to join you in practice, but getting hit with this would shatter a rib or break my arm."

"Ha! He told me that was part of the learning." I knocked my wooden blade against his, and he stumbled. "It seems Valiente didn't teach you how to keep your balance."

John smirked. "We trained with a different sort of blade. Something lighter, not claymores and broadswords."

"Oh?" I walked over to the chest and flung it open. "What weapon was it? A rapier? Even a tuck, perhaps?"

"Are you kidding?" Wide-eyed, John glared into the assortment of weaponry piled inside. "There's enough here to supply a small army."

"I know. Your grandfather was something else." John reached in, grabbing the rapier and leaving behind the heavy wooden practice sword. "He would clean them often. It should be in good order if you unsheathe it."

John pulled on the hilt, and the blade slid out of the scabbard with ease. "It's gorgeous."

"Technically it's yours." I closed the chest. "Test it out."

John looked across the room at the dummy and grinned. "I should."

I sat on the chest and watched him take his stance. It was so different than my own, but the weight of our blades and purpose of our training had been opposite. Lord Knight Paul had trained himself to fight against my kind, and we both knew it would be needed for me to take out Falco. I wasn't a bloodeater, but if his style kept the old man alive against the Viceroy, it would assure me victory. Meanwhile, Knight Valiente had taught John to be agile and strike with precision, not to cleave a limb. His blade was aimed to bleed an enemy out while parrying heavy strikes.

The way he leaned and rotated his body was like a dance. Each muscle stretched, tightening like the cords of a violin and the sword singing in response. *I can at least thank Valiente for teaching John such graceful swordsmanship.* He switched between front and side, a constant feint for an opponent to think they can strike and miss. Indeed, this was an important style considering John wanted to help protect a flock of nuns. With this, he could tire out an enemy and keep his stamina. Raised on a farm, he was at a great advantage.

"When are the nuns coming?" I thudded the tip of the training sword at my feet. "I know it was being discussed, and the snow delayed it."

"They were supposed to be here in time for tomorrow's service, but that was before the storm moved in." *Fwip!* He was still enjoying the well-balanced blade. "I imagine we will see them tomorrow some time, if not later."

"Do you know anyone who is coming?" I asked, and John's swing froze. He returned the sword to the sheath and turned to me with a pained expression. "What's with that look?"

"Valiente is in charge of this flock. They were the only ones willing to attempt the visit," John told me. The burning jealousy crept into my chest, and I pushed it back. He added, "I do know the Mother Superior Sonja. She is his canoness and he her canon."

"Forgive me. I don't know much about ranks within *The Church*," I said. John came close, dripping with sweat as he wiped his face on his shirt. "All I know is that you have seven knots until you are promoted and leap to ten knots like Bishop Marquis."

"Mother Superior is the head nun in a flock." John slid the rapier across the table, watching the light of the brazier dance across the decorative flourishes on the sheath. "Canon refers to the male partner to a nun, in turn, his canoness. In short, they work together to manage the flock. Traditionally, this role was between the Bishop and a Mother Superior, but the war has shifted these roles drastically."

"I see." Grabbing my shirt, I pulled it back on. "Let's get some rest. It may be a rough day tomorrow with the storm tearing the trees all to hell."

"Dante." John's eyes were still on the rapier. "Thank you."

"For what?" I lit the lantern and snuffed out the brazier, a smoky darkness between us filling the room.

"For taking care of the old man." There was an unsteady breath, "And for waiting on me. I was so afraid I'd come back, and you would be gone."

"If it makes you feel any better," I began, then swallowed hard, thankful for the deep shadows the lantern cast across John's face, smothering his expression and hiding his eyes from me, "it was terrifying to think you may not come back home at all."

His shoulders slumped, and I took the chance to slide through the shelves.

* * * * *

Basque's hearth was still warm by the first light of day. He was happy to have the wind gone and the snow stopped. Tree limbs lay scattered across the pathway, but it would have to wait to be cleared. The snow was packed in hard, making Basque more confident in his steps as he occasionally hopped over a tree trunk. John wrapped his arms around my stomach, and I laughed. He felt like an overgrown child clinging to me for dear life. In spring, I could manage to buy a smaller horse for him, teach him to ride, and free us both of the awkwardness this routine brought on. Basque was far too high and too big for a first-time rider. The service would have to start late, but many had feared there wouldn't be any at all. Even within the town, the storm lifted shingles from the houses, knocked over a chimney or two, and left wagons and carts toppled over.

Waiting at the church doors was Viceroy Falco. No one had seen him for some time and my hands tightened on the reins as we approached. He was planning something, but none of us knew what he would try next with so much going wrong for him. At best, he was an animal starting to feel cornered in his own territory, and he would bite at any moment.

"No mask?" He gave a slimy grin and lifted an eyebrow. "What if King Traibon shows up today?"

I ignored him, putting my focus on helping John dismount, and I left Basque to his hay and water. Nikolas had come and gone, breaking ice from the troughs and leaving the hay ready. They had expected us late, but they pitied us for having to face Falco today. Not a soul dared to wait for the church to open its doors with a monster standing guard. The two city guards shifted, nervous from the tension growing in the air now that I had arrived.

"Viceroy Falco!" John threw his arms out as if greeting a long-lost friend. "Where in the heavens have you been?"

"Around." He gave John an unamused look. "But the storm brought me back home, no less. You do know we have a war to tend to?"

"I haven't forgotten." John was unlocking the doors, pushing them open and gesturing for him to enter. "It's the reason why I am here."

"Still no nuns." Viceroy Falco walked in with John, peering about the church. "And no hearths for heating the room. I thought you'd get more done with the place while I was away."

"He's been busy." I was close on John's heel, afraid to leave the two alone. "King Traibon has come for many visits and John's first priority is the people."

"Is that so?" There was a sparkle in Falco's eye, a dangerous gleam. A chill rattled through me. *He isn't phased in the slightest that my father might know I'm back now.* "It's a shame I have missed all the wondrous interactions."

A crowd had gathered at the open doors, and John waved them in, his smile bright. "Come! Come in! I apologize for the late start!"

"I take it your father knows, Dante?" Falco hummed, a strange excitement in his voice.

Why do I feel like this is going according to his plans, not mine?

I frowned, but John stepped between our glares. "Take your seat, Viceroy. I am already behind schedule, and many of us have repairs to start after last night."

He narrowed his eyes at John. "As you wish, my dear priest."

John was climbing on the pulpit, but Falco grabbed my arm. His lips brushed against my ear, "Why don't you give up on this charity case and come back to me? You can't keep this farce rolling much longer, my Prince."

It was a demand. I tried to break away from his grip but failed.

"Do you not have a gift for me today?" he cooed, nuzzling me, and John glared down on us with a heated expression. "Have you at least brought me my Lady?"

"No." I dug my fingers into his wrist, and Falco let go. "It's gone, lost forever to you and me and the world."

He sneered, opening his mouth only to have John interrupt, "Viceroy, please take your seat."

The weight of the bitter maroon eyes from Falco was amusing and terrifying. He wouldn't do anything to me or John in the public eye. People had spotted us on Basque and were pouring in behind us, eager to see both the sermon and how John would handle the Viceroy. He struggled to keep in their good graces as it was. The sermon went on, and I noticed the city guard was thicker and more watchful. As for the patrons, they were quiet and shifted nervously with the

Viceroy back. In fact, Glensdale as a whole had recoiled with his presence back in the open.

I exchanged heated glares with Falco, unable to hear the words John preached. Heads nodded, and hands raised in praise, but all I could focus on was the wolf in sheep's clothing. He toyed with me, licking a fang and mouthing: *You tasted so sweet.* He gave a side glance at John and added a playful: *He looks delicious.* It was one taunt after another, and there was nothing I could do but grip the longsword at my hip. In my mind, all I could hear was John's words. *You fucking run him through.* Falco's eyes dropped, locking on the sheath. I watched as his brow lowered and his smile faded. There was a twitch and snarl; he knew who the weapon's owner was and some part of me hoped he recalled the bite of the old man's claymore.

Falco doesn't handle pain well. It was the old man complimenting me on handling the bee stings and blisters I had earned that first year. *I nipped him with that broadsword, and he froze, and I nipped him again. First his side and then his cheek. I don't think he knew what open flesh felt like until I filleted him with my claymore. Countering, he knocked the broadsword from my left hand, broke the fingers good that time. He didn't know I could wield a claymore one-handed. That was how I got him.*

John was on the last part, the repetitive "good graces to all" and "see you next week" bit when the church doors swung open. Captain Ruth marched down the aisle, her armor sparkling with the color of the stained-glass windows. She halted in front of John, who stood silently along with the room of people, no one sure as to what was unfolding. Falco smiled, a wicked toothy curve and mouthed: *I wanted to see your face.* Dread filled me as Ruth shot me a quick look before bowing.

"Forgive me, Father John." She stood upright. "The King demands your presence this instant."

"Y-yes. Right away." John's book thudded closed, and he turned to his congregation. "Forgive me. I am needed elsewhere."

The city guards started to escort the people out. Viceroy Falco approached Ruth, and she ignored him, instructing guards to insure his safety. She gripped my arm and rushed me into the office. She slammed the door so it was just the two of us, and I paled.

I found myself muttering, "Is he still alive?"

"Barely." She covered her mouth, searching the room and back to my face. "Where's your mask? You need to have it on in order to get you into the mansion. We need to avoid any further drama, but he is calling for John and you. I just need to be able to get you passed everyone as quickly as I can with as little fuss. Granted, I don't know how far the rumors about you have gotten with the household staff."

I turned to my satchel on the cot and within it, my mask. "He's being poisoned by Falco."

"I suspected, but nothing we've tried has been able to combat the poison." The vial was still there with the strange liquid, and I held it up for her. "What is that?"

"The cure. I hope." Rushing over, I put it in her hand and gave her my long sword. "We both know I can't have these on me. Can you carry them for now?"

"I can do that much, but how long have you had this?" She peered at the liquid, curious. "Are you sure it will work?"

"The Assassin's Guild gave it to me when they first approached me. I was afraid to offer it sooner, unsure if it was an antidote." She nodded, agreeing she would have made the same decision. "But if he's on his death bed, it'll either finish the job or revive him."

"It's worth a try at this stage." She echoed my thoughts and grabbed the door as I pulled on my mask. "What makes you suspect Falco?"

"He's power hungry." Throwing the satchel over a shoulder, I followed her to where one guard waited with John. "And the fact he was here to see how I would take the news of my father's death. He mouthed it across the room to me, among other unpleasantries."

"How typical of him." Ruth waved for John to follow, pointing to give her the rapier on his hip. "They say *Le Chien Enragé* will have servants bring him a chair and a goblet of freshly drawn blood, so he can watch the throws of death or even the final moments of the plague. He's notorious for timing them out, so he watches one fade as the next begins."

John gave me a grave look, and I shook my head; *I don't need your pity.* Outside the church, the royal carriage waited, and we entered. Captain Ruth shut the door and mounted her own horse. Sitting across one another, I saw how John's breath lingered in the frigid air while my own stayed hidden behind my mask. He opened his mouth, and I lifted my hand, signaling him to stay quiet. I needed to prepare myself for what waited for me in my long-abandoned home.

You can't die, old man. I'm not ready to be King.

CHAPTER 21

Confessions

The carriage halted, sliding on the ice for a brief moment. My nerves were tight, and I fought back the waves of nausea. The mansion was grey and aged under the overcast winter sky, and inside, my father was dying. Ruth opened the carriage doors, and we followed her, silent and obedient. As we walked into the foyer, John looked humbled by the height of the vaulted ceilings. Every part of the interior was filled with tapestries and elegant furniture meant for display. Maids and butlers lined up, heads bowed, a sign we were honored guests.

"Weren't the churches similar in Captiva?" I asked, curious by his reaction and frightened by my own wealth. "Surely they were larger."

"Larger, yes." He met my gaze for only a moment before returning to soak in more details. "But horribly bare. Everything there is stone, wood, and if lucky, marble. Here, this is..."

I shoved John's back, pushing him to follow Captain Ruth and not wanting to hear anymore. My heart was racing, fear tangling into the building anxiety in my chest. Unlike him, I had seen it all a million times and grown numb to it all, until now. Swallowing, *this isn't the time to dawdle.* She led us up the grand stairwell, and we began the labyrinth of turns through the halls. It was a smart design, always brightly lit with lanterns, but each turn looked identical to the one we had just walked. The placement of portraits, the armor on display, the furniture and unmarked doors were skillfully duplicated. Once as a child, I had scuffed the handle of a chair, and it was immediately replaced. This was how a mansion protected its occupants and more so, bought them time to escape. The only hint as to where to go was the people in the portraits. The question left at this point was whether the visitor followed a pointed hand, the direction they faced, or the line of sight. My father always said, *Look your enemy in the eye and never let them go.*

The final turn put us down a dead end where large black double doors waited. Golden lions and stags bordered the edges, rubies and emeralds dotting their eyes. Two guardians of the royal family stood out front. Ruth waved, and they smiled, waving back. As we approached, one hugged her, and the other offered to shake John's hand, then my own. It took a moment to recognize the faces under the elaborate helms: Ruth's brother Brandon and his childhood friend Ryan.

"We're glad you made it back so fast." Brandon let go of Captain Ruth and glared in my direction with a curious look. "He's hanging in there for now, sis."

She nodded, turning her attention to us. "Let's get you two in there. We can catch up afterward."

"Catch up?" Ryan looked confused, and she waved him off. "Open the doors and let them in?" he asked.

"A-alone with the King?" Brandon scratched his jaw. "Are you sure?"

She grabbed her brother's shoulder, pulling him closer as

she whispered in his ear. His eyes shot to me, face red with a look of contempt. She was pinching his ear now, her whisper harsher, and he slapped her fingers off. With a heavy sigh, his expression faded to one of remorse. Whatever she had to say about my overall situation was enough to give him a change of heart.

"Fine. Let's open the door, Ryan." They nodded to one another and tugged the doors open, the hinges squeaking from the weight.

Ruth turned, grabbing my hand to give me back the vial. "Let's pray this is a cure, Dante."

I nodded and followed John into the dark room. Adorning the walls was the fabric which filled the church's own; he hadn't changed anything in the last ten years. The doors creaked again, a stream of light from the hall shrinking at my feet and disappearing when they shut with a thud. On one wall was a massive fireplace, its fire low and glowing with hot coals. Opposite this, on the other side of a smattering of chairs and tables, was my father's grandiose bed and canopy. John wasted no time to join my father's side, and I saw the fragile hand reach for the one offered.

I couldn't breathe. I couldn't move. *How could he let it come to this?* My chest tight with anxiety, I looked away, fighting the tears building. *How could I let it come to this?*

Murmuring buzzed between them, but the beating of my heart made the words inaudible. My throat tight with fear, I managed to take a step, bumping into a chair. I steadied my balance on it, memories of playing here as a child rattling through me. My eyes turned away from the bed and fell on the warm glow of the hearth. The last of the orange flames danced until they no longer existed. Another ache clawed across my chest. I looked down at the vial in my hand, the liquid inside sloshing from top to bottom.

I don't think Madame Plasket would give me poison. She

prefers the blood to flow like wine. She likes the bladed arts more than anything. Why didn't I think about it sooner? The Guild never kills by any other means...

John's hand gripped my shoulder, and I flinched. "It's now or never."

Nodding, I steadied my breathing. It was the most intense march of my life, approaching my father's death bed. Kneeling, I stared at the hand resting on the blankets. The pale fingers glowed in the darkness, reaching up to pull the mask away. I let him, unlike before. *I promised to come back, after all.* My eye shifted, meeting the glow of my father's maroon eyes in their sunken sockets. It pained me to see him like this. He had deteriorated so fast since the last visit in the church. We dropped the mask, letting it clatter to the ground where I knelt. His hand was icy against my cheek, and I fought the tears biting at me. Anger and regret filled me, but here he was, smiling.

"I'm–" I tried to speak, but he pressed his fingers to my lips.

He shushed me, inhaling deep, "If you are wondering why I haven't taken out Falco, I can't. A magical blood pact was made long ago and killing him would assure my death. Hence why he's poisoned me because he's putting his own life on the line keeping me on the edge of death."

I took his hand into my own and pressed my forehead against the cold flesh. All I wanted was his warmth to return, his strength to allow him to cross a room with breathtaking grace once more. A tear escaped and painted the fabric of his blanket like a drop of blood.

"Dante, you never took blood from *La Dame d'Croc?*" he asked. I squeezed his hand and shook my head, feeling ashamed to have to tell him no. "Good."

I snapped my eyes up, and he gave a coy smile. *He has a plan.* "What do I not know? What plan do you have for me, Father?"

"It's a blood oath. It's designed so one family lineage must be gone for it to cease. Falco is the last of his family as you and I are the last of ours." He frowned, squeezing my fingers. "I suspect he killed your mother, and now, I wonder, your brother and sister from over a hundred years ago."

"What are the stipulations? Magic is a forgotten art, and I imagine it's taken you some time to solve." I let go of his hand and rubbed his forehead. "I need to know, Father."

"Listen well. I don't have the patience or strength to repeat myself to you." He smacked my hand away, and I laughed. "He must die by the *Fanged Lady*. Your blood must be across the blade and pierce his heart to break the spell. The wielder can't be a bloodeater under the blade's curse, and thankfully, you've avoided the temptation. Dante, you are too precious to suffer for something you wanted no part of. Granted, there was a simpler solution, but we lost that when we lost Ashton." He was struggling to sit up, and I aided him.

"Wasn't Ashton a bloodeater?" At last, I was learning the missing pieces from a source I trusted. "Why was he different?"

"He was a true daemon, a guardian who was given blood from his keeper and made stronger." Inhaling, he caught his breath and continued, "The blade mimics this bond, but it is no match against the real thing. There were more like Ashton, before the uprising, but as the distrust between human and daemons dissolved, no more came after him, mainly because we went from equals and protectors to slaves and fodder. Anyhow, the unique thing about Ashton is he only craved and took blood from one man, and that man gave Ashton his freedom willingly. The only other person would be Frank, but that has to do with how they broke the spell."

"Broke the spell?" He was drowning me in a sea of information I didn't know what to do with nor how to comprehend. "The spell from the dagger?"

He smiled, patting my arm, "You do remember the stories about the seven nights and the great immortal? The trials we now perform for..." He started coughing, wheezing with a horrible rattle, and I abandoned the history lesson.

I have the information on how to kill Viceroy, but now I need to tend to the damage at hand.

Opening his hand, I pressed the vial there, and he looked down, "What's this?"

"I was told by a trusted source it's the antidote for what ails you. I pray it isn't too late."

A sparkle came to his eyes. "I may sleep like the dead after I take it if it gets rid of this godforsaken pain. It can be assumed Madame Plasket has gotten involved and found a solution?"

"You never cease to amaze me." Covering my face with my hands, I marveled over the foresight the man still possessed after being poisoned for such a long time. "How do you know all of this?"

He chuckled, urging me to help him open the vial. "It's my city. I was a guardian of the royal family when we discovered it and took over Glensdale. It comes with living for two or so centuries."

"I don't know if I want to live that long." Working the cork off, I winced at the pungent smell.

"Ugh, smells like horse piss." Despite the declaration, he gulped the mysterious liquid down and eased back into his bed. "I have delivered the message and set the chess pieces into play. It's up to you to finish what I have started, Dante."

Kissing his hand in the tradition taught to me as a sign of affection and royalty, I replied, "I will see to it that Falco fails."

His hand turned, gripping my jaw with renewed strength. "Is it true?" he whispered, his eyes searching my own.

My forehead creased, confused by the shift in him, as if he had almost forgotten to address something.

His eyes shot to John and back to me, "Is it true?"

"That I declared myself a servant and John is my keeper? Yes." I swallowed, my heartbeat racing. *Why do I get the feeling this isn't what he's asking of me?* His fingers tightened and nostalgic fear from my childhood rushed back. *I'm in trouble again.* "That he's in love with me? Yes."

He lowered his voice, "And have you told him?"

I looked to John. He was crouched at the fire, putting fresh logs in and giving the flames a chance to thrive again. My eyes came back to my father's. "How can I? He's a priest, and if it was discovered... there would be war against *The House* and *The Church*. You know this."

"It's not easy, being a Prince or a priest." His fingers let go, leaving my jaw aching. "He knows that you're not his servant and he isn't truly a keeper. That he is nothing more than the Prince's Priest playing pretend for your sake."

"Prince's Priest," I echoed the words, the concept strange.

"It's the title given to him by the people in Glensdale." Sighing, he patted my hand. "You are a Prince, and you may take anything you desire and not one soul can stop you. Not one person here will deny you for taking John all for yourself."

My face flushed. *How much does he know?* "How..." I couldn't get the words out, and he pointed to his nightstand.

"The drawer." A smile crept across his face. "He's a smart man and outspoken at that. I approve."

Fingers trembling, I opened the drawer to see the half-open letter. I recognized the writing; it was John's own. Pulling the pages out, I read in silence. This was the letter he had sent to Ruth to give to my father his first day in Glensdale. I covered my mouth, my eyes jumping back to the start and reading it again with more care:

Captain Ruth & King Traibon,

First, my apologies on the method in which this letter has found you. Be reassured, Captain Ruth, my heart is not yours, but belongs to someone far more precious, Dante. He is indeed alive and well.

King Traibon. I do not write to you as a priest, but as a man who is in love with your son. I have reasons to be concerned about his safety.

Please be advised Viceroy Falco claims he would invite you to my first service, but here is my invitation instead since it's clearly all to send Dante into a panic. I understand the Viceroy has a jaded reputation, and I will not leave anything to chance. My grandfather took Dante in. Perhaps you recall meeting Lord Knight Paul when you made the pact to give him land and allow him to retire in peace? The assassin sent to kill my grandfather failed, though Falco took my father and mother in retribution. Still, I harbor no ill-will toward you, Glensdale, or Dante for the crimes Falco has committed. So, please do me the honor of allowing me to invite you to my first sermon.

I pray I will see you in person, and I promise Dante will be there as my Sword and Shield. Let us discuss matters in private afterward, face to face if you wish. As for whether Dante will make himself known to you, I don't know. It isn't my place to intervene in your relationship. I just know he never spoke ill of you, and because of this, I decided to reach out to you.

Dante is precious to me. I know as his father you feel the same. My only wish is for you to know I love him, knowing that I can't have him, and that I need your help to protect him from Viceroy Falco.

Best regards and kindest apologies,

John Thompson

Folding the paper, I slipped it back into the drawer. I didn't know how to reply to it.

A confession to my father before ever speaking a word to me first. John, you're a stubborn asshole.

Still covering my mouth, I searched the air for answers. My father was grinning wide, knowing full well I was struggling to grasp my emotions. I had fought so hard to hide my feelings, yet it seemed John had been better at hiding his feelings from me than I had from him.

Those first weeks when you were back, I wondered if you missed me, if you remembered that last day together. You never forgot. That's why you came back and why you were so calculating for my sake. This whole time you were just shy of screaming your confession from the tallest tree. And here I sit, barely able to tell you yes to the simplest questions, afraid the smallest crack will tell you how I feel and how I yearn for you.

"I'm a coward." Muttering under my hand, I looked to my father, and he shrugged.

"It's an easy matter for him to speak from the heart." He laughed, his eyes growing heavy with sleep as a sense of relief washed over his face. "Being a priest lets him get away with that. You, on the other hand, have a country to run, and speaking from the heart is often seen as a weakness."

"But I'm not a Prince anymore." It sounded childish coming off my tongue.

I flinched as my father's hand flashed by my cheek, shoving the hood down to expose my braid. "You still have sixteen knots. Why did you decide to keep it?"

Pulling it out for him to see, I gave him a measured look. "I cut it off, but it grows back against my will."

He laughed. "So it does."

"Who will take my place?"

His fingers stroked the knots. "Ruth."

"Does she know?" I raised my eyebrows, imagining how much of a fit she would throw over the idea.

"No." Another grin of mischief. "But she'll know soon enough. She doesn't think her position as Captain and her brother being my immediate guard a mere coincidence – she's catching on to your old man's games rather fast. *The House* is in need of a true lady's touch, not the cursed blade

203

we were built from. You think she'll manage to make peace with *The Court* and *The Tower?*"

"Is that what you're hoping for?" I was pulling myself to my feet, his eyes closing.

"Yes, I grow tired of war." His hand lashed out, fingers tight on my hand before relaxing and falling to the bed. "Farewell, my precious Dante..."

He was out but breathing. Weeks of sleep and healing would be in order to make up for a decade of slow poisoning, but from the color flooding back into his face, I was sure he'd live. Walking to the fireplace, I flopped into the old chair I often claimed in the days of my youth. John stood, looking to the bed and back to me, his face filled with worry. I shook my head, a silent message: *He's not dead.* Sighing, John sat down, covering his face. He was letting all the tension flow out of him.

"The letter," I glared at him, wondering what he'd say.

His hands pulled downward, and he eyed me, his mouth hidden behind his fingers. "The one I sent him?" John leaned back, his face sinking behind the curved lip of the chair's back, hiding his expression completely. "What of it?"

"What did it say?" I wanted to hear him say it. *I understand how you felt that day you wanted answers from me. This raw honesty between us that we keep denying one another, it's what we're missing, needing.*

"That I loved you, couldn't have you, and needed his help to protect you." It was blunt, John's voice steady and sharp with each syllable. There was a long silence before he added, "Are you ready to go home?"

"N-no." The weight of my emotions pressed against my chest. "Let me stay here a bit longer. Some part of me misses this."

"It's a beautiful place." His voice was weak now, envious and jealous in tone. "I wish I could have seen you in those days when you embraced your title of Prince."

204

Do you really want me here and not by your side so easily? Bitter emotions spat poison into my heart. *Surely you know the weight of those words, John?*

The flames licked upward in the hearth. My father's chest rose and fell with a hint of a rattle in his lungs. If the antidote worked, he would start to heal more every day in his comatose slumber. My fingers trailed along the swirling pattern on the old chair. Dirt was smudged in a few places, and yet my father never allowed them to replace it or clean it. It was in these small gestures he showed his affection toward me, and now I realized my fears had been wrong. He knew I would never betray him, not in the sense I had thought.

How wrong was I to think he wasn't tired of war? I didn't think of how he felt about bloodeating and the Madness. There wasn't once, in all those small private moments between us that I thought to ask him. Here I am, right where he hoped I would be, right where my life is both complete and scattered. I want to give away my heart, and his only concern is to reprimand me for not taking it for myself.

I huffed, releasing a small chuckle.

"What's so amusing?" John's voice returned to normal.

"My father," I replied. "He can be unusual at times."

"I imagine that's where you get it from then," he groaned, standing to stretch.

I furrowed my brow. "What do you mean by that?"

John motioned to the room. "Who in the world hangs his father's bedroom tapestries in a church of all places?"

My face flushed, but we broke the tension with laughter. "You're right. How could he not know it was me after that!"

Glancing over, I could see my father's lips curving upward. Even in his sleep, he could hear the happiness we brought one another.

The Prince's Priest. What an interesting title you've earned, John.

CHAPTER 22

Darkest Night of Winter

Pushing out of the doors, I met the gazes of Ruth, Brandon, and Ryan. The guards paled. I had left the mask on the floor, abandoning all the secrecy. Before them stood their long-lost Prince. I was back, and Glensdale needed to know that during these trying times. John closed the doors behind me. When he turned, taking in the reactions on their faces, he burst into laughter. Ruth joined him, enjoying the noticeable fear and confusion held in their expressions. I looked to the ceiling, shaking my head, part of me cursing for not thinking to grab the mask.

"D-dante." Brandon broke from his shock, closing the gap between us, wrapping his arms around me. "It's really you! You're here and alive! The rumors. I wasn't..."

"Yes, it's me." I patted his back. "Sorry to make things so complicated."

"We thought you were dead." Ryan rubbed his eyes. "But your father refused to hold a funeral, so I should have taken that as a hint. He's such a witty old man."

"If it makes you feel any better, I think he knew more about my whereabouts and choices than I did." Peeling Brandon off me, I took them both by the shoulder. "Listen, he'll need tons of rest. His body has been in bad shape, but he'll recover after a few weeks. Whoever he's been drinking blood from needs to be swapped with someone else. The key is not to reveal who the new slave will be to Falco."

Brandon lifted an eyebrow. "Well, Falco manages the slaves now."

"What do you think he's doing, Dante?" Ruth crossed her arms, pondering the ideas flowing through her own mind. "Even still, I am sure a citizen or servant would do his majesty this favor of giving him blood. No more slaves that have a connection to the Viceroy moving forward."

"I think the poison he's using is harmless to humans." Their eyes widened; it hadn't crossed their minds something like this existed. "My source knew it, but they are in the business of being aware of these things. In short, he's feeding the blood slaves something they aren't reacting to, but instead, taints their blood and thus, poisoning my father. Does he let anyone else drink from the chosen slaves?"

"Never." Ryan's face twisted; he was pissed. "I can't believe he would go that far. Has Viceroy Falco lost his mind?"

"He's power hungry." Ruth handed my sword back to me as well as John's rapier.

"Well, that should give you a chance to find evidence and take counter measures, right?" John sighed, relieved to be armed again. His fingers tugged on the back of my shirt. "We should head home, come up with a plan of our own, Dante."

"R-Right." His fingers let go, and we followed Ruth down the halls.

Fear filled the servants who recognized me as the man from the portraits. Their Prince was back from the dead, and a shudder fell upon them. A smile crept across my face. Falco would know I no longer hid my identity, and the rules of his game would change into my favor. Staring at John's back, I was reminded of his bravery. He was a branded man who had taken vows, and yet still he was willing to confess to a King he was in love with his son, the Prince. This was the spirit I'd fallen in love with over and over again.

How can I ever keep up with a strong-willed man like him?

We reached the grand stairwell, and once more, the servants lined up. Ruth motioned for me to go first. Inhaling, I knew what she was doing. I started down the steps, and in a waterfall fashion, they knelt before me. It was so strange to be back after so long. There were whispers flowing between them as I glided past without a word or glance. It was ill-mannered to acknowledge them, and I hated the tradition of it all. The doors opened, and a burst of wintry night air welcomed me back to the outside world as Prince Dante for the first time in over ten years.

Basque strained on his reins, giving two soldiers the fight of their lives. He halted, one man tumbling over. Ears high, Basque snorted steam from his nose and neighed at John and me, *Where have you been!* It was his way of showing his disapproval of our absence and our decision to allow cretins to handle him. The soldiers at the entrance started to salute Captain Ruth when they caught sight of my braid slapping against my chest. I watched them glance up to my face, stunned and kneeling in a panic. If only they knew how many times they had shaken my hand or invited me to a drink despite the mask and silence. With a single motion of my hand, I gave them reprieve to stand up off the snow and ice.

"You didn't have to bring the horse over." I approached Basque, and he took the sugar cubes from my hand.

"We didn't," remarked the soldier on the ground. "The behemoth launched himself over one gate and through the other. Ran full steam to the front doors here like a hound on a fox."

John and I looked at one another, grinning at the idea he came running after us.

"It's true." The other soldier gave the reins back to me. "He's a monster and how you ever tamed that asshole is beyond me."

Basque nudged John who scratched his chin, remarking, "He's too smart for his own good."

"We'll be seeing you around after this, I hope." Ruth's voice brought everyone's attention to her. "Right, Prince Dante Traibon?"

Rubbing my forehead, I relented, "Yes, I'll be coming in and out of town. No more masks; no more silent treatment. Please respect the fact I have given up this life and taken to being nothing more than another citizen of Glensdale. I'll leave matters in your hands, but know that I am here if needed until my father's health recovers."

John shot me a glance, but we both knew how scandalous it would have been to declare myself nothing more than a servant to a human priest still wearing sixteen knots. For now, this should suffice until we could figure out what to do with Falco and what to do with my status.

"For now." Ruth's eyes narrowed with a smirk on her face. "One day, I hope you might change your mind. If a big decision comes up, don't be shocked to see me come knocking on your door."

Snorting, my breath boiled in puffs of steam. I pulled myself onto the saddle, sliding forward and offering a hand to help John on behind me. He cupped my shoulders, the soldiers muttering around us. Two men on a horse was an odd arrangement and impractical, though unlike most cases, Basque could handle the weight of two full grown men. Ignoring them, I nodded a goodbye to Ruth and squeezed my knees around Basque. He launched forward, happy to be heading home with both of his companions.

Not a word was spoken between us as we passed the last of the city braziers, slipped through the gates, and faded into the woods. A lantern on a staff laid across my thighs provided some light thanks to the guard at the gate who gave it up for our sake. Basque needed little guidance on what to do, easily finding his footing and skirting around the storm's debris, careful of the riders on his back. Snow started to fall, and I was thankful the wind hadn't returned with it. The night wrapped around us, and trees faded in and out of view. Sleep was weighing on me, my eyelids feeling heavy, and I fought to keep one eye open.

A rush of warmth wrapped around my stomach. John hugged me, and my nerves burned in my throat. His cheek nuzzled between my shoulder blades, hot against the muscles tensing under it. He heaved a hard sigh, his chest rising and falling against me. The pain ripping into me was frustration and want clawing at one another. It was hard to breathe; his touch sent a fire across my soul and there was nothing I could do to stop it. John wiggled closer, my skin prickling as he shuffled his arms and hands once more. His fingers groped handfuls of my clothes. *I can almost see us together, on my bed, under him...* I shook the thoughts from my mind.

"Don't let me fall off," he mumbled into my back.

I dropped an arm down, holding his hands together like a belt. "You know I wouldn't do that."

He squeezed tighter, pressing himself against me once more. A wave of hungry lust tightened in my joints, and I held my breath. It was so warm being in his embrace, and it made my loins ache. My heart pounded in my ears, my blood rushing with excitement. Swallowing, I shuddered, and his cheek lifted off my back. Again, my body stiffened, and I pressed his arms into me, unsure if he was slipping or if I simply didn't want him to pull away.

"Are you cold?" His voice was a sleepy whisper as the

steam of his breath rolled over my shoulder.

"No." I cursed my luck, my fate, and our situation. "Just not used to you being so close."

"I'm sorry," he tried to pull his arms away, and I hugged them into my stomach. "D-dante?"

"I didn't say I didn't like it." My face growing hotter as snow melted against my cheeks, I let him see through a crack in the wall between us. "Get some rest; it's not much farther."

He kissed the nape of my neck, his lips like hot petals gracing my skin, and goosebumps rattled across me. The heat of his face pillowed between my shoulders, and I could breathe again. Tension in my muscles were starting to relax. For the first time, I let myself indulge in the heat of his body. John fell asleep in an instant, and I sighed. To feel so safe in my presence to let himself be completely open was a marvel to behold. For now, we at least had these small moments.

Basque shook his head and carried us into the familiar clearing of the farm. The cabin looked derelict in the snow, the windows lifeless and the field hidden in a blanket of white. He walked to his stable and stopped, curling his lip at the hearth, unhappy to see no fire inside. I patted John's arms, and he stirred against me, cuddling me like a cat. The night air cut between us as he dismounted, and I followed. Half asleep, our bodies did the tasks needed. The hearth was lit, Basque's saddle removed, and hay shuffled to keep the icy air at bay.

We burst through the cabin door, both our arms full of logs for the fire. We wanted to be free of the cold biting at our bodies. Even I started to shiver and chatter my teeth. The fireplace took some encouraging, the logs losing their battle to the growing flames miserably slow. Huddled shoulder to shoulder, we welcomed the rising heat. My clothes damp from the snow and ice, I turned and disappeared behind my bedroom door. My shirt thumped against the floor at my feet. I leaned back against the door ignoring the chill rattling through me. I glared down to the tanned skin of my chest with all its scars misplaced under the braid. No longer was this the body of a forgotten farmer, but a seasoned Prince who hadn't been afraid to walk his own path.

Covering my mouth, my father's words spurred me on. *You are a Prince, and you may take anything you desire.* I glared at my empty bed, my imagination filling the space with all the things I had denied myself to think about. My skin prickled again, the thought of allowing myself to walk out of this room and take John frightening and enthralling. Closing my eyes, swallowing down the emotions, I let my mind tread the places I hadn't dared for fear of knowing what lay there. These were taboo thoughts: forbidden love between royalty and clergymen beyond their role, their expectations, their vows.

Do I really want to tear down the last of this wall I tried so hard to keep? If I do this, if we do this, there will be no turning back. The Church will have a bounty on his head and wage war with The House. John's dream... I never asked him what it all entailed. And what of my own dream? All I've known in this wretched life is desire: to be with someone, to run away from my past, and to do something to change the world for daemon and human alike. I vowed to be royalty, but I also vowed to never become the bloodeater I was obligated to become.

How could John ask me to be his Barrier of Strength? He knew what that branding, that vow meant for him, for us. Was it an act of love in his eyes? Those stolen kisses still hot on my lips, the stroke of his tongue against mine, his lips against my neck...

I groaned, my arousal demanding to be let loose in physical form.

Has he ever been with someone? A woman or a man? Could it be he's saving himself for me?

The idea sent a shudder through me tangled with

excitement and dread.

Am I to be your first as Falco was for me?

A great weight came crushing down on me, heartache and desire in a cage clawing and biting at one another.

Why does this fact torture me so?

CHAPTER 23

Viceroy's Game

BOOM-BOOM-BOOM!

The cabin shook with the knocking against the door.

"HELP!" A man's voice echoed through the walls along with another flurry of knocks.

Who followed us so close on our heels? Did my father...

Swinging my bedroom door open, I watched as John's hand gripped the front door. Neither of us had the time to even catch our breath. The panic in the voice startled us both. Winter air slammed against me, and John stumbled back. A man wearing armor entered and, in his arms, a red-stained nun. John shut the door, shutting out the cold, and blood trailed across the floor as the knight entered the room. John cleared the table, and the knight laid the nun there just in time for his legs to buckle. The knight looked up at John, his windblown dark locks shifting to show the beaten face and desperate brown eyes.

"V-Valiente?" John's harrowing dread turned from him to the nun. "Sonja!"

I stood in the doorway, silent and unsure. *What are the*

odds? My stomach turned, a sickening wave rolling over my entire being. *Falco's changing the game to bring it back under his control...*

"John..." Valiente let his body slide to the floor. "Help her. Somehow, help her."

Snapping out of my trance, I crouched over Valiente. His armor had taken a beating and blood seeped from under his left shoulder pad. I wasted no time to searching for the buckles I knew kept the metal in place. A hand gripped my wrist, my eyes locking with Valiente's own. He was huffing, sweat from his pain dabbling his icy skin.

The fingers were tight and gathering strength, his whisper only falling on my ears, "Take care of Princess Sonja." He let go and brushed my hands away. "I can do this much." His fingers shuffled to unbuckle his own armor. "Help her."

I paled, standing to turn to John. "I thought you said he protected a nun." *Does he know?*

John's eyes shot up, confusion on his face as he gathered the clean rags from a small chest. "What are you talking about?"

Rushing to the table, I placed a hand on her forehead and cheek. The girl was burning a fever, her skin a rich dark earthy tone with pink lips like a rose bloom. She was gorgeous, but I had to know. Pulling the coif off her head, my stomach lurched. A braid uncoiled and sixteen knots rippled in her pitch-black hair. *A Princess indeed.* Gulping, I searched for the source of bleeding. Ripping the collar from her neck, I found the pulsing wound. Snatching a cloth from John's hands, I pressed it firm against the flow to slow the bleeding.

"I've got her. Check on Valiente." It stung to have to focus on my fellow royal and beg John to be with someone who had stolen a kiss from him. *This isn't the time to be jealous.* "He needs to drop the armor off and have those wounds stitched."

"B-but Sonja..." John's blue eyes were dancing in a panic. He had never seen anything like this, nor the amount of blood still threatening to paint the room.

"Princess Sonja," I corrected, and he paled. "We need to know what happened."

John dove to the floor beside Valiente. "Let me help."

"She's been bitten." Armor clanked to the floor, and the knight hissed in pain. "We were ambushed. A third showed and overpowered me. He grabbed her and latched on, fucking bastard!" Another piece of armor thudded on the floor, leaving him bare and bloody. "I didn't have the strength..." Valiente choked. "I should be dead."

The words rang in my ears, and I pulled back the cloth. Against the smooth skin of her delicate neck were fang marks. Nausea moved through me. I recognized those marks. My body had borne these same markings across my neck, my arms, and... my heart stung with regret and pity as I looked at the deep punctures of fangs with the smattering of incisors ripping and digging. Worse, I'd seen a man die from them. This was the mark of *Le Chien Enragé*, the ragged bite belonging to Falco. He had gone too far this time. This travesty would take a muted Civil War and send it screaming to life once more. The Princess whimpered in her ill-stricken state. It was only a matter of hours before the next stage of the Madness would start.

"Aren't you from here, daemon? You can fix this, can't you?" The question fell from Valiente's lips. "You can take the Madness away, right?"

John peered over his shoulder at me. "He can't. He's not a bloodeater."

"Then I've failed." Blood painted Valiente's skin, his wounds bleeding where flesh laid open in long ugly slices. "She'll tear herself apart."

John focused on the slash, clearing away blood so he could assess the damage. I leaned on the table, my eyes on the crimson mark across her dark skin. The three of us stood there, helpless and shaken by the state of the Princess. My mind raced, searching for all the pieces and all the answers I could imagine. The hairs on the back of my neck stood on end, my ears taking in the conversation from the floor.

"Why didn't you tell me you were a Guardian of the Royal Family?" Betrayal filled John's voice.

"I couldn't," grunted Valiente, leaning forward to reveal another slash. "The whole idea was to hide Princess Sonja."

"Then what the hell were you doing coming to Glensdale?" John marched to the small chest, pulling out needle and thread along with a jar of ointment. "Bringing her here was a suicide mission."

Valiente frowned. "It wasn't my place to disobey her either."

John flinched. "I see."

"That's the bitch of it all," I interjected, understanding Valiente's situation. "The balance of power and rank is fickle. I was fortunate to have cousins brave enough to twist my ear on occasion, but elsewhere..."

"Indeed brave." Valiente stared up at me, his eyes following the pendulum swing of my braid. "You're royalty? What's your name?"

I could see the cold reflection of my eyes glowing red in his own, "Dante."

John's cheeks flushed, but he said nothing. The needle in his fingers dove in and out of flesh. He pulled tight and repeated the motion again. Valiente winced, unable to speak until the work was finished on his shoulder, and John slid behind him.

"You never told me the man you loved was the Prince of Bloodeaters!" There was a sparkle in Valiente's eyes, and he grinned, fighting through the pain. "I don't feel so bad for the punch I got for stealing a kiss. Ha! I lost to a fucking Prince."

"I *was* a Prince." I wiped the sweat off Sonja's troubled face. "We'll need to tie her down soon. The fever is just the beginning."

John cut the last of the loose thread. "You're done."

"That was rather fast—and efficient." Valiente marveled over the job. "If I didn't know better, you've done this more than once."

Standing and wiping his hands on a blood-covered cloth, John confessed, "Comes with working on the farm."

Staring at Princess Sonja, I could hear Viceroy Falco's laughter. He planned this. The attack was the contract Madame Plasket turned down, and it was why he ventured out several times with only two guards. The ambush had been settled on. Bishop Marquis would have known who Sonja was and allowed this to unfold. He left the knight alive, another tidbit from Marquis: *John and Valiente are friends.* From there, it was about pushing the survivors, a wounded Guardian and his cursed Princess, to our doorstep. Falco would be back, hoping to find either me stricken or the Princess stricken with Madness. Perhaps he even hoped we would be dead in the next three or so days.

"I can do it." My words cut through the room.

"Do what?" John furrowed his brow. "What are you talking about?"

"The cleansing." I locked eyes with him. "It'll take the Madness away, but there's still a problem."

Valiente grunted, rising to his feet. "Let's do it n–"

John's hand rose, silencing him as he demanded, "What problem?"

"I'm not a bloodeater." Swallowing, my chest tightened as I forced the words out into the open. "It pulls the curse from her body and places it in mine. Without the magic from *La Dame d'Croc*, I will be inflicted with the Madness instead. Only a bloodeater is immune."

"Then it's not an option." John turned away, heading into his room, face red and fists tight with frustration.

"I'm willing to sacrifice myself to prevent war!" I shoved the rag into Valiente's hands and chased after him. "John!" He shut his door, but I jerked it open, hot on his heels. "You're not going to hide from me like this!" Slamming his bedroom door behind me, I glared at his back. "There's nothing else we can do. Once the Madness settles in her blood, not even a well-seasoned bloodeater can pull the curse. It's meant to be taken within hours of contracting it."

"Fucking Falco!" John threw a blood-soaked rag across the room.

"I'm going to do this." My voice came out eerily calm. "I won't let him have this war. He doesn't have the *Fanged Lady*, and if Father dies–"

"What if you were a bloodeater?" His voice dropped like a stone between us.

"W-what?" I blinked; it wasn't what I expected him to say.

"What if you were a bloodeater?" His shoulders tensed under his shirt, his voice darkening.

"John, I'm not. I can't..." Confusion tangled through me. *Something is wrong.* I answered, slow and calculating, "If I were... I could heal her, and no harm would befall her or me. But there would be..."

His head tilted to the ceiling, "I have it."

"Have what?" I whispered back, chills snaking up my spine. *I suspected, but...*

He crouched and reached under his bed. A finger slipped into the knothole of a plank, and with a firm jerk, the board came lose. I watched his hand glide into the darkness, and my heart caught in my throat. The room was dark, the flickering light of the fire danced across the floor from the crack under the door. Orange light caught on the item he pulled from its tomb. Familiar skulls laughed at me as if their only purpose on this earth was to haunt my most vulnerable moments. The archaic writing glowed red on the blade; it smelled the curse in the other room and demanded blood. John stood, spinning to face me. I pressed my back against the door, fear crawling through every part of me.

"Don't..." I was breaking.

"I went back for it, but after learning about it in the libraries at the Abbey, I..." He shook his head. "I understand why you took it and left it. No good could ever come from this magic."

"John, you can't do this." He took a step closer, the blade catching my stare. "I don't want to be one of them."

"You can't make me watch another person I love die from the Madness." An aching pulled at my soul. "Falco will not take you from me."

"It's not just that." I spoke with tender care, remorse drowning me. "It would mean that I would need blood often, and the only person here is you."

"I know," he whispered, taking another step closer, and I could see he was trembling. "A cut, right? That's all it takes is a cut from this cursed blade, and you drink the blood to–"

I reached for it, aiming to snatch it away, but he raised it to his neck.

"Where do I cut? My neck?" The blade dropped to his wrist. "My arm?" A flash of silver, his shirt ripping open as buttons cascaded to the floor between us. "My chest," the point pressed against his left breast, "or my heart?"

I shook my head. "A cut from *La Dame d'Croc* never heals completely. It stays a crimson colored scar, and a lick from a bloodeater will make it open as if the blade has stroked your skin once more. Falco would know. If he saw such a mark, he would know, and I... I know he'd destroy us both over it."

John brought the blade to his lips. There, his tongue rolled across its keen edge, drawing blood. I opened my mouth to reprimand him but found his lips hot against my own. The blade thudded against the floor at our feet, but I didn't care. His blood was thick, and his tongue dove between my teeth.

I swallowed, the sweet, enthralling sensation of it filling me. My tongue ventured forward, pushing back against his own. Another swallow, sweeter than the first, and I found myself hungry for him in every way possible. Fingers slid across my jaw and tangled with my hair. We played with one another, exploring the flavor and sensation it brought us to taste one another's lips, to dive into one another's mouths. I sucked his tongue, blood coming freely as I drank him in, and he moaned.

I twisted him around me with panting vigor and shoved his back against the door. We were breathless, boiling with desire. Anger waved back and forth, mixing with longing inside me. *I am a bloodeater.* My lips found his ear, a shiver shaking his entire body as the heat of my breath snaked across his neck. I bit and sucked his earlobe before I settled on what I wanted from him in this room of taboos. It was my turn to corrupt him as he had done to me.

My voice fell with provocation and desire. "You broke my vow. Now I'm going to break yours."

He stiffened as my fingers trailed down his neck and over his collarbone. Pinned between me and the door, he didn't stir or struggle. He wanted this too, his pounding pulse growing louder in my ears. *I'm a bloodeater because you couldn't let go of your love for me.* My fingers slid across his chest and bounced across the muscles of his abdomen. They followed the dark path leading to what I wanted, what I would take from him. Gripping his pants, I unbuckled them, and they fell to the floor. He watched me, silent and breathing hard. His skin prickled as my fingers met his cock. I trailed them from the tip of his hardened length, along the bottom, and back again. He swallowed, and I found myself smiling as I knelt before him.

He may have stolen the first kiss, but this I get to take for myself...

Again, I let my fingers flow over the velvet touch of him,

glaring up into those blue eyes. With each stroke, I watched his body tense with anticipation, and a throb of pleasure pressed into my palm. My tongue stretched from my lips, cupping him as I licked across his length and circled the head. His voice was ragged with longing, his arousal no longer under his control, but mine.

"Dante."

Kissing the tip, I took all of him into my mouth. His head knocked against the door. I pulled away, only to take him back in, and he thickened, hot on my tongue. A moan left his lips, and his fingers gripped my hair. *Our guilty pleasures will prevent a war.*

"Dante."

You broke my vow. He jerked my head back and away. I glared up at him, filled with lust and ire as he panted. He cursed under his breath. *I'm going to break yours. I promise.* My tongue lashed out like a flame, and he dove back into the wet fire of my mouth. Another moan, longer and deeper.

"Dante!"

His fingers gripped ever tighter, hips rocking, wanting more. Tugging me closer, he was on the cusp of an orgasm, his cock harder now. I began sucking, and he moaned, fighting the urge to fold over. My tongue wiggled, and he throbbed. Pulling off and away again, I wanted to see the pleasure written all over his face followed by agonizing want as I left him teetering so close to the edge of his breaking point. Cheeks flushed, sweat beaded across his pounding chest, he peered down at me.

"Look at me. Don't look away. I forbid it," John ordered. I did as he commanded, my eyes locking with his. "Take it all from me my *Barrière de Force.*"

I tilted my head, opening my mouth wide for him. He slid slowly onto the slippery slope of my tongue. The roof of my mouth guided him to the edge of my throat, and I hummed, and he moaned. I gently pulled away, my lips tickling the tip and tongue teasing him. He pushed himself back inside, and I leaned in, receiving all I could. Closing my lips around him, I sucked in and began to push and pull. Not once did we break our gaze with one another. He moaned and hardened again, teetering on the edge once more. Pressing my tongue hard against the underbelly, I flicked the tip before allowing him to dive in again.

My hands slid up his thighs, gripping his ass to push him farther, and it was all he could bear. The muscles in his body flexed, and the heat released from him. I swallowed, and his muscles stiffened. Letting go, gasping for air, I allowed him to sink to the floor before me, panting and silent. He couldn't take his eyes off me, soaking in the sweat on my own body and the tightness in my own pants. He reached over to touch my jaw, and I smacked his hand away. *I am a bloodeater, and he is a priest.* Wiping my mouth, I ignored my own throbbing. If I provoked it, John would have returned the physical affections, but I wanted him to feel pained and know why my soul ripped itself into pieces.

I stood, towering over him. Recognizing the contempt on my face, he moved to the side, allowing me to go through the door. Valiente turned, looking perplexed by the rosy color of my cheeks and the heavy breathing. His face flushed, realizing we had done more than confess. Far as Valiente knew, I would be taking in the Madness and dying within days. I watched as he padded the sweat from Princess Sonja, and he had taken the time to tie her hands and feet together. He understood the next stage would be a ravenous need to feed on blood, flesh, anything she could claw and bite with, like a wild animal starved beyond sanity.

She was a beautiful woman. Her body curved like the hills in the south, and her face was round with no harsh edges. It was a shame she might be left with the scars of her enemy's teeth on her throat. Waving Valiente off Princess Sonja, I leaned down and ran my tongue across the bite mark. Blood began to pulse out once more. Something magical now bound me to the blade, to the curse, and to the desire to feed. My tongue slid across my teeth, fangs starting to develop, a permanent change and mark of the bloodeater. The flavor of the curse lingered on my tongue, bitter and slimy. Inhaling deeply, I recited the spell I learned day in and day out in preparation for the day I would become the Prince of Bloodeaters:

> *"Une lune rouge décroît,*
> *Des flaques de sang pour la Dame.*
> *Les crocs goûtent la chair,*
> *Dévore la douleur de l'âme.*
>
> *Plaisir pour la folie,*
> *Mon corps sera à toi.*
> *Par les lèvres du désir,*
> *La malédiction sera à moi."*

Opening my jaw wide, I slid my fangs into her flesh, and excitement sped through my veins. One hard suck, and it came running into me. Sour decay filled my mouth, and I forced myself to swallow. After a moment, I pulled away, my stomach turning with the weight of the Madness entering my body. John's blood had been pleasant and sweet, making the sudden change jolting. Cleansing a curse running at the end of its time was said to be vile, and worse if given by a bite from another bloodeater. It was like devouring weeks-old garbage. Covering my mouth, I stumbled outside into the black of night. The snow fell heavier, and I lunged over the porch railing. My stomach couldn't handle the flavor of the curse. It rushed out of my system, yet my body shook with excitement.

I shivered as icy wind raked across my bare back and chest. I surged forward once more, my stomach rejecting its contents. This wasn't just the curse, but the inevitable change overtaking me. I had performed my feeding, I had proven I was keen to cast a spell, and now I belonged to the *Fanged Lady.* My heart thudded hard against my chest. *I've lost my ability to kill Falco.* As a bloodeater under the dagger's spell, I couldn't kill him without the magic claiming both my father and me.

There has to be another way.

A warm blanket landed heavily on top of me, and John leaned on the railing next to me. His eyes stared down at the black stains across the snow. He reached out as if to brush hair off my cheek, but I recoiled. He heaved a sigh, his elbows falling back to the railing with his hands clutching one another. Guilt weighed down on us both. Our first acts of love had been our undoing. Morals had been stripped away, and we were left numb. My tongue flicked my fangs, and an echo of John's taste fluttered to the surface.

What an annoyance. I've wanted John, but this terrifies me. Like a wolf yearning to eat.

"What does it mean?" He had listened to the spell, curious to know what I'd spoken.

> *"A red moon wanes,*
> *Blood spills for the Lady.*
> *Fangs taste flesh,*
> *Devour the soul's pain.*
> *Pleasure for madness,*
> *My body will be yours.*
> *By lips of desire,*
> *Curse will be mine."*

He nodded, taking in the words I spoke with care. "Falco

will be coming for her and for us."

"Yes." My breath floated in the air before the wind stole it away. "We need a plan."

"I know." John pulled himself off the railing and leaned into my ear. "And I have one. First, get some rest."

The heat of him so close made every part of my body ache with frustration. "I can't kill him now."

"I can still kill him." John nuzzled my head, but I shoved him away. *Never did I mean for you to spill blood, especially your own, for my sake.*

My eyes slid to him. "But I thought–" I straightened.

A bloodeater can't wield the blade, which means a human...

I understood, cupping his face and pressing my lips to his. Pulling away, I smiled. "You're a snake, and I love you for it."

John knew if he broke my vow, he would be letting go of his own. Instead, he gave me the strength only a bloodeater was known for, and he had the blade. My blood was his, and his blade was as good as my own. We shared another kiss, our lips parting to allow our tongues to play. The cut opened, blossoming like the sweetest of treasures, and I shivered. John pushed his tongue into my mouth, enjoying the suckling and rubbing. It would always be like this *Could it be I will never need to press these fangs into the man I love?*

Chapter 24

Breaking a Curse

I found it impossible to sleep. I tossed and turned, thoughts wandering to John on the other side of the wall. My body throbbed and ached, frustrated and changing in ways I didn't want to fathom. The threads within my muscles pulled tighter, responding faster to every notion to move. It was as if I was doubling back and taking a year's worth of bodybuilding and smashing it into a matter of hours. If I closed my eyes, my ears could hear heartbeats, sighs, and the whispering prayers of Valiente. I was so horribly thirsty. My stomach grumbled, my tongue cotton, and my throat dry. The only flavor I wanted was John's blood dancing across my tongue, and I fought the urges. Sweat soaked my sheets, the physical exertion frightening. I'd read about the change, even watched others undergo this process. It was my turn to face this sacred rite, but I would have to do it alone.

This isn't what I wanted, this toothy animal gnawing at my soul. I could still taste him in my mouth, feel his fingers in my hair, and it made me ravenous. Clutching blankets, I bit into them. Pain surged through my body. I remembered my father talking about this part, the part about those who refused to feed after receiving *La Dame d'Croc's* gift. Only King Traibon had managed to last beyond five days with the fever and pains without soothing it with blood. If I were in the mansion, there would be slaves eager to rush over to help quench the thirst until I made myself sick on blood. Granted, I aimed to attempt the tradition of breaking the curse and claiming legendary status.

I have no choice. I have to surpass this without feeding, or I will need to feed daily. I can't kill Falco... I can't follow through on any promises if I don't starve it out for seven days and seven nights. It's been done before. There's no one here to tempt me. I just have to avoid John until it's over.

Frank, the legendary immortal daemon, had taken his initial drink and locked himself away for seven days. On the seventh night, he emerged free of the Madness and still didn't take in blood. They say he left eating a red apple and was never seen again. The theory was he had proven himself stronger than the bite of the blade's curse. Tales of his uncanny strength echoed in the storybooks, but when he finally drank from his lover, he became a God. Still, no one knew what happened to him or where he went. If my days lost in books taught me anything, it was that there was truth in fiction. There was a reason the ritual of the Prince becoming a King included an attempt for seven days without blood. My father managed to go five days before my grandfather decided to let him feed.

Pain seared through my veins. Shivering in the wake of it, I never thought something could top being covered in bee stings, yet here I was. No amount of spit and herbs could undo the magic running through me, terrorizing my soul. I could hear John talking to Valiente and Princess Sonja. They were discussing leaving as soon as possible, despite the snow. John's pulse started to drown their words, and I was starving to sink my teeth into his flesh. It was arousing, and I shuddered. A darkness was suffocating me.

Is this the madness? This thirst and one's very being lit on fire?

"Dante." John came into the room, and I flinched. "What's wrong?"

I was balled on my bed, releasing my bite on the blanket. I answered him in a bitter tone, "I'm becoming a bloodeater. This is part of the process."

His eyes fell to the floor. "I'm sorry. You tried to tell me there was more."

"I'm so fucking thirsty." My head pounded, and his scent was overwhelming, like walking into a perfume shop. "And you smell amazing." He took a step toward me, and I flinched again, "Don't. It's hard enough."

"Do you need...?" Before he could finish, I shook my head.

"No, I don't want it. It's too soon to feed." My face stayed buried in the blankets, a sad attempt to dull my senses. "I will move myself down into the cellar; it may help. Can you take care of the farm until I am... better?"

"I've already tended to Basque. I think I'll let them take him when they leave." John turned away, leaning against the door with his arm. "But Princess Sonja would like to meet the daemon Prince who saved her."

"I just need some time, and I will greet her briefly. Until then, you should see if there's supplies they could use." Peering over the blankets, I stared at his back, longing for his flavor. "Falco. He'll come here. He may wait a few days, expecting me, or the Princess, to be dead or dying of the Madness."

John's shoulders slumped. "He's going to know we have the dagger when she's gone, and you are well."

"I know." Silence held the air between us, and I forced myself to speak. "You'll have to go to the service. If he thinks I'm not here, and it's just you, he might think I am trying to save her. It may buy us time."

"Do you really think he would believe you left me here defenseless?" It was that cold tone again. "I'll prep the cellar. Come out when you've gathered yourself, and Dante?"

"Yes?" He pulled away from the door, and we locked eyes.

"Don't be afraid to call me." Guilt filled him. "I forced this on you, and I am responsible for what happens to you. After all, I'm your keeper."

Before I could say anything, he fled the room. Rolling away, I stared at the cabin wall, the grains of the woods an unsolvable puzzle. Swallowing the dryness in my mouth, I let sleep take hold. My limbs were heavy, my head spinning into darkness. There in the searing wave was a woman's voice. She urged me to *Drink*, to *Take just a little* of my treat for myself, and for her sake.

Is this the voice of the Fanged Lady?

* * * * *

Startling out of my sleep, I felt daylight streaming through the window and across my eyes. The thirst was still there, the agonizing dryness in my mouth and the gut-tearing hunger that whispered *Drink* with the flavor of John's blood.

Remember how delicious he was? What harm would it be to take just a little? Again, the woman's voice tempted me.

Shivers trickled across my body. The struggle to get to my feet revealed how weak and drained every part of me felt. My legs threatened to buckle under me, my senses dull, and an intense chill ran through my veins. Shuffling across the room, I stopped at the door, taking in a deep breath. I held it and opened the door.

Princess Sonja turned to me as I entered, her green eyes bright and an essence of life warming her face. She had the coif laid on the table, and she was wearing the nun's tunic, clean of blood. Her excitement was confusing, and nowhere in the room did I see John or Valiente. My chest ached with jealousy and relief. I took a few steps from the doorway and wobbled, gripping the doorframe for support. She rushed to me, her hands like fire against my bare chest. I froze, staring at the delicate fingers.

"Are you alright?" She leaned her face down to catch my stare. "You've been asleep for two days. John is outside, and Valiente is helping with repairs after the blizzard, but I can get them for you."

My balance finally steady, I gripped her wrists, pulling her hands off my skin and pushing her back. "Forgive me, but being close to me is dangerous. It's my first time taking in the Madness, and it's always unstable."

Oh, perhaps this one will do? Just a little taste, cooed the *Fanged Lady.*

Taking the warning to heart, she backed up until she bumped into the table. "Thank you. If you hadn't been here, I would be... John let us know this was a huge sacrifice on your part. I was fortunate you were even here."

Her words faded under the throbbing of my head and the irritating thirst tugging at my soul. "Water," I croaked.

Spinning on her heel, she rushed to fill a cup and gave it to me. Greedy and eager, I slurped it down, but it did nothing for the sensation torturing me. Water wasn't enough. It wasn't the same; it wasn't the sweet alluring flavor of John's blood. I shoved the cup back, angry and frustrated. The stinging in my throat hadn't wavered. A hand on the wall, I stumbled toward the cellar door. I was wrestling with something dark within my own mind, and I dared not show how frightened I felt.

The *Fanged Lady* laughed, mocking me. *You're thirsty, but not for that, my dear Prince. What you crave has a name.... John, and a priest no doubt! How delightful.*

"I can help you." Sonja's voice was soft. "You're going to the cellar, right?"

I paused, huffing. "Yes. Can you open it?"

She was light on her feet, not a board creaking under her as she sped past. Like an attendant, she waited for me to reach the opening. Fingers stretched to aid me and again, I shoved her away. I shot her a look of warning. She had no idea how dangerous it was to be human and touch a daemon in transition.

In the back of my mind, the *Fanged Lady* tempted me with soothing whispers. *Do you not wonder how sweet she might taste on your tongue, my dear Prince?*

Shuffling past, I eased down the ladder and found myself breathless by the time my feet hit the ground.

"This is my fault. If I hadn't come..." She squatted at the opening, peering down at me. "Prince Dante, is there any way I can repay you for saving my life?"

Leaning against the ladder, I glanced up. "When my father is well, seek to meet with him. I promise you: he will sign a peace treaty after this is all done. The only person in Glensdale wanting war is the one who was at your throat, Viceroy Falco. Captain Ruth will see to it that you are safe; just tell her a stubborn cousin on the farm said so."

"So I've heard from John." Her fingers tightened their grip on her skirts. "Wouldn't it be wiser for us to unite the kingdoms by marriage?"

The muscles in my back tightened, and strangely, I found myself laughing. "You're right." *Of all the things to bring up at a time like this... is this the reason why she came?*

"What's so funny?" If her skin hadn't been such a beautiful dark shade, I would have seen her blushing. "Are you not the Prince of Glensdale?"

"I *was*." Smirking, I glanced back up at her. "But please understand, peace would only last a short while if we marry.

It would seem like it would work faster, until scandals and assassins came for us. It only lasts a single generation or two before the corrupt break it down."

Princess Sonja gave me a baffled look. "Once a Prince, always a Prince."

She thinks I am worried about my status. How thoughtful. Shaking my head, I poured forth my opinion in this political game she was unaware of: "In the past centuries, they married royalty because we're the easiest to overthrow and corrupt. We are disposable and so is the peace attached to a marriage. Instead, make a treaty that will tie the hands of anyone who shall rule either of our kingdoms. Including trade promises like wood for fish or along those lines helps as well. Then whether our royalty marry or die out is no longer involved. A treaty is kept by the people and those in charge. It is seen as a hostile act to be the first to break a well-written treaty, unless one has a very good reason to do so. This is why I believe it is a better solution."

"I-I see." The fingers relaxed, and she smiled. "You've been thinking about this far longer than I have."

Nodding, I told her, "Yes, a very long time and even did a lot of reading and research."

"Indeed." Standing, she smoothed out her skirts. "Well, Prince Dante, I will follow your advice on this matter. Your wisdom and counsel are greatly appreciated."

"Princess Sonja." She blinked and our eyes met. "I appreciate the bravery it must have taken to be willing to marry not only your enemy, but a bloodeater, if it came down to that in order to end the war. Not many are willing to sacrifice themselves for the greater cause."

She touched her neck, and I watched her shoulders shudder. "You were never an enemy. I made up my mind to come here with no assumptions in hopes of proposing peace. The same can be said about your bravery and all that you've endured in your efforts to stop the Madness for the world's sake."

"Again, I admire your courage." The burning hunger was coming back, my senses sparking to life again and fears wrapping my soul.

She would be such a delightful appetizer before John, no?

Cursing the *Fanged Lady* under my breath, I barked, "Now shut the cellar door. Forgive me, but I won't be able to see you off."

Swallowing, she gripped the door. "In that case, farewell, and I hope we meet again."

The cabin door opened, sunlight flashing between us. I could smell the sweat of John's body. "What's wrong?" Panic filled John's voice.

Salty and sweet, hummed the *Fanged Lady.*

He had been doing chores, and the scent invaded my senses and danced on my tongue. The agonizing need to eat—to eat John—rushed over me. I shook with the fears and reality of it all. *The Madness was her hunger for devouring the world.*

I doubled over, gripping my stomach. "Close it!"

Her eyes wide with fear, Sonja dropped the cellar door. The *Fanged Lady* screeched, as if she was fully aware of my intentions, and the hunger for John peaked. Covering my mouth, I stumbled through the shelves. Jars fell to the floor, but I had to hurry. *I remember seeing them here, in the arena just behind the dummies, isn't it?* Fumbling past the last slide and twist of shelves, I came into the hidden training room. John had been there. I found a cot with blankets and buckets within reach, one with water, and his scent all over it.

Feed on him and this will all end, bargained the voice as a wave of twisting pain rattled through me.

I fell face down on the cot and blankets, wallowing in John's scent and the comfort it created. Hissing filled my mind.

She doesn't want me to feel comfort. How amusing. Turning my head, I saw what I had come looking for and rushed to dig them out of the old hay-laden floor. Something dark stirred at my core, and I knew I needed to do this. *For John's sake.*

Cold in my fingers, I uncovered chains and shackles as old as I was. My fangs throbbed as if smelling John gave them their own life. Shaking my head, I latched onto my memories, gripping the shackles tight. The *Fanged Lady* waged war on my mind, ripping and clawing at my soul. I noticed the shackles but never did brave asking the old man about them. After all, he said so many times, *Never know when you'll need to go to war again.* The metal was rough against my skin, but I didn't care. This was to keep me here; this was to keep John safe. *Seven days.* No one else made it that far since Frank, but having John inside the cabin was sending my body and soul into a frenzy; it gave the *Fanged Lady* the push she needed to make my body betray my heart. I was hungry, and the only thing I wanted to eat was the sweet flavor I sucked from his tongue.

It was indeed good, she latched onto the memory, and I could taste his blood there on my tongue. *Just unshackle yourself and go to him. Dig your fangs into those pulsing veins. It's yours for the taking. He's offering himself to you. How dare you deny him!*

Goosebumps ran across my skin, the idea of his taste in my mouth again exciting and tantalizing. Gripping the cot, I slid it closer to the cool wall. My body was burning with the rising fever to feed. I searched beyond the footsteps and voices to single out John's heartbeat. I knew now how it was my father always knew where I was or what I whispered. This was an advantage of being a bloodeater. I curled onto the cot, hugging the blankets, and soaked in his scent. The soft *ba-bump, ba-bump, ba-bump* lulled me back to sleep. The *Fanged Lady's* words slurred in my mind.

CHAPTER 25

The Madness

I *don't know who or what I am anymore...*
John sat on the floor out of my reach. My body was no longer mine. I panted, drool dripping from my chin like a rabid dog. The Madness had taken me, and I had lost the days.

Seven nights... Seven days... where am I... so hungry...

My wrists were caked with blood where metal had rubbed my flesh raw. At some point, I had tossed the cot into the shelves, toppling them over. Worse, I had lost the ability to fight the urges. I even lost the ability to speak. My shoulders ached, a constant strain pressing on them as all my weight pulled in an attempt to get my fangs closer to the meal I desired.

The blue eyes stared, cold and pained. John's mouth drew tight, his breathing slow and shallow. I could smell he hadn't eaten in two days, but he still came to my nose as something delicious, something I couldn't live without. Grinning, I paced to the wall and back to the end of my chains. I couldn't tell how many times I had done this. All I remembered was willing myself to sleep and waking an animal.

"I thought you said you would be better." He sounded hurt, but it was the heat of his breath that excited me. "I thought if you became a bloodeater you wouldn't be affected by the Madness."

That's right. This flavor in my mouth...

My thoughts faded from me, like fluttering butterflies tossed in a storm. When he came to see me, I was gnawing on my arm. I was mad, frustrated, and so hungry. Since then, John sat there staring at me. In his hands was the *La Dame d'Croc,* and she sang to me. He noticed how moving it brought me to a quiet trance. It sang for me to eat, to drink, to worship it. She would scream for me to tear him apart, for her and her alone. Fear rattled my core. She couldn't have him; he was mine. I frowned, crawling to the wall. Covering my ears, I wanted her to be quiet, to go back to her whispers and stop the banshee's scream. Somewhere inside, I was still fighting, still clawing to bring myself back to the surface again and tell him it would be over soon.

Seven days.

"I'm not going to service tomorrow," he sighed, his voice mumbling between us as if unsure it would reach the old me. "I gave Basque to Princess Sonja. If any horse could get them home safely, that monster..." He choked, swallowing, and I grinned with unknown excitement. "Why would you do this? It's like seeing my parents tear themselves apart all over again." Salt filled the air, and I inhaled the scent of a tear escaping his eyes. "If feeding on me could have kept you..."

John bit his bottom lip, and a hint of sweet crimson hit my nose. Nerves sparked to life and I slammed at the end of the chains, hissing and snarling. This was all I knew to express my feelings. *If he doesn't go, Falco will know!* I pulled harder, but the chains didn't budge or creak. *And I am so hungry... and he is so delicious.* Hot blood ran down my arms; my thoughts fought against the animal. Inside I couldn't decide whether to eat him or to tell him to go. Opening my jaws presented a flash of newfound fangs, and no words could be found. My body wasn't mine, but the *Fanged Lady's* puppet. It was making sense now. This was a curse or a tribulation to prove our worth. How could anyone return from this?

"Falco may come, but don't worry." He lifted the dagger, and she cooed at his bloodlust. "I'll make him pay." She laughed, singing and dancing in his hands like a harlot. "I'll gladly make his heart bleed like he has done to mine."

Don't listen to her, John. Don't take my John from me. I dropped to my knees, panting. *I want to eat him; he's my food, not yours.* The pain of hunger numbed the ripping of muscles, ligaments, and flesh from my efforts to reach the morsel just out of reach. It hurt to see him so close, and yet I couldn't drink or eat from him. I wanted him. I wanted him so badly. A pop filled the air, and my right shoulder dislocated and deformed. Pain surged through me, and I buckled, my face against the dirt.

"I want to believe this isn't the Madness." He was mumbling under his breath, but my keen ears heard him as if his lips whispered into my ears. "If it is, you'll be dead soon. I'll be alone."

He pulled himself to his feet, and I watched, eyes wide. *Don't go! I just want a taste! ONE SMALL TASTE!* I whimpered like a dog left out in the snow.

"Dante, I love you." His heart was racing; the muscles in my body wanted to give chase. "If some part of you is in there..." The pained look again. "Please be in there. Please come back soon."

He left, and the room was dark again. Sweat painted my body, a fever burning me alive. A pyre of hunger and madness threatened to burn away the last of my soul. My food had left me. Rage filled me, and I wailed in contempt. No words could be formed, only bitter thoughts of the person this body used to know.

COME BACK! FEED ME! LET ME DEVOUR YOU!

* * * * *

The birds singing brought me awake, and I could hear the snow crunching as they hopped around. I had no desire to move. John sat there, asleep where he had been staring at me again. My throat was hoarse, but I had nothing to say. I was exhausted, drifting in and out of sleep. He'd taken the cot for himself and a blanket was draped over him. An aching in my chest made me sigh. This was a pain I knew and was happy to have back: longing and concern. A chill crawled across me. My fever had left at some point, and my body felt cold and hollow. The wounds I created on my wrists throbbed, and though the thirst was still there, I could wipe the drool from my chin. My right shoulder throbbed, and I groaned.

Where did I go? What became of me?

Sitting up, I peered around and found I had shoved blankets off against the wall. The chains scraped across the floor, and John stirred on the cot. *He shouldn't be here. I was dangerous, and if he misses service, Falco will come looking.* Banging my shoulder against the wall, I popped it into place again. Ever since I fell off my mare, it hadn't taken much during farming and sword practice to slip out. Leaning down, I grabbed what I wanted—*warmth.* Covering my shoulders in the blanket, I watched John sleep. He had left to tend to things but returned time and time again.

Something was unnatural about me. I'd been driven into the depths of the Madness, yet here I sat as if it had been a nightmare.

The shelves still lay on their sides, the broken jars untouched. Leaning against the cool cellar walls, I pored over the fragmented flashes. My tongue licked at my fangs, an unusual sensation I would have to adjust to having as they had grown larger, more carnivorous. Closing my eyes, I wanted to sleep more. There was no telling what day it was, but I could wait until John woke up. My senses dulled again, responding to my desire to turn down the volume on the world around me, and that too brought a wave of relief. Hearing heartbeats and smelling things at such an intense level had been exasperating. The cot creaked, and I froze.

John's eyes stared at me, confusion on his face. "Dante?"

I tried to say something, but my first attempt was nothing more than a rasp before I managed, "I'm sorry."

He sat up, alarmed. "Y-you're back?"

Jumping to his feet, he took a step toward me, and I panicked. "Don't!"

"Are you..." John's face twisted, making himself sit on the cot. "When does this stop?"

"Seventh night," I rasped.

"From when?" He covered his mouth. "From feeding? From after? Which is it?"

I don't know. Shaking my head, I shrugged.

His eyes gauged me before landing on the bleeding wrists wrapped in iron. "H-how do you feel now?"

"Hungry." I frowned. "Thirsty."

The silence between us was crushing. John was pale, weak from the worry he let take him over. It hurt seeing him like this, and I shuddered at the thought if I had died. He was sleeping here, hovering over each moment of the tribulation I faded in and out of. Panic filled me, and I realize I was missing a day or more in my head. Nothing was adding up. My senses responded; Valiente and Sonja's essence were fading from upstairs.

How long ago did they leave?

"What day?" I tried clearing my throat. "Service?"

"I didn't go." My heart pressed hard against my chest. "It

was this morning, and I didn't want to leave you."

Morning! "Dammit, John," I croaked, covering my face. "Falco will–"

My body gave out. Darkness swallowed me, and his reply fell mute. I wanted to crawl out of my own mind or even my own skin. With a clenched jaw, I fought against the tide of sleep. I could hear the thumping of his heartbeat and calm brought me to seeing him sitting there. Dreams clung to imagery, the heightened senses making me feel like a phantom haunting John's every move, every breath, and even the sweat sliding down his temple sent a thrill across me as if I were really watching it connect to other beads before falling beneath his beard.

CHAPTER 26

Internal Warfare

The dream faded in and out, taking turns from my darkness where I found myself lost with only the hissing voice for company. Lingering lustful thoughts levied me back to where I could feel John's warmth against me. I managed to crack an eye, only to see him in the corner. A blurred heap confirmed he still sat there just out of reach. We were both relying on the safety of my shackles. Shutting my eyes tight, I cursed under my breath, dreaming of lying beside him, watching over him, and lost in the poetry of the *tha-thump, tha-thump, tha–BANG-BANG-BANG!*

Knocking at the cabin door forced my eyes open for a fleeting moment. We glared at one another, paling. My senses were muddled, unable to smell who awaited there for him, and I struggled to settle my nerves.

What good are these senses if my emotions can derail them so easily?

My eyes closed against my will, and a chill slid up my spine. I tried to stir from my sleep, mixing dreams with the waking world. My senses chased after John, hearing the steps, the rise in his pulse, and even the change in his scent as he swallowed back the fear boiling to the surface.

Am I upstairs? Can John see me? No, maybe–BANG-BANG-BANG!

John left me there, chained. Fear filled me. A smell drifted down from outside, and I knew without a doubt who had come knocking. The hint of blood, daemon, and armor revealed my worst fears. *What will become of me? Of John?* I could only pray Ruth would be alarmed by our absence and come looking for us. *Please, let us live to see a new day...*

The *Fanged Lady* whispered with self-satisfaction. *He's come to get me at last. You will pay for breaking my curse, son of Traibon! I WILL HAVE BLOOD!*

John shut the cellar door with care, shoving something over it to hide my location. In the darkness of my mind, I could see it like a phantom following hot on his heels. Pausing, he ignored the knocking as he performed a short prayer. Reaching the door, John paused at another round of knocking, his weight creaking on the floor above. The metallic scent of the rapier dug at his hip. He had grabbed it from the table, and inside his coat, I could still hear the hissing of *La Dame d'Croc*.

The atmosphere shifted, heat lost to the wintry cold. John would see the two knights in armor who grinned with bloodlust in their eyes. I didn't need to see it; I could feel it, smell it, sense it with every fiber. His brow would fold, his eyes drifting over their shoulders to see Viceroy Falco on his horse at the edge of the property. A mixture of blood and manure told me he sat there, waiting at a safe distance in case we aimed to strike with an arrow. Knots hardened in my stomach.

"What do I owe the pleasure of this visit, Viceroy Falco?" John leaned on the doorway, trying to deter any signs of foul play. Clearing his throat, John coughed and rubbed the back of his neck, feigning illness or exhaustion.

Something like that wouldn't fool a tenacious bloodeater like Viceroy Falco. We can smell illness; we can hear your beating heart and fearful inhales, John. Even locked down here, through walls and doors. Curse these senses! No wonder he could read me so easily that first day back.

"You missed service today." Falco's horse sidled under him, the hooves crunching in the snow. "Are you well?"

Standing up, I strained to listen. My vision blurry, body heavy in a state of exhaustion and newfound strength all at once. I struggled, but my arms were pulled back by the chains. Burning rage filled me, and I pulled harder, desperate.

"No," John answered without hesitation and added another fruitless round of coughing. "My servant has run off with a woman into the woods. After tending to the farm alone, in the snow, I've fallen ill. What can I say? It's a downfall to being human. Did my message not reach Glensdale either?"

Really John? You can fucking feign ignorance to my face about even my father and yet you fall apart in front of Falco of all people.

"You lie."

No shit.

Falco's voice filled with excitement, the horse stepping closer. "But you have some guts to lie to my face and do so with such finesse. Well done, my dear priest. If you don't mind, we'll see if Dante eloped with the Princess or stayed close to home to be with his pet priest."

The guards reached for John, the creaking of leather and scraping of metal armor rattling me to my core. Every muscle tightened, my eyelids struggling to stay open. The guards were dragging John out and away. I needed to be free, but the keys weren't within my reach. Turning, I traced the chain to where it was attached to the ground.

He's too slow. I need to escape; I need to protect him! He'll underestimate them.

All John managed was to shove one back, but the other disabled him. John hadn't counted on Falco jumping straight to the point. One guard wrenched John's hand, and he dropped the rapier, cursing under his breath. His feet dragged across the cold snow, no shoes to protect them from the ice.

Dammit, he'll freeze to death!

Firm hands on his shoulders pressed John to his knees. The smell of sweat and sound of John's pounding heart told me his rage had peaked. Falco laughed, dismounting his horse, long strides closing the distance. With both hands, I braced myself and pulled up with all my strength. My right shoulder threatened to dislocate again, and I cursed it. The metal creaked. My heart skipped a beat at the spark of hope, renewing my strength.

I can see it, the way he toys with his prey and the relentless games he plays with a priest. This time he can smell me on his breath. Falco will know we've been together. He will make me pay for this. I've seen him do it before, watched like a lamb in the presence of a lion. Not this time...

Falco leaned down, gripping John's chin, turning his head to the right then the left, craning his neck as he did so. "If you think I was bitten, I am sorry to disappoint you," John sneered, earning him a narrowed glare. "As I said, they fled to the woods."

"Here's a fact your beloved Prince and you didn't know about." Falco's icy metal gauntlet slid inside John's laid open jacket and found the dagger. "As a bloodeater, I can hear her singing to me. She's quite demanding, in fact. Told me things, like how sweet you tasted and how angry she is with Dante for ignoring her."

John fought against the knights only to have his face slammed into the hard-packed snow. Ice bit into the flesh of his cheek. Again, he resisted, but they buried a knee in the center of his back, and he yelped. His breathing grew shallow as he struggled to inhale under the pressure. His body shivered from the frigid air and the snow pressing against his chest. I could hear the way his blood slowed, John's body heat draining from him. They pulled his arms behind him, rope wrapping and tightening against his wrists, digging into his skin.

I could see how Falco's eyes sparkled, his face glowing to have *La Dame d'Croc* in his hands. He slid it into his belt, his fingers tracing the skulls and vines like a lost lover. This was the moment he dreamed about for so long. The silence added to my agony. I froze from my tireless efforts, straining my senses and praying that Falco would continue to toy with John, or reminisce over the blade just a moment longer.

John squirmed, and Falco snapped back to the present, his eyes on my prize, *my priest*.

Positioning myself more carefully, I pulled up, hard and fast. The chain slipped, ripping my palms open. Blood hot on the frigid metal links started steaming in the cold air of the cellar.

"Where is she?" Falco kicked snow into John's face. "Where did you put her?"

He's looking for the Princess? How deep does his reach go? What backdoor deals has he made with Bishop Marquis?

"She who?" Falco needed information, and John wouldn't give it to him. "It's just a bunch of sour old men who live out here," John laughed, unnerving Falco and adding to his ire.

"Princess Sonja, the one dressed as a nun from *The Tower*." This time Falco's boot connected with John's cheek, blood from a split lip spattering across the snow.

Inhaling deeply, I froze. The scent of the blood invaded me, and I recognized it. *John!*

"Tell me where she is. I have no more patience for you or Dante. I have what I want." Falco's fingers tapped the skulls. "I'll skin and dress you like a rabbit. I'm sure Dante would take great pleasure in seeing you hung off the porch, stripped of cloth and skin. Where is she?"

"Why the fuck would I know anything about a Princess?" Falco delivered one more kick, splitting John's lip farther. Another slash of red painted the white canvas. Blood dripped steadily, but despite the pain, John held his smile, riding on the tailcoats of Falco's anger.

Panic filled me. I positioned my hands lower this time, fingers entangling with the metal chains.

"Stop playing the hero, Father John." Falco crouched, a finger pressing against the open wound. John wiggled under the crushing knee of the knight. Falco lifted his finger to his own lips, sliding the blood-soaked finger between them and sucking. "Oh, you're a sweet one. I know Princess Sonja didn't go home. I have men waiting in the pass for her, waiting to finish the job if she had. Where are you hiding her?"

With a scream of rage, I jerked on the chain, and it broke.

"I don't know where she is," growled John.

"Strip him down." Falco was stepping back, the guards yanking John up on his feet. "Let's see how long it takes a man to freeze to death, shall we? Or perhaps I'll find where the *Fanged Lady* has bitten you and have a taste?"

Again, I rushed for the cellar door only to be halted by the remaining chain. There were two, one for each arm.

"FUCK!" I clawed at my other wrist. "WHY!"

I heard John throw his weight into the guards, this way and that, desperate to gain some freedom. He knocked his head into the chin of one knight, but before he could knee the other, metal slid across John's throat.

The *Fanged Lady's* laughed at John's attempt to escape. *He is ours!* She hissed, taunting me. *I will be the one to taste him next.*

The past collided with the present, mortal wound, Falco's bite marks, and red painting the ground. My chest tightened.

John would be the next dead priest of Glensdale, and worse, the *Fanged Lady* would get her own share of the fun.

I'll never allow him to be marked twice by that wretched blade!

Falco laughed. "That fighting spirit is wonderful. I have a missing Princess, a daemon who hasn't shown himself, and no signs of Madness. The only thing I do have is a rebellious priest who is madly in love with a daemon whom I suspect is a bloodeater. I wonder, where did you choose to have your cut? Did he pick it or you, I wonder? Do tell..."

Blood splattered at my feet, palms and wrist ripped to shreds. I stepped back and threw myself forward, my other shoulder threatening to dislocate, if not break. Again, and again, and again. Sweat dripped from my chin; panting, I leaned on my knees. I tried to listen, to find John's heartbeat. It was there, but something was wrong. There would be a flutter, but it was slowing down as if too cold. Inhaling again, I took the chain in my hand, wrapping it around my arm, and pulled it toward me. *PING!*

Falco let the *Fanged Lady* slide down the center of John's torso, her elation reaching me. Her keen edge split the white undershirt with ease. Another cold steel blade snaked down the back of his neck and along his spine, splitting the coat and shirt with a firm tug. It was cruel, the icy metal against exposed skin as greedy hands ripped his clothes away. Despite the wintry air, he never flinched.

John's voice still held its cockiness as Falco searched his chest, "You won't find anything."

My strength this time proved too much for the metal, a link bending, snapping. Catching my breath, I searched the room. *I'll need a weapon.* Leaning against some armor was the claymore still wrapped in canvas. *Thank you, old man.* Ripping it free, I ran for the exit, launching myself over fallen shelves and broken glass. I climbed the ladder, but the cellar door wouldn't budge. Frantic, I put my shoulder into it.

"Oh, I'm not done looking." Falco continued the blade's descent, slipping the tip under the waist of John's pants.

The *Fanged Lady* cut through the leather belt and thick fabric. "Now you look desperate, Viceroy," John accused.

My panic fueled me. Ramming the cellar door, I knocked the object off.

"Do you know why you find yourself naked in the snow at sword point, John?" Falco circled around, his eyes taking in all of John, feasting on his prey, knowing this was the thing I wanted most. "Any guess as to why I would go this far?"

"N-n-no." John's teeth were chattering. "You have y-y-your blade. I have n-n-nothing else for you."

Pulling myself from the cellar, I found the fireplace held nothing more than coals. Seeing the cabin so neglected for the first time was jarring. *Oh John, how careless. The old man would have our hides over this.* Turning to the door, I found it blocked. *They either aimed to keep him out or keep me in.* I put all of my weight into the front door, aiming to knock it off its hinges.

With a fingertip circling a skull on the blade, Falco leaned into John's ear and whispered, "Because she says she's tasted your blood. That Dante wouldn't give her more, and he is gone from her reach. Did he really sacrifice himself for you, priest? You have been a thorn in my side, meddling where you don't belong, and here I find out you had my sword and lover held captive this whole time. You owe me."

I heard John answer sternly, "She's a liar."

Falco laughed. The door wouldn't give. I pressed against a crack in the door, watching as Falco's icy gauntlets snaked across John's bare chest. The fingers trailed down his abdomen, and John closed his eyes. A smile crept on Falco's face, metal armor gripping him, and John grunted from the unpleasant harshness of it. Viceroy Falco ran his tongue across John's neck and inhaled his scent.

I misjudged Falco. He wants us both.

"What would Dante think if I took you for mine?" Falco's lips tickled at John's ear, his hot breath wafting in clouds in the frigid air. A look of dread filled John's face. "Seeing you naked, tasting your sweat, your blood. Yes, I could shave your head and break you in how I see fit. Normally, I don't care for slaves with so many scars and cuts, but you wear them well, Father John. Why should I waste something so delicious, so pleasing to the eyes? You're so much better than your predecessors. Bishop Marquis chose well this time."

John remained silent.

"Oh, there's that flash of anger and contempt." Falco let go and circled around. Cold fingers followed in his wake, over John's hip as he began to shiver. "Nothing to say to that, huh?" Falco's fingers traced the branded cross rippling across John's back, and he laughed. "And strangely, Bishop Marquis did a wonderful job. Though I'm disappointed." Starting at the nape of John's neck, Falco's fingers pressed into the middle of John's back, stopping at the lower end of the crucifix. "The poison he soaked on it was supposed to kill you, or at least keep it from healing. Could it be you figured it out?"

John tensed. "I thought-t-t the p-poison you were f-f-f-feeding the slaves w-was only harmful t-t-to d-daemons?"

"Oh, so you know about that? My, my!" Falco gripped John's ass and whispered into his ear, "Who on earth did you get that information from? Hmm?"

I dug my fingers into the wooden panels of the old oak door. My muscles strained, still tired from breaking the chains. *If I can just lift it, it'll fall off the hinges...* Another tug and the door creaked, a hinge coming loose. *Two more...*

John's heart raced. "Dante f-f-figured it o-o-out. He treated the wounds."

"Oh, did he now? Shame he's not here," Falco cooed. "Well,

it's only harmless as long as it's not heated beyond a certain point. Then it changes and becomes quite the opposite, harmless to daemon and deadly to humans."

Again, I jerked up and the last two hinges slid off. The door rocked back onto me. I sidled, letting it fall to the floor with a heavy thud.

"This is most interesting," I could hear Falco hum. "I don't see a mark anywhere. She is screaming, but she only knows she has tasted your flesh."

I froze on the porch, dragging the claymore with me, both hands tight on its hilt. *I'm going to finish what the old man started.*

"S-s-sorry t-to disappoint you." John's body was shaking, his feet turning blue and his body losing to the cold.

Falco rushed forward, his tongue licking across John's bloody lip. "Such a succulent flavor, not even your parents tasted this sweet."

John spat across Falco's face. "Someone needs to put you down, *Le Chien Enragé.*"

"So much fight. I can't wait to put you on your knees and fuck you until you submit, priest." Wiping spit from his face, Falco leaned in, whispering into John's ear, "You should have seen Dante's face that first time I entered him."

Where is John?

"Falco!" John lunged forward, but the guards caught his arms. "You'll pay for everything you've done to me and Dante. I'll run you through! I SWEAR IT!"

CHAPTER 27

Immortal Bloodeater

Falco froze. The grin on his face fell, his eyes wide as I met his gaze. They fell to the claymore, and he took a step back. *Good. I hope you remember the bite of this blade.*

The steam rolling from my mouth cleared. My stomach twisted. John was naked and fell on his side as the guards let go and pulled their blades. They paused in their game of beating him. The snow was stained red with his blood, his face bruised, his body trembling, and his heart slowing. Gritting my fangs, I steadied myself. *They will pay with their lives.* Chains dragged behind me like the screeching of banshees. *Death is coming.* No longer was I concerned about my hunger or my exhaustion. I rushed the guards.

"ARRGGGHHH!"

One raised his sword. My first swing with the claymore and the blood let it slide in my grip. Cursing my luck, I swung out, the chain wrapping around his neck, and I pulled him to me. The other's sword came down on me, and I was thankful for the shackles on my wrists. I gripped the chin of the first guard, yanking. *Snap!* He fell limp at my feet, and I stepped out of the arching sweep of the remaining knight's blade. My heel tapped against John's rapier, and I swooped it up. It wasn't my preferred weapon, but I knew I had him. He stumbled over his dead companion, and I stepped forward. The rapier slid through his neck with ease. Blood gurgled in his throat, dribbling out of the corner of his mouth. I pulled the weapon out, and he dropped face down.

"Dante!" Viceroy Falco's voice earned my heated glare. "Nice of you to join us!"

I skidded between him and John. Smiling, Falco was delighted by this. "It's over, Falco," I said.

"Ha!" He pulled his sword out of its sheath, giggling with excitement. "He is a handsome man. What's with the bracelets, my love? Rather adventurous of you two, no?"

The rapier slashed out, and he parried it, but I earned some distance between him and John. I refused to speak. All I wanted was for him to be dead, and John to be safe. Again, I took a strong stance and a step forward, and I spun his sword to the side. He didn't let go, but his face flushed. I distracted him long enough to pull the dagger from his belt and toss it in the snow behind me. I could hear it shrieking, but it no longer pulled at me, no longer possessed me. My body was my own, the curse broken.

"Dammit, Dante! Give her back!" A hard, angry swing came down on me; the contact of it made the rapier vibrate, shaking it from my grip.

The old man shouted within me. *Don't let me see you drop it again until it breaks!*

"Ha! You were never good with light swords." Falco lunged forward, and I redirected the point with the metal cuff.

The point of his sword sliced my shoulder, but I didn't waver. I deserved that much for allowing him to jar my weapon from me. Knocking it off course again with the shackle, sparks flew. I leaped back, frustrated that I didn't have the claymore. Falco lifted his eyebrows, a smirk teasing me. He brought the bloodied tip to his lips and ran his tongue across the red treat. His eyes rolled back, eyelids fluttering, and he moaned.

"Oh, this taste is so interesting, Dante." Another slide of his tongue, and he looked drunk from his sampling. "What is this new flavor you've become? No sour taste of mother's curse. How alluring!"

"Dante!" John's voice made me twist, the claymore landing at my feet.

Falco's grin faltered. He had forgotten about the priest. My heart ached; John had ripped the heavy fur cloak and boots off the dead guardsman, but he scooped up the *Fanged Lady* and cut the ropes on his wrists during the commotion.

Our eyes locked, and John commanded, "Fucking run him through."

Snow crunched; Falco was closing the gap between us. He swung down on me, but I grabbed the hilt with my right hand, and with ease jerked the claymore up for a haphazard block. He grunted, the muscles in my arm twitching under the weight of the hit, and he backed off. Shifting my stance, holding firm to the claymore, I pushed him back and away. At some point, my palms stopped bleeding, healing some. Shaking my head, I needed to focus. I tightened my grip, muscles in my back burning, and I swung down. The vibration in his sword changed into a glint of alarm on his face. He barely had enough power to redirect it.

His eyes were wide, seeing the hilt and the etching on the blade. "That old man still mocks me even now."

I grinned, and Falco jabbed at me. Blocking, I shifted and let go of the hilt, freeing my left hand to counter my balance. The hard-packed snow with the weight of the large blade proved tricky. A bitter thought mused. *You should have trained me in the snow. This is hard to handle two-handed, old man.*

"One armed and with a heavier blade." Falco's breath floated between us, "I am impre–"

The blade swung more easily than the rapier, my balance welcoming its weight and complimenting my body. All those years of training for this weapon brought fright to Falco's eyes. I wouldn't give him any more time to taunt me. Falco parried, the blade warping and struggling to redirect the claymore. He knew I could snap his blade with the force of my swing. He side-stepped, redirecting my blow, and I ducked under his counterstrike, landing an elbow in his ribs. The whole time I would pace myself, see how far I had pushed him away from John before ducking again. I landed a heel across his ankle, and he gritted his teeth. His swing faltered; his body more concerned with falling. I had missed my chance to slice him open, so I put all my force into the upswing of the pommel. It met his chin with a hard knock, and he stumbled backward, stunned.

"Oof!" Falco retreated, blood dripping from his busted chin, and his face twisted with rage.

I don't think he's ever seen his own blood before that... The old man knew what he had been training me for: this moment, to finish what he started. "What's the matter? Afraid of your own blood, Falco?"

"Shut your mouth, cur." He looked wild, staring at his bloodied fingertips. "How dare you... you insolent brat? I should have killed you in my bed all those ages ago."

We glared at one another through steaming clouds of breath. A wintry breeze cleared the way, and I charged again. An upward swing, but he parried. A downward fall of my pommel, and he twisted. I countered, a strike forward, and my blade bit at an opening in his armor. Leaping back, he reached in and sneered at his blood. *If only I had come in from the side...* We had gained more than enough distance from the cabin, and I could focus more. John would be safer the farther the fight slid away.

"That wretched meat bag taught you his fucking fighting style!" Anger blinded Falco.

He came at me, clumsy and wild, the swing desperate. I faked a parry, his swing flinching as it slid off my torso. I swapped to my left hand, my dominant hand. Turning my wrist, the pommel smashed across his fingers, and he dropped his sword. I spun, keeping the momentum and the claymore *thunked* into his thighs, and he fell back. The blade had connected to the bone there, and I prayed it'd broken it. My hand slipped, the leather binding too old to handle sweat, but I had him. Leaping forward, I was on top of him, my hands on his throat as we hit the snow. He struggled under my weight, but I had far more mass and strength for once. Straddling his stomach, Falco's ribs bit into my thighs and behind me his legs flailed. My fingers tightened, his eyes bulging, and he gasped.

"Your father!" It was all he managed, but it was enough for my hands to let go. He smiled, huffing up at me like he had won. "Kill me, and your father dies with me. *Mother* will always protect me!"

Something cold slid through my gut. Painful and burning, it pushed through my back and out my stomach, swift and precise. Looking down, steam wafted up from the tip of the *Fanged Lady,* painted red with my blood. My heart pounded, and the cold hand on my back told me everything.

"I'm sorry..." John's breath fell hot against my shoulder as he pushed the dagger farther. "I would never betray you." He shoved me down, and the blade travelled with me. "I promised. I promised I would kill him, for you."

Trembling, my eyes stared down at Falco. The point of the dagger dove deep into his chest. His heart had been pierced. Relief waved over me. He knew the stipulations, the importance of my blood, and the fact a bloodeater couldn't be the one holding the blade. *He wouldn't leave it to chance...* John ripped the *Fanged Lady* from me. Gripping my stomach, I felt the hot blood gushing between my fingers. The pain dizzying, I tried to stand, and I fell back. John's arms embraced me. It was over. The heat in Falco's body faded, his eyes lifeless, and the *Fanged Lady* lay silent.

"Dante," John pressed his hand over mine, blood staining our locked fingers. "Please don't leave me."

I smirked. "You shouldn't say that so often. You're making me look bad."

"DANTE! JOHN!" Captain Ruth came bursting through the woods on her white horse. "SHIT! We're too late!"

"John!" Valiente was close on her heels, Basque's nostrils flaring at the scene before him. "What the hell happened?"

"D-dante's wounded." John shuddered, muscles tensing. "We need to do something! Help him first."

A loud whistle unfolded from Ruth's lips, and she turned to us. "We found several guardsmen in the woods, and we had to fight our way here, but to think Viceroy Falco would go this far..."

"Why are you still here, Valiente?" My eyelids were heavy, the pain still burning under our hands. *Is it the wound, or am I still feeling exhausted from breaking the curse? I just want to sleep now...*

"You shouldn't talk, Dante." Valiente sounded sad, but relented. "Princess Sonja decided to ask your father for safe passage. We didn't realize he was recovering from an attack by Falco as well, and when we discussed things with Ruth, it seemed best to first locate the Viceroy."

"He showed up at the church, but you two didn't." Ruth knelt over Falco's body, her fingers closing his lifeless eyes. "He seemed ruffled, according to my guards, and that's when Princess Sonja insisted we investigate. Glad she gave us the push! This got ugly."

"I don't care about that!" John's shout caught everyone's attention. "Someone help me stop the bleeding..."

Ruth stood, huffing, before she gave him an answer. "No one can do anything. You're already putting pressure on it." He pressed down harder, and I grunted. "The only time I've seen something like that be healed was in the medic tents where bloodeaters would feed on the slaves, and it would stop the bleeding and bolster the healing process."

John's hand patted my cheeks, his skin hot with my blood. I cracked my eyes open; it took so much effort to open them to see the panic in those blue eyes. His fear was raw for the first time and strangely, it made me grin. I wanted to say something, anything to wash that look off his face, but I couldn't find the energy. My eyelids were so heavy.

Leaning down, he whispered, "Kiss me. It may be our last..."

Something inside me came to life at the thought. *Our last kiss...* and I reached for his head, pressing his lips down to mine. My tongue slid inside; the cut opened as the tip rode along the ridge of the wound. John pushed me out, and his own lashed out into my mouth, urging me to take it all. Sweet and hot, I sucked and drank, taking his blood into me. There was no thirst or want, but something tingling and sharp like the buzz buttons. This time it wasn't grass or salt but electrifying just the same. Our hands left my wound. I just needed a little more. I could feel the new instinct driving me. *Just a little more and all will be okay again.* John broke away, his hand sliding down my chest and smudging the blood away. No wound remained.

"So you're the last of the bloodeaters," Ruth smirked. "Do you want to go inside and clean up? You look like a sex slave with the shackles on, all shirtless like that."

I leaned forward to sit up, and John's arm pulled me back against him, skin touching skin. My face flushed; *how could I forget?*

"We both need to clean up. Will you take care of this mess?" John's voice was rushed, panicked even.

"I have to log this and bring the Viceroy's body back as evidence." She waved a few city guards over and allowed them to sweep Falco's body away. "What was the murder weapon?"

"*La Dame d'Croc,*" I answered, sliding into John to shield him further. John was still naked under the cloak, though warmer than the moment I had broken through the front door.

"It's there, half buried in the snow where I tossed it." John nodded in its direction.

Everyone turned to look, but John jerked me up to my feet. He shoved me through the broken cabin door and into my room. I would have refused, but I noticed the chest and cellar door I rammed had blocked his door completely.

"Do y-y-you think the s-s-saw me?" John snatched the blanket from my bed.

"Saw you?" I pulled him into me, trying to weasel into the covers to give direct contact to let my body warm his. "How could anyone not see?"

"Dammit." He muttered, leaning in me as his body slowed its shaking. "That was Valiente with Ruth, was it not?"

My face flushed, jealousy pushing pass logic. "He can look, but I've already laid claim."

John laughed. "Can't you hear them from here?"

I puffed out my cheeks. "Stop fretting over that. Let's get you warmed up and dressed."

* * * * *

"I was going to say, I'm a little surprised they found the dagger." Ruth slid the weapon into her belt. "Guess they needed a moment alone?"

"Uh," Valiente's paused before declaring, "I think John's naked."

Rut's steps crunched in the snow. "Well, seeing someone shredded a priest's garments during this battle, I think you might be right on that one."

CHAPTER 28

Broken Vows

Falco was dead. And with him, the *Fanged Lady* started to decay where it sat on display. My father was still alive, but he was left weak. In fact, many of the bloodeaters had lost their sense of thirst and even their power waned. On the battlefield, there were reports of survivors of the Madness increasing every day. Whatever *La Dame d'Croc* was, its curse over Grandemere had been broken though there were places where no change had been reported. The cabin was a mess. We were still in the dead of winter, and with John's injuries, I folded and came back home. Glensdale was back to the city I remembered, the streets alive, and with the treaty with *The Tower* and *The House* signed, the murmuring of peace started to spread, but we still needed to find safe passage for Sonja and her knight Valiente.

"So this is what the inside of a Prince's room looks like?" John slipped through the door. "Did I interrupt you? I can leave?"

"You may stay. Lock my door behind you either way. I don't mind you, but the others are annoying." Laying on my bed, I read through a book on magical items, flipping aimlessly in hopes of revealing talking blades or cursed items with souls. There were hints here and there. Flipping the book over to see the cover, I realized it wasn't a book from either home. "Where did you find this book, John?"

"I stole it." John shrugged. "From *the Church*."

"Why on earth would they need books on how to create and destroy magical weapons?" He plucked the book from me and tossed it on the nightstand.

"They have one, if not more, weapons like the *Fanged Lady*." He flopped down beside me, shirt loose and hair still wet from a hot bath as its golden locks lay over his shoulder unbraided. "Has anyone found Bishop Marquis?"

"I said that man was a clever one," I retorted. John's hand slid across my bare chest, and I rolled away and off the bed. "John, you do realize staying with me means you can't be a priest?"

"Am I not the Prince's Priest?" I flinched, and he smiled. "No one knows I broke my vow."

I laughed. "You kissed me in front of everyone. Hard to take that one back, John."

"I saved your life." Turning away, he stretched himself out across my bed. "I never knew you slept on something so soft. How the hell did you ever adjust?"

"After working the field, you're too tired to care." There was an assortment of oils, perfumes, and colognes on the dresser. "Hard to imagine I used to fret over which of these to wear or mix."

Curious, John rolled off the bed and picked through the bottles. I watched as he popped open the various shaped glass containers, no one like the other. Leaning in, he'd inhale, sniffing each. The various faces and reactions as John's face twisted filled me with delight.

He shuddered from one round bottle. "This is so pungent."

"This one is meant to be mixed with water." I reached around him, pouring water in a saucer. "Just a tiny drop. In fact, I think this was my favorite."

A drop rippled in the water, and he leaned in, sniffing with caution. "Okay, that is nice. I think I remember this smell when we first met. It doesn't fade fast, does it?"

"Yeah, I wore it a lot, so I guess it was this one."

"How do you put it on?" John had never been exposed to such a luxury.

"Here." I dabbed my fingers in the water and went to reach for John's neck, but he gripped my wrist. "What's wrong?"

"I want you to wear it." His cheeks red, he turned back to exploring the bottles. "It's a nice scent for you."

I could feel the heat in my own face as I dabbed my wrists and neck. It was exciting to know he had remembered the scent and moreso to have him request I wear it. A grin snaked across my face, this moment intriguing. He reached for a familiar bottle of oil, and my chest ached. Popping the cork, John smelled it. After another sniff, he swirled it and turned to me. I flushed red, waiting for the question I knew was coming, heart racing. *We've already crossed the line, we've both broken our vows and confessed our feelings. He's mine to have, as I'm his. Do I dare...?*

"It has no scent," John announced, picking up on my stiffness. "What is this used for? Do you mix it like the water?"

I shook my head, my mouth dry as I whispered, "I can show you."

"Show me?" John handed the bottle to me, and my blood rushed. "What does it do?"

"Take off your shirt," I commanded.

He did so, dropping it to the floor.

"And your pants." Again, he did as I commanded with a smirk on his face.

My eyes flowed down, and I realized he was aroused and

getting hard. *You didn't come by my room just to say hello, now did you John?* Dribbling some oil in my palm, I rubbed my hands together. As I stepped closer, he backstepped against the dresser. The bottles all clanked against one another. *Yet, you're nervous, and it just makes me want to take you here and now.*

"Did I scar you for life from last time?" I lifted an eyebrow, the oil heating in my palms. *The way he looked down at me and hardened on my tongue...* The memories were still vivid and my loins ached at the idea I had denied myself further pleasure in a moment of rage. "That night, I was angry, but tonight we..."

"That's not it." His voice was abrupt. "I just... shouldn't I do something for you?"

I moved in closer, my lips kissing his. His tongue demanded to enter my mouth, but I denied him. Pulling away, I nuzzled his neck, kissing and sucking. He shuddered, trapped between me and the dresser as bottles rattled again. My knuckles tickled down his center, riding the trail downward until the bottom of my hands cupped his cock. He inhaled, holding his breath frozen there. I pressed my thumb firm against the underside, my fingers rippling over the lip of his head. John moaned, growing hard in my palm as I stroked him, slow and firm. His cheeks grew red, and his eyes closed tightly as he hummed.

His hands gripped the dresser, white knuckled, and his heart beat like the wings of a hummingbird. I continued sucking along his collarbone, his body hot under my lips. Trembling fingers were trailing across my ribs now, across my hips where he tugged at my pants. I tightened my grip, my thumb circling the tip. He leaned into me, his chin pressing into my shoulder. I returned to sucking at his neck, indulging in the control I had over his body. Tightening my grip, I pressed my thumb harder against the underbelly, riding his hardened length to the tip and back down again. His chin pressed harder into my shoulder, and I laughed, amused.

"Break me," he huffed, his hand reaching into my pants, hot fingers wrapping around me. "I want my vows broken all the way so I can be with you, and only you." He mimicked my motions and I groaned. His thumb circling the tip of my cock, he whispered, "Break me all the way with this, Dante."

Desire surged through me. I let my pants fall, and I turned him, his face on the bed. The chill of oil dripped across his firm ass. My hand rubbed along him, passing over the entrance and under where I grasped his balls. He moaned again, breathing hard. A shudder waved over him. He'd never done this with anyone. This was meant for me and me alone. His body tensed, and I sighed. Leaning forward, my cock pressing into his slippery lower back, I reached around his hip and started to stroke him again. He tried to stand, but my hand cupped the back of his neck and pressed him back down. His moaning increased, and he began relaxing again.

"I want to hear you ask me one more time." My words made his cock stiffen in my palm.

"Fucking break me." He was breathless, his hand cupping my own cock as I stroked his hardening length.

I let go of his neck, snaking my fingers down his spine. As I slid down the center of his lower back, he shuddered and hardened in my hand once more. He wanted this physically and emotionally. The oil slippery, I pressed my thumb into him. Again, he stiffened in my grip and moaned. My body throbbed with desire, and I couldn't fight my need to take him any longer. Gripping his hips, I pressed the tip firmly against him, and I pushed, slowly. He tensed around me, and I moaned. I pushed forward again, and he relaxed, letting me all the way inside. I stayed there, enjoying the heat of being inside him. My hands slid back over his hips, kissing his backside. Grabbing his cock once more, I rewarded him, stroking hard and fast. I could feel the tension melting, his body hot with ecstasy.

"What are you waiting for?" he rasped, lost in lustful delight.

I pressed against him, my hands retreating to his hips once more. Pulling back, I almost left his warmth before I pushed all the way in, and he yelped. His fingers gripped at the blankets under him. Another thrust warranted a yelp turned moan. The oil rode inside him along my cock, each stroke easier than the last. I enjoyed the way I rubbed inside him, picking up speed, moaning more and more, fingers digging into the bony hips in my palms. John rubbed his cock, pushing against me as sweat glistened across us. My eyes unglazed, and I glared at the branded cross and its flourishes. Selfish desire took hold of me. I pulled his hands up above him, my weight pushing firmly into him, throbbing inside. He was panting, squeezing and releasing, driving me to my peak.

"I get to cum first." I rocked my hips against him, moaning, "As your *Barrière de Force,* I get to hold you down and cum first."

He moaned, "You promise?"

I pushed harder, faster. Peaking, an explosion of undying pleasure ripped through my core. My grip waned, and I fell forward, flushed and lost in in my orgasm. John wasted no time pulling away. He shoved me to my knees, gripping my hair as he pushed himself into my mouth. Hot and sticky with oil, he slid to the back of my throat and out again. I was still throbbing all over but sucked the hard cock, eager to satisfy him in the same way he had allowed me. I wanted him. He moaned, the muscles of his length flinching on my tongue as he released the hot liquid of his orgasm. I swallowed and continued sucking. He fell backward on the bed, trying to pull me off.

"It's too much," he huffed.

I pulled away, crawling over top of him, our satisfied cocks rubbing one another.

My lips found his ear, "Are you broken?"

"Y-yes," he gasped, rolling me over. "I am yours, my Prince."

Wrapping my arms around him, I nuzzled him from behind. "You have a funny way of showing your love, John."

"You're one to talk." Breathless, he sighed, "It's a shame this will only add to our problems."

I sobered, his words bringing our pleasure back to the ground. "I don't know how long we can keep this secret."

"Any word on what we will be doing about Princess Sonja?" his voice lowered, a whisper now. "We can't just send anyone with them."

"You're right." My eyes caught the book on the table. "Are there more books like that in the catacombs?"

John held his breath in thought before relenting, "More than I could read through in three years. Why?"

"I want to know more about soul weapons," I confessed.

His body tensed. "It's a dangerous magic. I think the *Fanged Lady* was one and there are more out there."

"That's what I'm afraid of." I kissed the nape of his neck, and he shuddered. "How about we escort Princess Sonja and Valiente back to Captiva City?"

He shuffled, rolling so he could meet my eyes. "Are you sure? Falco has men placed everywhere."

"We can see if anyone else will accompany us, the more the merrier. At present, we have three men skilled with swords. Adding one more would benefit us." He searched my face. "What's the matter?"

"Is there anyone we can trust?"

"Looks like I'll be paying Madame Plasket a visit." I kissed him, this time allowing him to enter my mouth, delighting in the taste of his blood.

To Be Continued...

MORE TO COME

Traibon Family Saga

The Prince's Priest

The Priest's Assassin

The Assassin's Saint

The Saint's Bloodeater

The Bloodeater's Lover

The Lover's King

The King's Priest

ABOUT THE AUTHOR

V.C. Willis

Willis is an avid reader of male romances, whether its series like C.S. Pacat's Captive Prince Trilogy, a standalone novel such as The Song of Achilles by Madeline Miller or diving into the many mangas they've discovered published and independent artist and authors. With a passion for the characters, worlds, and plots in these fellow Fantasy Romances, V.C. Willis is still left thirsty for more and has taken up the pen to fill the gap in their own reading selection. Wither the debut novel, The Prince's Priest, a saga of two men who are broody in their own right and love each other, the aim is to introduce works with no other underlying motives. Enjoy sexual tension, raw romance, and amazing worlds. A touch of magic and paranormal should be expected as under other pen names this writer has earned their share of accolades and awards.

4 Horsemen Publications
Erotica

Grayson Ace
How I Got Here
First Year Out of the Closet
You're Only a Top
You're Only a Bottom

Leo Sparx
Claiming Alexander
Taming Alexander
Saving Alexander

Dalia Lance
My Home on Whore Island
Slumming It on Slut Street
Training of the Tramp
72% Match

Ali Whippe
Office Hours
Tutoring Center
Athletics
Extra Credit

CPSIA information can be obtained
at www.ICGtesting.com
Printed in the USA
LVHW090904210820
663747LV00001B/176